Samaritans

Jonathan Lynn

First published 2017 by Endeavour Press Ltd.

Jonathan Lynn authored the bestselling books The Complete Yes Minister and The Complete Yes, Prime Minister, based on the multi-award-winning BBC series, created and co-written with Antony Jay. The books sold more than a million copies in hardback, have been translated into numerous languages and are still in print nearly 30 years later. Other books include the novel Mayday, and Comedy Rules.

His films as director include Clue, Nuns on the Run (both of which he wrote), My Cousin Vinny, and several other hits. Awards include the BAFTA Writers Award, Writers Guild (twice), Broadcasting Press Guild (twice), NAACP Image Award, Environmental Media Award, Ace Award (Best Comedy Series on US cable), and a Special Award from the Campaign For Freedom of Information.

PRAISE FOR *SAMARITANS*

"Jonathan Lynn, already a comedy legend, has reinforced his storied reputation with this coruscating, wrathful, passionate, hilarious and astonishingly timely novel. It's wonderful! I was hooked, mouth open, heart pounding. The catastrophic state of medical care is his story but *Samaritans* can be read too as a wider allegory, a discourse on a politics of greed, dis-entitlement, deregulation and social brutality that has run quite mad."
STEPHEN FRY

"Jonathan Lynn tackles the US healthcare system in satirical splendour. I laughed out loud. It is both hilarious and scary at the same time! Nobody does it better."
BARBARA BROCCOLI

"Given the extraordinarily complicated and often grim circumstances that have become the hallmark of the American healthcare system, I would not have thought it possible to find comedy in what is so often nothing less than calamity. But that was before I was treated to Jonathan Lynn's satirical and remarkably revealing exposé of the twisted pretzel that is American healthcare. It is with the highest confidence that I recommend this book, with particularity, to those Members of Congress who remain committed to making access to life saving care far too difficult for far too many people. It is my fondest hope that they might laugh their way to the education they so sorely require."
RICK UNGAR, Co-Host of Steele&Ungar, Sirius XM POTUS Channel, Senior Contributor for Politics & Healthcare Policy, Forbes Magazine

"In *Samaritans* Jonathan Lynn utilizes his legendary comedy genius to enjoy making us laugh at an absurdity, as he subtlety awakens us to the fact that the absurd is the reality, and that the joke is on us for not having noticed. This is a book that is as politically and socially important as is it is entertaining."
MURIEL GRAY, past Chair of the Orange Fiction Prize

"Jonathan Lynn takes on the US medical system with the same probing laser he applied to 'Yes Minister' and wryly proves that malpractice makes profit. Ingenious and funny."
MAUREEN LIPMAN

"Make America great again."
Donald J Trump

TABLE OF CONTENTS

1

Max Green worked in an industry that some people said existed purely to exploit people's greed. Max knew better. He worked in Vegas, the entertainment capital of America. There are many different approaches to entertainment, and gambling was one of them. Sure, most people lost money there but all entertainment comes at a price. Max had no sympathy for buyers' remorse. It was their choice. It's a free country. They didn't have to gamble.

"I understand that you can't pay," he used say to desperate people who were begging him to give them a break, in the days when he worked the casino floor. "But you should have thought of that. Everybody knows that the odds favor the house, it's no big secret, what are you, stupid? Or do you just want something for nothing? You shouldn't play unless you can afford it. That means, afford to lose. What do you think, you think this is a federal building, you think we're offering welfare here?"

Max didn't believe in welfare. He believed in freedom of choice and taking responsibility for your own actions. He had no time for handouts. He had no time for spongers. He had worked his way out of poverty, and he couldn't see why the fuck anybody else couldn't do it.

He had a better job now, way above the casino floor. But there was no route to the very top. He wanted to run his own shop.

On the way out of Vegas, at McCarran Airport, he phoned his mom. "I'm going for a meeting about a possible big new job," he said.

"At another casino?" asked his mother.

"Not exactly." Max smiled. "But... in a way."

"You'll make more money?"

"Much less," he said. "At first."

"Less? Why do you want it then? Are you in trouble where you are?"

"No, Mom. I'm doing great. But there's no chance of real advancement where I am. At this new job I'd be the CEO. I could make serious money if they do what I tell them."

"Where would you be going?"

"DC. A big medical center."

"A *medical* center." She sounded bemused but impressed.

"Mom, you wanted me to be a doctor. If I get this job, I'll be the doctors' boss."

"That sounds good. I'm sorry it's less money, but how much do you really need? You have plenty, you're not even married—"

"Don't start."

"No, all I'm saying is, it's good to give back." She always said that. "And how could you ever make more money at a hospital than you make now?"

"It's complicated. I'll tell you if I get it."

"Okay. Are you going to tell your father?"

"You know I'm not. I don't understand why you keep asking that. I don't want to have anything to do with him."

"Don't say that. He's your father."

"He left you penniless. You never talk to him, why should I?"

"Okay. Good luck with your interview."

"It's not an interview," he said before hanging up. "It's a meeting."

*

By the time Max reached DC it was a steaming summer day. He took a taxi from Reagan Airport, named after a president he revered. He was excited about the opportunity to live and work so near the center of government. His spirits rose at the sight of the reflecting pool and the Washington Monument, and the Capitol dome rising out of the haze. He asked the driver to stop and wait while he stood for a while on the sidewalk, admiring the Lincoln Memorial. According to Wikipedia (he had looked it up), Lincoln would be twenty-eight feet tall if he stood up. He was built on the same gigantic scale as the Vegas Strip.

The blacktop outside the Samaritans Medical Center was softening in places and spots of tar stuck to the soles of his handmade brogues. The main entrance was the portal to a different aspect of DC. The wooden signs, barely clinging to the grubby, rough-poured concrete sixties façade, were faded and spattered with bird shit. Cigarette butts littered the sidewalk and the gutter. If appointed, he would make a start on his direct marketing right here.

Columbia Heights was a mixed neighborhood. Not that far from the White House and Capitol Hill as the crow flies if the crow flew straight, but a million miles if measured by influence and wealth. It used to be a high-crime area but, after being ravaged by riots not so long ago, efforts had been made to revive it. Crime had diminished now, but careful people still hesitated to walk around alone at night and they kept a watchful eye out if they did.

Samaritans had a good brand name for a hospital, but that wasn't enough to keep it afloat. Max had learned from his due diligence that the last CEO had suffered a nervous collapse. After a few weeks in rehab he threw in the towel, exhausted by the seemingly limitless deterioration of the fabric of the building and endless fights over money with the city, the Department of Health, the insurance companies and the board. The board hired headhunters to find and entice a new chief. They came up with a bunch of people who weren't interested.

And one who was.

A chubby young Latina escorted Max to a small anteroom on the second floor, with naugahyde chairs and institutional green paint on the walls, applied carelessly with splashes over the edges of the light switches. A bunch of grubby yellow and pink plastic tulips stood forlornly on the deeply scarred coffee table.

He glanced with approval at the smart young man in his late thirties reflected back at him from the flaking wall mirror – taller than average, slim, tanned and dressed in an electric-blue mohair two-piece, fashionably tight.

The local news anchor addressed them from an old lumpy TV, then gave way to a reporter shouting to make himself heard above the sound of gunfire against a backdrop of arid ocher mountains. "Where's that?" Max asked, without caring much about the answer.

"Where's what?"

"That war. On the TV."

She shrugged, sharing his disinterest.

"When we stamp out those fuckers in one place they just show up in another," he said. "It's like playing Whac-A-Mole. I'm bored of it."

"Me too," she said. "Wanna coffee?"

She handed him a paper cup containing warm brown water with a faint coffee flavor and left him in the company of a self-confident attorney on TV who was, according to a caption, *Victor Stone, Trial Lawyer*. "I have won most of my cases," Stone was boasting, "but, you know, funny thing, I practically never go to trial. By the time I'm finished with the pretrial process, my opponents are usually desperate to settle out of court, rather than allowing me to annihilate them on the stand." His smile reminded Max of the alligators on the golf course in West Palm Beach near his mom's assisted living apartment.

A smooth, pink-faced, well-upholstered elderly gentleman in an expensive Brooks Brothers suit popped his head around the door. He had round, tortoiseshell-style glasses perched on the bridge of his nose. Despite his neatly parted white hair he resembled a very large eleven-year-old.

"Mr Green?"

"That's me," Max said.

"I'm David Soper, Chairman of the Board of Governors of Samaritans. It's nice to meet you."

"Thank you." Max turned the charm dial full up. "It's an honor to meet you, sir."

Soper looked pleased. "I must admit I was surprised by your letter of application."

"In a good way, I hope?"

"Very much so. That's why you're here. Come along, bring your coffee."

Max left his coffee and followed Soper through to where the search committee members were seated around a long, slightly scratched, reproduction mahogany table. The boardroom was old-fashioned, oak-paneled and run-down, with threadbare olive-green carpeting. Air conditioners rattled quietly in windows whose paint was flaking off the frames.

"Committee, this is Mr Max Green."

Max smiled, waved and sat.

"That's quite an outfit," said a gruff old member of the board in a baggy, worsted pinstripe.

"Thank you," said Max, slightly surprised by the compliment, especially from one so conservatively dressed. "It's a Valentino."

"Isn't that in February?"

Everyone graciously made allowances.

"Mr Green," Soper said. "Let me start by putting you fully in the picture. Like most hospitals, Samaritans Health Center is beset by rising costs and poor management. Since the so-called health care reforms the government is squeezing us even further on Medicare and we all know it's going to get worse if they ever repeal the Affordable Care Act. Though we don't know how, exactly. Or when. We have come to depend on Obamacare but it's not enough to cover all our outgoings. We have been making cutbacks where we can, but it seems that something more radical is needed – and, frankly, we don't quite know what."

Max nodded with interest, even though he knew all this. He had also, at first glance, seen that Soper was wealthy. He could tell from the shoes, and the diamond-encrusted Rolex confirmed it. As far as the chairman was concerned, Max was confident he would be preaching to the converted.

"So perhaps, Mr Green," Soper continued, "you could explain to us how you would approach things if we were to appoint you. The search committee would be interested to hear what makes you think you can handle this job when your previous experience has been in such a... different... world?"

"Well, you know—" Max reached for his most confident and reassuring smile, "—it's not really that different. I went to business school, maybe the best, Wharton. Terrific. Believe me. On scholarship. As you know, I'm currently running the Lions' Den Casino in Vegas, the hotel operations side. Other than the fact it's a casino, and ten times the size of this hospital, the rules for financial success are pretty much the same. It's all about volume. Check-in, checkout, bed occupancy, number of dinners served. It's numbers, that's all."

"Hmm..." said Soper.

"How many beds can the hospital fill? That's the question. And the answer should be: all of them. A bed is like an airplane or theater seat. You sell it that night, or never."

An elderly blonde spoke up from the far end of the boardroom table. "Mr Green, my name is Jacqueline Goodman."

"Hi, Jacqueline. Good to meet with you."

Was she sixty-five or eighty, Max wondered? Her skin was stretched so tightly from her eyes to her temples that there was no longer any way of telling. But it was clear that she had a lot of miles on her and a couple of serious diamonds on her too. His smile widened. "Call me Max."

Her smile seemed a little thin. "Thank you... Max... I'm afraid I have to disagree with you. It cannot be just about numbers. After all, this is a hospital, not a gambling institution."

"Right," Max agreed instantly. "But what I'm saying is, the number of beds we fill equals the number of inpatients we can treat. And that's where much of the profit will come from."

"Profit?" She raised her eyebrows as far as plastic surgery would allow. "What profit?"

Soper jumped in. "I must agree with Mrs Goodman. We can't just be about profits – even if there were any, which frankly seems beyond the bounds of probability. We have ethical responsibilities here. We have to make serious savings, but we must continue to care for our community."

"Sure. What I meant was, it's about the number of beds we can fill, *balanced* with our ethical responsibilities." People around the table nodded. "There's no conflict. I don't see a moral dilemma. A service business is about volume and, whether we like it or not, health care is in the marketplace now. It's all about the bottom line. You have to increase the margin. The business plan must be *robust*. Look at all the hospitals that have gone under because they couldn't make ends meet. Altruism's fine, but if you want to stay in business you got to make the hospital pay."

No one on the board felt they could disagree with that. A small, worried-looking man with a little ginger mustache and faded red hair raised his hand. The chairman nodded at him. "Mr Coward?"

"Uh – yes, thank you, Mr Chairman. Mr Green, I'm Fred Coward. Why would you leave Las Vegas for this job? We can only offer a much lower salary than I understand you're currently receiving."

"Good question," Max said. He always believed in complimenting the questioner if he could. Be positive. Dale Carnegie 101. "I'll tell you why. Vegas is not doing so well. Bed occupancy's down. Why? Because it's a resort. It's a luxury. We're going through tough times and nobody has to gamble. But health care? That's a necessity. The one indispensable industry. Sooner or later everybody needs it. With more and more old people hangin' in there, medicine is the business of the future."

"Is that the only reason?"

"No." Max spoke with the passion of a true believer. "I know I can turn this hospital around. My father died in a place like this after two months in Intensive Care. The hospital lost money on him. I want to give something back."

"So you want to join the Samaritans family?" asked Soper, oozing sympathy.

"Yes. I really do." Fearing that he might have sounded a little too eager, he added, "After a conversation about my stock option package, of course: my bonuses and dividends."

"I thought you wanted to give back..." Jacqueline Goodman's right eyebrow elevated a centimeter.

He smiled at her. Always smile. Never tell people they're wrong. "I do. But there's nothing wrong with being properly rewarded for giving back, is there?"

"Absolutely right." Soper's face had become even pinker with enthusiasm.

"That's the American way, right?" said Max.

Mrs Goodman persisted. "What kind of reward do you have in mind?"

"All I ask," said Max, "when I get Samaritans out of the red and into the black, is a fair slice of the profits."

"Profits?" Once again, the members of the search committee smiled sadly at each other. One or two actually laughed.

Max didn't see what was so funny. "Management is management," he said. "There's only two kinds: good and bad. I'm good. What Samaritans needs is..."

He glanced at their expectant faces.

"Bouncebackability."

2

Max was in his comfortable Vegas office at The Lions' Den a couple of days later when Soper phoned him. The lion-shaped front of the hotel offered a view over the Strip, all the way up to the MGM Grand and the black, pyramid-shaped casino, the Luxor. His window, on the other hand, was high up at the ass-end of the lion, under the tail with a view over the parking lot.

"The board liked you," said Soper. "But what I want to know is, how *do* you plan to make Samaritans profitable?"

"You know the Hospital Corporation of America?" said Max. "It owned or operated a hundred and seventy-six hospitals and ninety-two freestanding surgery centers in twenty-one states."

"Yes. Wasn't it eventually bought out for about thirty billion?"

"Thirty-one. That's what made me interested in health care."

The chairman hesitated. "But… didn't I read somewhere that it pleaded guilty to a whole bunch of criminal counts?"

"You did. Fourteen of them. Filing fraudulent Medicare reports and paying doctors kickbacks for referrals. That's what's so great, don't you see? It paid more than two billion dollars in fines and penalties, by far the largest fraud settlement in US history, and they *still* sold it for over thirty billion. How great is that!"

"I see."

"And the chairman, Rick Scott, became Governor of Florida. He still is."

"My goodness, so he is!"

Max had thought long and hard about men who make big money. He had long believed that they were the ones who perceived opportunities that were there for everyone to see, but which are only spotted, seized and acted upon by a true entrepreneur. Max knew he was one of those. He was passionate about his plans for the hospital. "Samaritans could be the basis of a new health empire."

"But we're a non-profit," said Soper. "We take care of everyone who needs us."

"Well, that's obviously got to stop," said Max. "What do you think you're running, some kind of charity?"

"That *is* what we're running, yes."

"Don't you know that seventy-seven per cent of all US *non*-profit hospitals make a profit?"

Soper paused. "I didn't know that, no."

Max wasn't totally surprised by the chairman's ignorance. He had looked Soper up online and found he was CEO of a corporation that supplied electronic parts of computerized weapons systems to the marines and other branches of the military. He wasn't a full-time hospital chairman, just a part-time do-gooder with exceptionally high net worth. His chairmanship appeared to be an attempt to give something back.

"Why shouldn't Samaritans be one of the profit-making non-profits?" Max asked. "Some non-profits are banking hundreds of millions a year. Ascension Health has almost $7.5 billion in the bank. Tax free. Northwestern Memorial in Chicago has so much cash they opened a new women's hospital with a marble lobby and rooms with forty-two inch flat screen TVs."

"Did it keep its tax-exempt status?"

"Yep. And the CEO's salary was ten million, last year."

Soper cleared his throat. "I - I hope that's not what you would expect us to pay you?"

"Of course not." Max hastened to reassure him. "Well, not initially, anyway."

"I see. Um… look, Max… I don't know how to put this, but…"

Max knew that Soper had no objection to high salaries for CEOs. He guessed that the chairman was wondering what was in it for himself. "We'll be partners," he promised. "I'll take care of you. Trust me. We'll make Samaritans great again."

"I'll talk to the board," Soper said.

The fish was hooked.

*

David Soper put down the telephone with the satisfaction that another box checked always gave him – particularly when that particular box contained a fruitful combination of philanthropy and self-interest. It was turning into a very productive day.

He'd had meetings that morning at the Pentagon and the State Department, about sales to an assortment of consumers in and around the Persian Gulf. The unraveling of assorted Muslim regimes and the breaking and remaking of alliances all over the Middle East and North Africa was making him wealthier than even he had imagined possible.

His pals in high places, with whom he had enjoyed an exceptionally chummy and convivial lunch at the Hay-Adams, a luxurious and discreet boutique hotel a stone's throw from the White House, revealed that several of the weapons systems to which his privately owned corporation supplied electronics were being sold to both sides – and, in a few splendid cases where there were more than two sides, to *all* sides. Iraq, Syria, Libya and Yemen were all densely populated with multiple, well-funded customers, locked in apparently never-ending internecine conflict.

David Soper was untroubled by death raining down from Middle Eastern skies because serious terrorists were almost certainly being hit. He had a clear conscience. It wasn't up to him to decide when to unleash these weapons. He gave no orders to use them. He simply helped manufacture the means by which America could defend herself and her interests, and remain leader of the free world. Not that killing Muslims who were killing each other gave him moral qualms – on the contrary, what could be the harm in helping them out? So long as they were killing each other, they might not have so much time to kill Americans.

*

Max heard from him a week later. "The job is yours if you want it."

Max flew back to DC immediately. Soper's Bentley picked him up at arrivals and they met some distance from the hospital, at Charlie Palmer's Steaks on Constitution Avenue.

"Welcome aboard." Soper offered him a big, pudgy, perfectly manicured hand.

Max wondered if there had been any objections to his appointment. He had debated with himself whether asking would show weakness, but decided to go for it. Samaritans would be hard to turn the place around without the full support of the board.

"There were some dissenters," Soper acknowledged. "But I persuaded them that we need new blood and a new approach."

"Can you tell me who they were?"

"I think you can guess. But don't worry about it."

Max tried not to, but he couldn't let it go. "How did you persuade them?"

"It wasn't hard. I told them, 'You've all seen his references – an MBA from Wharton Business School – top notch. He really could be the man to tackle our financial problems. We'd be lucky to get him.'"

"Thank you," said Max. "I'm honored."

Soper ordered a bottle of Joseph Phelps Insignia, a cabernet from California which was listed at $850. Max liked his style. He wondered who would be paying for it. He hoped it was the Defense Department. Then Soper ordered a New York steak for himself, with a baked potato and string beans. Max ordered oysters followed by prime rib, with mashed potatoes and sautéed spinach. He was feeling good. Great wine, delicious food, discreet service, crisp white linen table cloths, tables far apart, just the way he liked things.

"So how do we start?" asked Soper as they clinked glasses. "I really don't know enough about all this; it's not my full-time job. This chairmanship is my contribution to the community."

"For which you deserve to be properly compensated, in my opinion."

His eyes glistened. "I've no objection to that, if Samaritans can afford it."

"We need to think outside the box."

"Everybody says that," said the chairman. "But what do you mean?"

"We need a mission statement. Every business needs a mission statement."

"With respect, Max, we're a hospital. Everyone knows our mission."

"With respect, Mr Chairman, knowing we're a hospital is not enough. There's a lot of competition around here. We need to position ourselves just right, so that we have a competitive advantage. Just like you do in your business."

"I see."

"Here's the way I see it. In many respects, a hospital is like a hotel. First off, to bring the customers in it needs star attractions. Casinos hire Elton John, Britney Spears, Cher, Tom Jones. At a hospital, patients come to see the doctors, right? So that's who I figure our star attractions must be."

"Doctors? Star attractions?" repeated the chairman, not yet convinced. "Oka-y…"

"They must be billed, marketed, advertised." Soper didn't respond, he just blinked, several times, so Max continued. "My question for you is: What kind of doctors are a draw? For Joe Public, I mean."

"A draw? For Joe Public?" These were clearly alien notions to Soper. "I never thought about that. We don't really have billing at hospitals."

"Well, not that kind of billing…" Max smiled.

"No." The chairman chuckled.

"What I'm asking is, which doctors are the stars?"

"Well," said Soper, "surgery is the most dramatic part of the hospital. It's life or death. The surgeons must be the stars. That's where the biggest profits are."

This made sense to Max. Every medical TV doctor show he had ever seen had stories that revolved around surgery. "Any particular type?"

"Well, all of them, really. But the most glamorous right now are the cardiothoracic and neurosurgeons. Then there's plastic, ophthalmic, gastrointestinal, orthopedic… High fees, fast turnover, and mostly excellent publicity. You know, the ones who appear routinely on those 'best doctors' lists."

"Then that's who we need to hire," said Max. "Surgeons with big reputations. We can start to make Samaritans the hospital of choice for upscale patients, celebrity patients, patients in the news. Just think how great it would have been for you if Cheney had been given his pacemaker here at Samaritans. That would have really increased your market share. You'd have been truly buzzworthy."

"Buzzworthy?" The chairman eyed Max with caution. The word seemed new to him. "That's all very well. But how do you propose we find the money for these doctors?"

"By making cuts. Austerity. It's just like the national budget. You of all people must understand – the government finds the money for defense by cutting entitlements. We need to slice away the fat."

Soper still looked skeptical, so Max continued selling. "We do want the best, don't we? We want this to be a *great* hospital, right, not just a solvent one?"

"Yes, indeed. But our budget could hardly be more austere than it is already."

"We'll see," said Max. "And finding enough money can't just be done by austerity. Obviously we're going to need more revenue as well."

"Wait a minute," said the chairman. "Let's talk about these cuts first. Where would we find them?"

"Gimme a break, buddy! I haven't seen the budgets yet."

"No, I know. You're right. But I assure you we've cut to the bone already."

Max sipped his Insignia and smiled. "I doubt it. As you know, rule one of management is that there's always wastage. Five per cent at least, often a lot more."

"Maybe…"

Max saw that more reassurance was called for. "Don't worry about it, David. I haven't even started looking yet. And if we really can't cut wastage, we'll cut services instead."

Soper's brow furrowed even more. "Services? What kind?"

"There are so many to choose from. We'll have to be radical. But we could begin with the medical staff. The doctors."

"Wait! You want to cut *doctors*? You just said they're the most important people."

"Some are. Some are vital, some are merely important, and some hardly matter! I'm sure you agree that Samaritans shouldn't be providing employment to doctors we don't need, or doctors who are overpriced. I'm willing to pay above the prevailing norm for the stars, but the supporting cast had better get ready to tighten their belts. We need more bang for our buck. Man, this prime rib is real good!" He sliced off a chunk of medium rare and stuffed it in his mouth. "De-licious!"

Soper looked dazed. "Supporting cast?" He took a gulp of sumptuous red wine.

Max waited till his mouth was emptier before asking his next question. "Tell me – which doctors are the ones that the public don't care about?"

"*Don't* care about? Well, pathologists, I guess…"

Max was excited. "Fuckin' A! That's it! You got it, man! When I was a patient I didn't give a shit who the geek in the basement was, looking at slides. I never even asked."

"I guess nobody does," acknowledged Soper.

Max could see he was making progress. "Tell me about your day job, Dave," he said.

Soper's next forkful froze halfway to his mouth. Then he relaxed. "My real work is in the defense sector. What we have in common with health care," he continued with a pious air, "is that we are all devoted to the safety of our fellow Americans."

"Exactly," Max agreed. "Safety. That's what I'm talking about. Health is just safety by another name."

"It is. But it's more than that. In the defense industries, just like in health care, we don't just keep Americans safe, we provide hundreds of thousands of jobs. The global war on terror has lasted sixteen years so far and shows healthy signs of expansion."

"That's wonderful!"

"Yes. Of course, nobody wants war…"

"Of course not."

"But it does mean that the defense industries will not only be able to continue creating manufacturing jobs, there will also be all those service jobs as well, in military bases, in swing states. And the provision of these jobs means that ordinary people who would otherwise be unemployed can live well, without entitlements and handouts."

This was music to Max's ears. He saw again how much he and Soper had in common. "But I presume that your shareholders have benefitted as well."

"Hugely. But ordinary people benefit too, in their pension plans, and because of all the income and work that manufacturing armaments has created. And the soldiers too; most of them would be unemployed if they weren't in the military."

"Right," said Max. "They take nearly as big a risk as the shareholders."

"Agreed. And we must never forget the downside," Soper added with solemnity. "Some heroes unfortunately die for us. For freedom and the American way of life. They make the ultimate sacrifice for their country."

"It's tragic," said Max. "But you can't make an omelette without breaking eggs."

"You know who said that?" asked Soper.

Max didn't.

"Frederick the Great of Prussia."

"No kidding!" Max felt it was appropriate to express astonishment although he had never heard of Frederick. Or Prussia. "He was *truly* great," he added. "And our fallen heroes must be honored."

"But the good thing is," said Soper, "that we suffer fewer deaths now than in any previous wars in history. That's because the weapons are smarter than ever before. A source of great pride to me."

"Let me ask you something. It's a moral question." Max paused. He liked moral questions. "Are you concerned about the moral implications of dropping all those bombs when they might hit innocent people?"

"Not at all," said the chairman. People always asked him this and he found it slightly irritating. "We kill terrorists. Of course there's occasionally some collateral damage, but it can't be helped."

"Right." They were talking the same language. "Any venture involves some collateral damage." Max was referring to his plans for Samaritans.

"And they're almost all Muslims."

"You can't please everyone," said Max.

"Quite. Furthermore, if they retaliate it only extends the conflict, which is good for all of us here in the homeland. From an economic point of view, at least."

"Right. So there's no contradiction between chairing a company that makes deadly weapons and chairing a company that provides health care?"

Soper frowned. "What an extraordinary idea! Both are entirely necessary. Health care, like defense, is an intrinsic ingredient of the political landscape and a permanent part of our way of life."

"And both have to be driven by economic realities."

"Of course. What isn't?"

"So!" continued Max, "that's why we have to talk about the pathologists. They'll be our collateral damage, that's all."

"I see..." Soper gave a faint smile.

"*Why* do they have a low value in the marketplace?" Max continued rhetorically. "It's because they're not profit centers. They're not rainmakers. We need *rainmakers*."

"I get it," said the chairman. "You don't need to explain. And it's probably not just pathologists we can downsize. What you're suggesting must be true of a lot of the other doctors too."

"That's right. The schleppers. If the surgeons are the stars, I'm guessing that the – excuse me – the supporting cast must be the ones who treat chronic illnesses. Am I right?"

"You are."

"Now – who else, other than a surgeon, would be a profit center?"

"Well…" Soper thought for a moment. "Dermatologists are good value, for instance. I'm told they can see a patient every five to ten minutes."

"Great productivity," Max agreed. "Really great! But let's start by hiring some big-name surgeons and promoting the shit out of them."

"Mainly," Soper pointed out, "we'd have to sell them to the medical profession around here. For referrals."

"Right! Indirect marketing."

"But…" Once more, the chairman's face clouded. "This is all easier said than done…" It was becoming clear to Max that, wearing his hospital hat, Soper might be a glass-half-empty man. "The best surgeons have jobs already, obviously."

"Of course they do, if they're the best!" Max tried not to show his impatience. "So, we simply offer the best doctors we can find *more*, and more benefits than they're getting right now. Doctors respond to money, better than most people in fact. Look at the AMA – money is all it's ever cared about."

Max was right, and it wasn't just greed. His research told him that the median education debt for medical school graduates was $170,000, and eighty-six per cent of young doctors had education debt. Many owed more than three hundred thousand. Plus interest. And this didn't even include the debt on a four-year undergraduate degree.

"No wonder they all want to be plastic surgeons and dermatologists," mused Soper when Max shared this with him.

"All we need to do," Max continued, "is identify our targets. I'll get a medical headhunter."

Soper was pleased. "I knew we hired the right man. Some more Insignia?"

They finished the bottle, agreeing jovially that red wine was good for their hearts.

3

Max's headhunters heard that an outstanding young cardiothoracic surgeon at Hammersmith Hospital in London, Dr Andrew Sharp, was looking for a position in the States. He was, they explained, in his early thirties and a rising star. Max was stunned to hear that the heart–lung bypass machine had been invented at Hammersmith and not in the US and the Hammersmith Heart Unit, said the headhunters, was still hot shit and so was Dr Sharp. His boss, Professor Ross thought Sharp was cocky, disrespectful and oblivious to everything except his own needs, though he was said to have exceptional technical skill and was looking for serious money at a major US hospital. Samaritans, the headhunters implied, might not be prestigious enough for him.

Max liked the sound of all this. *A star! Just what I'm looking for.* Max had hosted plenty of stars at The Lions' Den and he'd had no problems: he just gave them whatever they wanted. If you kept them happy, they performed for you. Max decided to step up, even though Professor Roth had reportedly threatened to fire him from Hammersmith because he broke the hospital record for the fastest heart transplant. Roth said that attitude was not in the patient's interest.

*

Max, on the other hand, was delighted: here was a man who understood that time was money, a man who could raise productivity. He paid for Sharp to fly to a meeting in DC. Business class. All the way from London.

A limo driver greeted the surgeon at the airport and Max met him in the hospital lobby. He was the real deal, Max could see that at once. Slim, tousled hair, blue eyes, he looked barely out of college although he was in his thirties. The complete star package.

"Dr Sharp, I'm Max Green, CEO of Samaritans Medical Center. It's a pleasure, a sincere pleasure, and an *honor*, to meet you. And I mean that most sincerely." Max was giving Sharp his special, prolonged, doubly sincere, two-fisted handshake.

"Thanks for the limo," said Sharp, extracting his hand from Max's grip and glancing around the dingy lobby. "Sorry I'm late, the flight was delayed."

"Par for the course," said Max. "Friday afternoons, the skies around here are jammed with doctors going off for the weekend in their private planes."

Sharp focused intently on Max. "Private planes, you said?"

"All the top doctors around here have them," he said. It wasn't true, but hey! "Let me show you around. I haven't been here long myself. This lobby is going to be completely renovated, by the way, it's a little shabby, don't you think?"

"It is a bit depressing."

"We're fixing it. We have many special facilities at Samaritans for the exclusive use of doctors. By the way, you get free use of that limo for airport runs and big occasions..."

"I do?"

"And free membership of our spa and gym. Everything that great doctors like you deserve." Sharp was looking even more interested.

They creaked up to the second floor in the old elevator. Max was excited. First off, Sharp sounded English which was automatically classy. "You English? You sound English."

"I am. And American. I have an English schoolteacher mum and a redneck dad in Kansas City. They divorced. I was brought up over there by my mum."

"But you have a license here?"

"Yes. I got my MD at Northwestern."

"Tell me," said Max as they came out of the elevator and strolled along the corridor, sunlight pouring in through the old, tall windows that needed a wash. "Why are you leaving Hammersmith?"

"Money, really. And Professor Roth."

"What didn't he like about you?"

"Apparently I was disrespectful."

"Were you?"

Andrew Sharp grinned. "I guess so."

"Why?"

"I didn't like the system."

"The National Health Service?"

"Yes. In some places it still offers the best care for urgent or life-threatening illness but successive governments have been starving the NHS of funds and slowly dismantling it for years now – long waiting lists, massive bureaucratic obstacles to anything new or unusual, incessant government intervention and change. The government no longer has a legal obligation to provide hospital services throughout England. Nor does anybody else. Britain has all the disadvantages of government control *and* the marketplace. Here, it's simple: private enterprise, market forces. Freedom."

Max's spirits were uplifted. A kindred spirit. He had to persuade him to come to Samaritans. He opened a door. "My office. Like it?"

It was furnished like a high roller suite at Vegas. "It's big," said Andrew, looking around with curiosity. He glanced at the pictures on the walls.

"Nude but tasteful – I told the designer Renoir, Modigliani – you know, in case members of the board drop by. Sit down. Make yourself at home. You want an office like this? I can do that for you."

Andrew shrugged.

"So, were you and your boss on really bad terms?" said Max.

"Not till I resigned, no."

"Then what?"

"Not so great. But always polite. A soft answer turneth away Roth,"

"It's no good quoting Shakespeare at me," said Max. "We didn't have any of that shit in the trailer I grew up in."

Andrew was too polite to tell him it wasn't Shakespeare. "Did you have any books?"

"Sure. The Bible. School text books. I was always great at math. I can read numbers the way most people read Tom Clancy."

"No kidding."

"You must have been pretty good at math and science yourself?"

"Not bad. I went to Westminster School. One of the best. Small classes, individualized teaching."

"Your folks had money?"

"None at all. I was a scholarship kid. I did pretty well. My housemaster told me I was gifted but lacking in empathy. The school shrink said I had no social skills and was tactless with others, but as I didn't have much empathy it obviously didn't bother me."

"Funny, I was told that too," said Max.

They both laughed. New best friends.

"I guess that's why I became a surgeon," said Andrew. "You don't see the patients much. Not when they're awake, anyway."

"So what finally made you leave?"

"Roth said if I didn't stay he'd give me a lukewarm reference. Blackmail. It had the opposite effect he intended. I thought, 'Fuck you, I'm outta here.' He warned me I'd end up at a crap hospital unless I had a good reference from him. Well, maybe so in the UK. But I wanted to come back to America so I guess that's why I'm here, crap hospital or not."

"This is no longer a crap hospital," said Max. And if it was, he really didn't appreciate hearing it from other people. "I'm in charge now. We are stepping up quality control. We don't yet have a cardiothoracic unit of international repute, but we will – because you, my friend, will create it and run it. American health care is the best in the world, everyone knows that. I will give you all the resources you want. As much money as you need. You won't ever want to go back to Hammersmith because you will be your own boss, at an even better place – right here. That's why I wanted *you*."

Later that day, Max called Professor Roth for a reference.

"To be frank, Mr Green, from what I've heard, Samaritans has not had the highest reputation in recent years, but I hear you're trying to turn things around. Dr Sharp is a superb surgeon but he's a loose cannon. He cares about his surgery but, paradoxically, I'm not sure how much he cares about the patients."

"Well, he's a surgeon," said Max. "Par for the course."

"Um… yes…" said Roth, who was also a surgeon. "Not necessarily."

Max considered it a perfectly good reference. He phoned Andrew Sharp and gave him an edited version of the conversation. "But you have to help me out."

"How?" asked Andrew.

"I will offer you an absolutely top salary. In return, I need reports on everything of interest that happens in the surgical department, anything that could possibly affect the financial well-being of the hospital."

Andrew promised to keep Max fully informed. It was a double whammy. Now Max had a star surgeon *and* someone to rat on the rest of them. Perfect!

4

Cathy Lockhart was phoned by Human Resources. The new CEO wanted to meet her. She was surprised and curious. Everyone knew that he had come from Vegas, and was wondering why the board had hired him. He had breezed through her section the previous month, but she hadn't met him and nor had any of her colleagues in Billings. He looked cool, though.

She was really surprised by Mr Green's office, which had soft black leather furniture and a white shagpile carpet. "Fancy-schmancy, very upscale, like it?" he said as he greeted her. "I brought the decorator over from Vegas."

She didn't like it. She felt uncomfortable. She wondered what this was really about. The answer was immediately forthcoming.

"I noticed you last month. I asked about you and I hear good things. I've selected you to work for Dr Andrew Sharp. He's a surgeon. He'll need a secretary. I'd like you to be in Dr Sharp's office when he arrives on Monday. I think you'll like him, he's a cool dude and one of the finest cardiothoracic surgeons on the planet."

"Thank you," she said.

She felt deeply relieved. In Billings she had supplied the information that helped Samaritans seize money from uninsured patients who had undergone emergency surgery. Samaritans did have a financial aid fund, but under the rules the patient's entire household income could be taken into account. One of Cathy's recent cases concerned a truck driver, with two small children, earning $30,000 a year. The bill for his emergency peritonitis surgery was $14,000, more than half of his annual take-home pay, but he received no financial aid because together with his wife he earned too much. Cathy briefed the attorney, who demanded full payment plus legal costs, another $4000. With her help, Samaritans won a judgment that took ten per cent off the top of the truck driver's paychecks, after tax. It didn't leave his family much to live on.

She didn't like her job.

Unfortunately, ten per cent of his wages was not enough to pay the bill, so Cathy then had to get a judgment against the truck driver's wife. She worked in a supermarket. Samaritans seized twenty-five per cent of her wages. That still didn't cover it and in the last couple of months – since Max Green was appointed CEO, in fact – a lien was placed against their home. By this time the truck driver and his wife had paid $15000, but as Samaritans was charging nine per cent interest they still had $10,000 left to pay.

The truck driver started experiencing chest pain. Cathy explained to him that Samaritans was glad to help with this, and he was given all possible tests. In next to no time the chest pains were diagnosed as a symptom of stress – and the truck driver owed Samaritans yet another ten grand. Now Cathy was starting to hate herself.

Trying to deal with the alternately enraged and depressed truck driver and his desperate phone calls, she was suffering from stress as well. Her heart went out to the man and his wife, who had paid $19,000 towards an original bill of $14,000 and now owed $25,000 more, but she was powerless to help them. Fortunately, as an employee of Samaritans, she had insurance to deal with her own anxiety and insomnia, but she was haunted by theirs. Working for a surgeon sounded like a great improvement – until the moment Max said, "Monday morning, wear a short, tight skirt. And show a little cleavage, okay?"

She told herself that Max was from Vegas, that she wanted a job that did not involve demanding money from people who had none, that she wouldn't have to talk to hideous lawyers, and she needed the raise.

The following Monday at 8 a.m. she waited with Max in Andrew Sharp's remodeled office. By incorporating two other rooms and demolishing the walls between, Max had created a space like a junior suite at the Mirage. Cathy had never been to Vegas, but she had seen plenty of casino hotels on TV.

He arrived punctually. "This is your office," said Max. "As promised. Pretty great, huh?"

"It's a bit grandiose for me, isn't it?" Andrew said. Cathy saw disappointment flicker across Max's face.

"Total luxury," said Max. "We think our chief cardiothoracic surgeon deserves something special."

"Nice. Thanks." Andrew didn't even seem to notice the big basket of fruit and cookies that Cathy had been instructed to order and place on the coffee table.

Max pointed to the wall. "Look, tasteful print. Monet, Manet, one of those two, I can't remember which. Can anyone really tell the difference or are they the same person spelled differently?"

Andrew was unable to enlighten him. "I know more about video games than impressionist painters."

"And talking of special," Max said, "this is your secretary, Cathy Lockhart."

As Andrew turned towards her she felt the blood rush to her cheeks. She had followed Max's instructions to the letter and was wearing a postage stamp miniskirt and a blouse with one-too-many open buttons.

"Hi, Cathy," he said. "I'm Andrew Sharp."

"I know," she said. It was not a warm greeting, she was aware of that. But she was worried that even "pleased to meet you" would have given him the wrong idea, considering what she was wearing.

"Here's your wet bar, refrigerator, entertainment center, TV, stereo..." Max could see Andrew didn't look that interested. "Andrew, buddy-boy, the lawyers have done your contract. Before we sign it, is there anything else you want?"

"Well, since you ask, I'll need a car."

"I'll get you a company car. What sort of vehicle did you have in mind?"

He grinned. "How about a Porsche?"

Cathy thought he must be joking. But she wasn't sure. And Max didn't even pause to draw breath. "Okay. You got it!"

Andrew saw the incredulity on Cathy's face. Max looked around and saw it too. "Excuse us, honey. Give us the room. We have to talk."

She hurried to the door, relieved to be leaving.

"Get me a coffee, please, babe," said Andrew.

"My name's Cathy," she said, and closed the door behind her.

"She's feisty," Andrew said. "She's cool."

Cathy stood outside the door in a daze. Surely they must be joking? So many of the hospital workers were on minimum wage and had to rely on food stamps and other entitlements just to get by, and she herself could only just make ends meet. "So that's settled?" she heard Max asking, "You're happy to join the Samaritans family?"

"Yep," said Andrew. "I guess the Porsche took care of any doubts I had."

Cathy sighed and went to get his coffee.

*

The two men walked along to Max's office. To Max's surprise Milton Weiner, Chief of Surgery, was waiting there. Weary and dispirited, with a lined face, sallow skin, and wispy thinning hair, fifty-eight years old and visibly worn out.

"Milton!" said Max. "Do we have an appointment?"

"Twenty minutes ago." His eyes flickered from Max's light gray shiny suit to the greasy-looking product in his perfectly combed, slicked back hair.

"Sorry," said Max. "Something genuinely important came up."

"A meeting with your Chief of Surgery isn't important?"

"Not *as* important, no," Max replied. "Dr Sharp here has just arrived. Andrew, this is Milton Weiner."

"Hi." They shook hands.

Weiner turned back to Max. "We have to talk."

"Go ahead."

"In private." He raised his eyebrows in Andrew Sharp's direction.

"Andrew's our new chief cardio surgeon. You can say anything in front of him." Weiner hesitated.

"Go ahead, Milty. What is it?"

"Very well," said Weiner. "Max, what I wanted to talk to you about is… we're approaching crisis point: more financial pressure, more mistakes."

Max nodded to show sympathy.

"I believe," Weiner continued, "that it's partly because surgical patients are no longer admitted the night before, so we have no time to talk with them, discuss their problems."

"Discuss their problems?" Max was surprised. "What does that achieve? Nothing more than bonding between doctor and patient, right?"

"But that's important."

"Is it?"

"Well, it also allows us to double-check for intercurrent illness, lab abnormalities, review pertinent medical studies…"

"I see," Max said, still nodding, tilting his head sympathetically to one side. "So… this is a real moral dilemma?"

"Exactly."

"But… we have no choice."

Weiner's face fell. "Why not?"

"Dr Weiner, how long have you been Chief of Surgery here?"

"Eighteen years."

"I gather that surgical techniques have completely changed in the last decade. Do you think you're still on top of this job? Same-day surgery's the norm now, and I'd hate to think my chief was getting out of touch."

Weiner was shocked. "I – uh… I thought we wanted to keep our beds filled."

"Yes, but hotel charges aren't enough. We need to be giving treatment to our patients when they're in our beds. Admitting them the night before means they occupy beds while bringing in virtually no extra revenue."

"But if it makes them feel better—"

"You're close to retirement, right? Just a couple more years, you'll get your full pension?"

"Yes."

"Wonderful," said Max. "I really hope you make it."

Weiner eyed him, and said, "You know – thinking about it again – same-day surgery does seem to work pretty well most of the time."

"I think so."

Max turned to Sharp as Weiner faded out of the room. "He worries too much, right?"

"I think so. I don't want to talk to the patients the night before. All they'd do is tell me they're sick!"

"You know that already, right?"

"I know that already!"

They chuckled. Confident that he had made the right choice, he was sure that Andrew Sharp was going to be his ally in the forthcoming struggle. And a major profit center. What was the price of a Porsche when considered in the great scheme of things?

5

Max knew that running Samaritans alone would not be enough, and he had given much thought to the question of creating his future empire.

For some years past, every time he looked at the Wall Street Journal or the business section of the New York Times he saw reports of hospital consolidations. Mount Sinai Medical Center, one of the largest and oldest non-profit hospitals in NYC, bought the parent company of three other New York hospitals: Beth Israel Medical Center, St Luke's Hospital and Roosevelt Hospital. In Dallas, Tenet Healthcare, which operated in ten states, bought Vanguard Health Systems of Nashville, a network of twenty-eight hospitals that included the Detroit Medical Center. And two big for-profit hospital chains, Community Health Systems of Tennessee and Health Management Associates of Florida, had combined in a $7.6 billion deal.

Booz and Company, a consulting firm he trusted, predicted that one fifth of the nation's five thousand hospitals would merge within the next five to seven years. And the Catholic hospitals too were already doing it as fast as they could: Trinity Health and Catholic Health East had joined to create an eighty-two hospital group in twenty-one states, and Ascension Health, the largest non-profit Catholic franchise, had added thirty-five hospitals to their existing network of seventy-eight. Financially solid, Max saw it had the benefit of helping to create further limitations on birth control as well.

Max phoned a buddy at his old bank, a mergers and acquisitions consultant. The hospitals were all doing it, his pal said, because increasing their size increased their negotiating clout with the insurance companies. Some were trying to reduce costs and improve care in the process, but that didn't interest Max so much. Driving up profits was the thing.

He set out his stall to Chairman Soper at their next lunch meeting. "We are at risk," he began as soon as they sat down.

"I know. From bankruptcy. That's why we hired you." Soper graciously accepted the wine list from the respectful sommelier.

"No. Worse. We are at risk of losing our independence. And the big money! We need to get our act together before other medical centers start thinking about buying *us*. We have no choice. The hospital business is dog eat dog. We're all getting lower payments from the federal government, we have fewer patient nights in the hospital. We are paid even less than we used to be under the Affordable Care Act and who knows what the government will do next, and the insurance companies are killing us. We need horizontal integration."

"Mergers and acquisitions?"

"Right. Size is our savior. The bigger we are, the more the cost per patient can be reduced. Costs like billing can be amortized. We can make economies of scale. We will have more money to devote to investing in electronic medical records systems and we can keep the patients from being readmitted for the same illnesses, which costs us valuable revenue. And when we control most of the hospitals in our region, we can change our pricing strategy and hugely increase our charges. And our profits."

"I like that," said Soper. He summoned the wine waiter, "A bottle of Opus One, please."

The waiter bowed and backed away.

"But it might give us a problem under antitrust laws," Soper continued. "We can get into trouble if there's no competition. And before we can even consider any of this, we have to be financially viable ourselves."

"I agree," said Max, but he was satisfied that he had taken a step towards winning the chairman's concurrence. Meanwhile, his top priority was a meeting with Bill More, Executive Vice-President of American Health Insurance Corporation, one of Samaritans' biggest customers.

He took Blanche Nunn, the hospital's risk assessor, along with him. She was in her forties but had kept herself in great shape. Max, who liked to categorize, decided at first glance that Blanche had graduated from babe to cougar. She had navy-blue eyes that she used on people with hypnotic effect when she wanted something from them. She focused them on Max the moment she saw him.

They drove to American Health in his Jaguar. The engine purred. So did Blanche, in praise of the soft leather seats, the walnut dashboard and the magnificent sound system.

"Blanche, I need you to brain-dump. What's our average markup at Samaritans?"

She had the answer at her fingertips. "Ballpark, a hundred and seventy per cent. We charge sixty dollars for tongue depressors, which cost us nothing, fifty dollars for a thermometer—"

"Fifty? A thermometer only costs five dollars at Walmart. That's a markup of a thousand per cent, not a hundred and seventy."

"You asked me for the average markup."

Max was excited. Maybe there were other possible markups of a thousand per cent. Perhaps plenty. He asked her to start looking. Blanche said she knew the people at American Health pretty well and had given a lot of thought about how to handle the meeting. She told Max her new idea. He liked it and told her to write down a number that could work.

*

"Where shall we start?" Max said, once they had all introduced themselves and sat down.

They were in Bill More's corner office, high up, with an expansive view of the Capitol through the wide picture window. Bill had medium fair hair with a neat straight parting. He was medium height, medium weight and he wore a medium blue suit. His face was almost featureless in its forgetability, but fortunately he wore trendy round glasses with yellow plastic frames which, together with his blue-and-white polka-dotted bow tie, ensured that he would not be a complete blank in Max's visual memory.

Bill was impatient to get the meeting going and he jumped right in. "Max, I know you're new there but, to be frank, Samaritans Hospital has been a bit of a thorn in our side."

"We don't want that," said Max.

"No, you don't."

Max and Blanche, glancing at each other, were both aware of the not-so-subtle threat.

"For the last few years Samaritans seems to have been run exclusively for the benefit of its patients."

"I know," Max said. "Shocking, isn't it?"

"That's why we have these problems, Bill," Blanche said. "We have to get rid of our deficit."

Bill wasn't that interested in Samaritans' problems. "Of course," he said, "we are helping people to get health care. We care very much about our members…"

"Of course, of course," said Max and Blanche.

"But we are also an insurance company. A business. And there is the little matter of the shareholders."

The mention of the shareholders indicated that the conversation had taken a solemn, if not sacred, turn. Max nodded. "The bottom line."

"The bottom line," repeated Bill, pleased that Max understood. "Exactly."

"The interests of the shareholders are paramount," said Max. It was the first thing he ever learned at business school.

"And where do the patients fit in, in your opinion?" asked Bill.

"Well, they don't bring much to the table. Not financially."

"You're right," said Bill. "But they are the reason we're there."

"Of course," Max said. "Look, I'm new to all this, but I've been asking myself some pretty fundamental questions. Like, what *is* health care? Yes, it's a business. But it's not just a business, it's much more than that. It's care for our fellow human beings."

Bill's eyes glinted behind his yellow-framed glasses. "So?"

"So it seems to me that we have the immense privilege of being in a business where *everyone* profits. Because health is wealth."

"You're absolutely right," Bill said. Max was talking his language. "Which is why we have to be rigorous about cost control, otherwise the wealth gets spread a little... thin... if you know what I mean."

"I know exactly what you mean," said Max.

"So American Health needs deeper discounts from Samaritans."

Max assumed an expression that was both apologetic and sincere, perfected since watching one of his heroes, Ted Cruz, on television. "Deeper discounts would be a problem, Bill. Medicare is squeezing us already, it pays us even less per patient than you do."

"Must you take Medicare patients?"

"It's a real drag, but yes, we must. We need seniors, that's where the volume business is."

Bill knew that, but he shrugged. "It's up to you. We can take our business elsewhere. You cost us too much right now."

Max wasn't worried. He knew this was all part of the dance. "Let me ask you this, Bill. What's your set price for a routine colonoscopy?"

Bill laughed out loud and sat back in his leather swivel chair. Max didn't see what was so funny. He glanced at Blanche, who was giving him a particularly intense stare with those navy-blue orbs. He wondered if he had said something stupid.

"I can see you're new to all this," said Bill, slowly swinging in the big brown chair. "There's no such thing as a set price. We have different prices at every hospital. And within one hospital we might have six different prices, depending on which of our company's many policies the patients have purchased. We might have sold thirty or forty different insurance packages. Add in the competition – the other insurance companies – and your hospital might get a hundred different prices for the same procedure."

Max nodded. So a medical procedure *was* priced like a room in Vegas or an airline ticket: you charged whatever you could get at that moment. "Okay," he said, "I get it. But that makes my budgeting hard. Have you ever thought about a flat rate?"

"A flat rate?" Bill sat forward, interested.

Max longed to play poker with him; so many tells, the guy would be a sitting duck. "Blanche and I have worked out how we can do all your surgery for two years for your five hundred thousand members. For this number."

She folded the piece of paper she was holding and handed it to him. Max handed it on to Bill. Bill read it and his eyebrows shot up. "You can deliver on this?"

"I believe we can."

"With the help of our Lord Jesus Christ," said Blanche, a development that Max had not foreseen. Both he and Bill turned to stare at her. Max recovered first.

"Absolutely!" he said. He was delighted with Blanche. *She's really smart*, he thought. It's always helpful to invoke Jesus. Unless you're negotiating with Jews or Muslims. But Bill was an obvious WASP.

"Send the paperwork," said Bill.

They all stood up and shook hands. "With God's help," said Max, newly pious, "the word Samaritans will shine like a beacon over this great city of ours, telling people exactly who we are."

"Amen," said Blanche.

"Amen," said Bill.

"Amen," repeated Max. "I think we understand each other."

"I think we do," said Bill. "Great branding."

6

As they sped back to earth in the high-speed elevator Blanche asked: "Why would he agree to pay so much, without even putting up a fight?"

"It's less expensive than maintaining an entire department to investigate every suspicious claim. Much cheaper just to pay us. And it costs them nothing anyway, they just pass the cost on through higher premiums."

"Makes sense."

Max wondered if what Blanche had said was for real, or if Jesus was just part of her negotiating strategy. "So – uh – you've been born again?"

"Yes."

"Then let me ask you a moral question," Max said. He never tired of moral questions. "What do you think we should do if our uninsured patients can't pay the bills?"

"Same as your last business did, I expect."

"Break their legs?"

She smiled. "No, silly. Use a collection agency."

"You mean, bankrupt them?"

"If we have to. Otherwise everyone will want health care, whether they can afford it or not."

"You're exactly right," Max said. "People can't have what they can't afford. That's what got America into this economic mess – everybody wanting something for nothing. There's no morality in that, is there?"

"None at all."

"Look into that please."

Blanche had passed the test. In the car, driving back to Samaritans, he asked her about the pricing in more detail. "Suppose a surgeon is removing a gall bladder. How much does he charge? Ballpark?"

"Ballpark? Three grand? Maybe four. Plus the anesthesiologist, maybe another fifteen hundred."

"We need to get that number up. Way up. The hospital needs to bill far more than that."

Blanche hastened to reassure him. "Oh, we do. Far more! You asked me about the doctor's fees. I didn't include the assistant surgeon. And there's so many other things we charge for."

"Like what?"

"We bundle the bills."

"Explain bundle."

"I'll show you."

When they got back to the hospital she took him straight to the ER. A smell of disinfectant mingled with vomit and urine. The color in everyone's faces was drained by cold, flickering fluorescents in the waiting area and the corridors were crowded with listless, despairing people, waiting hour after hour. Occasional urgent-care patients – victims of road accidents, heart attacks or random shootings – were hurried in on gurneys and attended to more-or-less immediately. Max was by nature an optimist, but even he found this a depressing place.

"Look around," said Blanche with enthusiasm. Unlike Max, she was exhilarated by the emergency room and its financial possibilities. "We charge separately for absolutely everything you can see going on. Evaluating the patient, use of the operating room, use of the operating table, use of instruments, use of instrument *tray*, use of sterilizer, dressings, anesthesia, IV, Band-Aids, biopsy, a *second* biopsy to make sure the first biopsy is correct, lab charges, use of wheelchair, hire of person to wheel the wheelchair, *additional* lab charges, recovery room, linens in recovery room, dressings on wounds, heating, lighting, the overhead... We can get gall bladder surgery up to sixty grand! We do it all the time."

"Nothing back door about it?"

"Unethical, do you mean?" Blanche was shocked at the mere suggestion. "No way! We're not hiding anything. It's all itemized. Everyone does it. In Florida one hospital recently billed around forty thousand dollars to remove a gall bladder with minimally invasive surgery, but where a friend of mine works in Orange Park Florida they charged ninety-one thousand for the same procedure. That's fifty grand more! We're somewhere in between, but I'm sure we can find ways to put ours up."

"Blanche, tell me, which part of the hospital produces the biggest losses?"

"This part. Right here. The ER."

"Why is that? If we do so well out of bundling?"

"We bundle everywhere in the hospital but too many patients in the ER don't pay anything at all, and we're legally obligated to treat them if their lives could be in danger."

"No way around that?"

"No. And the fixed costs are so high."

Max had seen and heard enough. "That's our whole problem. We have to reduce them. So do a study on the ER. Figure out what we'd save if we closed it down."

He headed for the exit. He hated the place.

*

Blanche gave much thought to the study about closing the ER and, although it was an idea she did not favor, she began work on the project with pleasure because she was in love with data. It gave her more pleasure than almost anything else in her life: Jesus, sex and data, in that order. As she researched unpaid bills over the preceding five years she was able to confirm that debt collection was one of Samaritans' biggest issues, especially when it came to ER patients. Many had no insurance. The data showed this was a major problem all over the country, not unique to Samaritans nor easy to solve because the government had interfered.

She explained it to Max. "There was a recent federal government rule that discourages non-profit hospitals from using aggressive tactics to collect payments from low-income patients."

"Why?"

"I can't imagine."

"How do they define aggressive tactics?"

"Anything that would actually make people pay," said Blanche. "There are five hundred community hospitals in the United States which provide nearly forty billion dollars-worth of care that nobody reimburses if the patient doesn't pay."

"Five *hundred*? Forty *billion* dollars?"

"Yes. We can't use strong-arm tactics any more. If we do, they can place our non-profit status in jeopardy with the IRS. Not to mention the colossal PR problem if the press find out. So we now have to determine whether a patient is eligible for assistance before we refer a case to a debt

43

collector or send negative information to a credit agency or place a lien on a patient's home, file a lawsuit or seek a court order to seize a patient's earnings. We're hog-tied."

"Wait a minute." He thought for a moment. "You know, in Vegas, we used a real good collection company. Velvet Glove Inc. Well known for its iron fist. See if they have any ideas."

"I'll check them out," she said. And when she discovered they had a subsidiary, MediReckoning, she proposed to Max that they outsource all their debt collection to it, not just the hard cases, and close down Samaritans' Billings Department entirely. He saw the force of the idea and within a couple of weeks the relevant staff were transferred from Samaritans to MediReckoning. This took them off the hospital's books, which was an extra plus. It looked like a big economy.

They set up a whole new set of rules. Collection agencies were usually hired by hospitals to pursue patients if they were discharged and then failed to pay but, after considering the problem carefully, Max decided it made more sense to get the collection agency involved right from the start. A number of mysterious new employees appeared in the ER. Nobody knew who they were, but some patients, especially readmissions who owed money to the hospital, were now asked to make payments before receiving any treatment. Interest could be added later if it was incurred.

While implementing this scheme, Max learned that Velvet Glove and MediReckoning, both of which were publicly traded, had reported $34.7 million in profits the previous year and he immediately bought stock in the company. The stock continued to rise. Max regarded it as one of the best deals he'd made since he came to DC. He was grateful to Blanche who, he felt, was becoming quite indispensable.

The paradoxical contradiction between providing health care and threatening the sick caused him no concern. He had a hospital to run.

7

Jordan Waters, the nurse receptionist in the ER, had been too busy to take much notice of Blanche Nunn and Max Green. She knew Max was the CEO and she liked to keep in with Blanche, who was always slipping in and out with her iPad and checklists, but right now she was focused on a frail, elderly, African-American woman who reminded her of her mom. She watched the woman make her way slowly and painfully to the counter. She wore a shabby black coat, a little frayed at the collar, and one of the cuffs had been neatly darned. Her shoes were black leather, creased and worn but they still had a little carefully preserved shine on them. Jordan knew the type.

"Pardon me." The old lady blinked at Jordan from behind her large, thick, square-framed glasses. "Can you help me please?"

"Sure. My name's Jordan Waters." She had been trained to tell all arriving patients her name. Nobody ever cared, but she told them anyway. That was the rule. "What do you need?"

The woman's head was shaking a little, and her hands were too. Her hair was gray and thinning. She didn't look well.

"My hip and my back are real painful."

Why not? thought Jordan. *You're entitled. My hips and back are painful too, after standing here all day, and I'm half your age.* "You have insurance?" she asked.

Swollen arthritic fingers fumbled in a handbag and eventually found a wallet.

Jordan was impatient; there were other people waiting to be seen. "You on Medicare, dear?"

"No, I'm only sixty-three." The insurance card finally appeared. She smiled. "I know, I look a lot older."

"You're Mrs May Jefferson?" asked Jordan, reading the card.

"Yes I am."

"Do you have a driver's license?"

"I didn't need one. I came by bus."

"We need ID."

"I just gave you my insurance card. Won't that do?"

45

"Photo ID. We need to verify you are who you say you are."

"Why wouldn't I be?" Mrs Jefferson gave a wry smile. "I don't think anyone else would want to pretend to be me."

"You with American Health?"

"Yes."

"I'll check it out. Take a seat." She hurried away.

"Okay," said Mrs Jefferson but nobody heard. She sat carefully down on an orange molded plastic chair.

After a while Jordan reappeared. "While we're waiting for authorization, I'll take your blood pressure."

"Thank you." Mrs Jefferson started chatting. The loneliness came off her in waves. "I had a hard life. I was born in Birmingham, Alabama, you know."

"That's interesting," said Jordan, although her interest in Mrs Jefferson's bio was strictly limited. "Who referred you here?"

"I referred myself. Can't afford no doctor. I came up here in the sixties with my mom. I was still in high school. It wasn't easy."

"School's hard," agreed Jordan, wrapping the sleeve of the sphygmomanometer around Mrs Jefferson's arm and squeezing the little rubber bulb.

"No, the schoolwork wasn't hard. But I was surrounded by troops and white children who spat at me. Then my daddy disappeared. Never found out what happened to him."

Jordan took her blood pressure again.

"So my mom and I got on a Trailways bus. We put the few belongings we could carry in a battered leather suitcase – I clutched it the whole way – and we headed north to Washington DC. To escape the racism, you know."

Jordan did know.

"Why you keep taking my blood pressure?" she asked, as Jordan checked it for the third time. "Is there something wrong with your machine?"

"No, there's something wrong with your blood pressure."

She made a note of the dangerously high numbers and shoved a thermometer in Mrs Jefferson's mouth, hoping that would shut her up. It did, but not for long.

"Of course, it didn't quite work out that way but we felt a lot safer in DC. Then, when I was sixteen, just when things were starting to go better, Mom was taken ill and she didn't have no health insurance and she died pretty soon after. Cancer, they said."

"I'm sorry for your loss," said Jordan automatically.

"Oh that's all right, it was a long time ago."

"Where do you work, Mrs Jefferson?"

"The pastor at her church helped my mom get a job as a cleaner, working for a janitorial business. I've worked there ever since."

"Would you write down your name, address and employer on this form, please?" Jordan handed her a cheap, leaky blue ballpoint, chained to a metal clipboard.

"When my daughter Angie was born, I worked a night shift so I could get home in time get her up, give her breakfast and take her to school. Then I worked a second job, a daytime shift as a waitress, and I was home again in time to be there for my little one when she got home after school."

"That's very nice. Just write down your main employer, okay?"

"I was determined that Angie would have the opportunities that I never had. I wanted her to experience the American Dream."

"Just fill in the form, please."

"I don't have an address. Can't afford it. I live in a shelter, Valley Place, they call it transitional housing. Transitional to what?"

"I don't know." Jordan had heard this kind of story many times before.

"There's no housing I can afford in this city, I've worked all my life but it's out of my reach. But I have faith in God. Although my life's been full of disappointment there's no bitterness in my heart."

"Good for you." Jordan was trying to be as patient as she could.

"I have kept my job and played by the rules."

"So your daughter is your next-of-kin? Put her phone number in there." Jordan pointed to the allotted space.

"I wanted to send Angie to college, but in the end there was no money for that, so she joined the Army Reserve. They promised her they'd get her a college degree. Well, she did get a degree but she also got call-up papers, first to Iraq and then to Afghanistan."

"Just write in her phone number."

"I'm telling you, I can't. She's in Afghanistan."

"Oh. I see. So who would we phone in an emergency?"

"Well, Angie can't come home to help me. And my sweet granddaughter LaTanya is in New York working at McDonalds for ten dollars and fifty cents an hour. Used to be seven twenty-five but they just put it up. Not enough though, she gets food stamps, otherwise she couldn't get by."

"Is there nobody else? A neighbor, maybe?"

"I don't know. I guess, maybe the pastor at my church?"

"Great. Write down his name and phone number."

"I know his name. Not his phone number."

Jordan sighed. She had no time for all this. "Look, just put down his name and the name and address of the church, okay?" She hoped she hadn't sounded too impatient.

"Okay. But can you do something to help my pain to go away?"

"I expect someone can. A doctor will see you."

"When?"

"As soon as there's one available."

"What does that mean?"

"I'm sorry, Mrs Jefferson, but it may be a long wait. We're real busy today."

8

It was Andrew Sharp's first morning in the operating room. He arrived at 6.45, changed and was scrubbing up at the sink when he sensed a lack of activity around him. It would be for the usual reason: the whole team hadn't arrived and somebody was covering for whoever was missing. He asked a theater nurse if everyone was present; he wanted to get started on time.

"An excellent question, Dr Sharp, if I may say so," said a young woman scrubbing up at the next sink.

"Who are you?"

"Dr Emily Craven. I'm the resident. Deeply honored to meet you, sir."

"Fine," said Andrew.

"I'm so excited to work for you, Dr Sharp," she said. "I've heard all about you. Your extraordinary dexterity in cardiothoracic surgery."

"Oh. Okay…" She was laying it on a bit thick, he thought, but stories about his surgical dexterity were unarguably true.

She was all scrubbed up and ready to go and Andrew couldn't see much of her except her eager, shining eyes. "By the way, we may not be able to start on time."

"Why? What's not ready? Who isn't here?"

Emily evaded the question. "I'll call the head nurse," she said.

Sheila McIntyre bustled in. "Is there a problem, Dr Sharp?"

"I hate starting late. It's hard enough to stay on schedule. Is someone not here?"

"I'll check."

"Sheila, Dr Sharp wants everyone to be punctual," Emily said.

Sheila stopped at the door and turned. "Great idea! Nobody ever thought of that before."

Andrew murmured a gentle reproof. "I can speak for myself, thanks, Dr Craven."

"Of course, sir. I'm just trying to help."

"Yes," he said. "Thank you." He followed in Sheila's footsteps to the ladies' locker room just in time to catch sight of a woman hurrying in from the corridor.

"You're a bit late," he heard Sheila say in a motherly way. "And the new butcher has just made it very clear that he likes people to be punctual."

Then he heard a voice that was unforgettable, a whiskey-soaked, smoky Diana Krall kind of voice. "So tell him to start without me."

"As you're the anesthesiologist," said Sheila, "I'm not sure that's such a good idea."

Andrew moved into the open doorway. "I know that voice," he said with a big smile.

Lori Diesel turned and stared. She must be in her mid-thirties now, but hadn't changed a bit. Slim, muscular, a marathon runner with twinkly green eyes and a long sharp nose, she was scrambling out of her clothes and into her scrubs.

Emily stood close behind him and muttered quietly in his ear, "That's Dr Diesel. She's always late."

Andrew said, "Hi. I'm the new butcher."

"Andrew!"

"Lori Diesel, as I live and breathe! I should have guessed it was you we were waiting for. Still can't get up in the morning?"

"How the hell are you, babe?" She smiled at him with obvious affection.

"Oh. I guess you two have met before," said Emily, recalibrating quickly.

"Northwestern Medical School," said Andrew.

"And assorted cheap motels," added Lori. "Sorry I'm late, I overslept. I was trying out a new prescription."

"With great success, apparently."

"Yup, I woke up and I didn't vomit. I think I've discovered the ultimate cure for a vodka martini overdose."

"You'd be the expert." He kissed her on the cheek and turned back towards the scrub room.

He could hear Sheila's voice as he walked away down the corridor. "Why didn't you tell him you were a couple of minutes late because you were up all night on an emergency triple bypass?"

"That's so boring," growled Lori. "I try to put people to sleep with drugs, not conversation."

Emily Craven scampered back to the sink alongside Andrew as he continued scrubbing up. "Lori Diesel's lovely, isn't she?"

"Yes. Very." He finished scrubbing-up and strolled into the OR where a nurse stood waiting with a green gown for him to step into. She placed a mask over his face.

Andrew had asked for all the Mozart piano concertos to play in sequence during the operation. Research indicated that even heavily sedated patients could hear and soothing music seemed to contribute to a good outcome.

Everyone gathered round the table after the patient was wheeled in and anesthetized. "Good morning ladies and gentlemen," Andrew said. "A tricky case. The diagnosis is end-stage dilated cardiomyopathy. Hemochromatosis caused the heart failure. Plus, he has a panel reactive antibody, caused by a transfusion sometime in the past. We got a donor this morning. We don't have much time." He turned to the theater nurse. "Give the scalpel to the resident."

"Scalpel," said the nurse as she handed it to Emily.

"Now, Dr Craven, you can go ahead and make the incision."

Blood squirted up from the patient. Andrew ducked and dodged it.

"Whoops!" said Emily.

"Emily, let me explain something. 'Whoops!' is one word we never say in surgery."

"Sorry sir. And may I say that I really appreciate the force and clarity of your—"

"Thank you. But I think I'll take over. In fact, I think I'll try for the hospital heart transplant record today. Check the clock." He started sawing open the chest bone. Blood everywhere. He couldn't see. "Suction," he called.

"Suction," repeated the circulating nurse, vacuuming like hell.

"Sponge."

"Sponge," she said, sponging.

"Clamp," he called.

"Clamp," repeated the nurse.

Emily felt the need to participate again. "I really respect your strength, your confidence, your sense of authority."

Lori looked up from her dials, eyes wide. Andrew saw the nurses glance at each other, but Emily remained oblivious.

"Suction," Andrew said again. The blood was getting everywhere.

"Suction," came the echo.

Lori said, "Do you really need that with her around?"

Everyone tried not to laugh.

"Emily, hold this." Sharp gave her the saw.

"Yes sir. Just tell me what you want and I'm there for you."

"More suction," said Lori.

9

Once a week in every hospital there's a meeting to discuss the screw-ups. It's called the morbidity and mortality meeting. At Samaritans the entire surgical department gathered in an old lecture room. Senior surgeons, and those with cases under discussion, sat on the low platform up front. The rest tried to stay awake in the main body of the hall.

When he heard about the M&M meetings, a few weeks after he arrived, Max showed up to one. Milton Weiner was in the chair, ready to start. "Welcome," he said to Max with a limp handshake and a pallid smile which made it clear that he wasn't pleased to see him. He took Max aside and explained that everything they would be discussing was confidential.

"I get that," said Max. "It's medical."

"So what that means, Mr Green," Weiner explained patiently, "is that you can't be here."

"Why not? I won't talk about it. I understand about medical confidences."

Weiner was unmoving. "I'm sorry, but I'm afraid you must leave. Now."

"I ain't leaving, buddy." Somehow Max managed to use the word buddy as a threat.

Weiner braced himself for an attack. "We cannot talk about our patients with you here."

"They're my patients too. I run this hospital."

"They're not your patients. You are not a doctor. And no one will be honest if you are present."

"Why not?"

"Because you are the management. And this is where we discuss our mistakes."

"Blamestorming's cool with me."

"We are not here to ascribe blame, we are here to learn and improve."

"I get it, this is the Band-Aid meeting, but I should be here. I'm the one that pays for the Band-Aids."

It was obvious to Max that he had no interest in giving patients any information about surgical mistakes. Information could lead to lawsuits against Samaritans. However, as several other surgeons joined the conversation he saw that they were far too defensive to admit mistakes in front of their employer. Though courteous, they made it clear that there would be no meeting unless Max left. So he did.

He went straight to his office and phoned his old security people in Vegas. He was determined to know exactly what went on in the M&M meetings. It was nothing to do with breaking medical confidence, he reasoned. Samaritans was financially liable. After a decent interval of two or three weeks, so as not to arouse suspicion, the lecture room would be closed by the Buildings Department for "structural repairs", which meant the installation of discreet CCTV. An enhanced system with mics for recording sound.

*

Weiner opened the proceedings. "It is once again my doubtful pleasure to welcome you to the M&M meeting to discuss the week's surgical… um… complications, in the hope that we can prevent similar problems in future. I should remind you, as always, that this is a closed-door assembly and everything said here is in total confidence. I hope we are all clear what that means?"

Dr Plummer answered for all of them. "It means that by tomorrow half the hospital will know everything we said," he rumbled. The dark bags under his red, watery eyes told people everything they needed to know about his anxiety and exhaustion.

"There have indeed been too many leaks," said Weiner. "So let's *really* try to keep it confidential today. Lawsuits at this place have been increasing exponentially, and some of the mistakes on today's agenda are even more embarrassing than usual."

Gloom enveloped the room. "The bigger problem," said Dr Duff, a burly, balding orthopedist, "is that somebody is leaking information from this meeting. I'm being sued again."

"Oh God…" Weiner moaned, addressing nobody in particular, and certainly not the Almighty.

"Who's suing you?" asked Plummer.

"Victor Stone."

"That ambulance chaser?" said Dr Singh, a bearded resident with a Mumbai accent. "He's suing me too!"

"And me," said Plummer.

"Me too," said Dr Embers. She rasped like Jimmy Durante. The skeletal pathologist had emerged from the fluorescent recesses of the basement lab, the smell of cigarettes emanating out of every pore. Her laptop was poised to project the pictures when required.

"I have never been sued before," said Dr Singh.

This remark caused some mild interest. "You'll get used to it," somebody muttered.

"All right," said Weiner. "We'll start with your case, Dr Singh. A patient who collapsed four hours after surgery. From a hernia, for God's sake?"

Andrew looked up from his doodle. "Was the patient in bed?"

"No," said Weiner. "On a bus. Dr Singh, since it was your case, would you care to comment?"

Dr Singh swallowed and stood up. "The surgery itself went well. Hernias are supposed to be sent home the same day. Hospital policy. So we sent her home. On the bus. It was a bouncy ride, and unfortunately the hernia... popped out... again."

There was silence while everybody contemplated this unfortunate turn of events.

"Any questions?" asked Weiner when nobody spoke.

"Which bus was it?" inquired Dr Embers. Everyone stared at her, confused by the startling irrelevance of the question.

"The eighty-seven, I believe," said Dr Singh.

"A new policy is clearly needed," said Weiner.

"Right." Andrew nodded. "After a hernia op, patients mustn't go home on the eighty-seven bus."

"Unless they buy a round-trip ticket," added Lori. They grinned at each other.

Weiner was not amused. "So that's yet another patient who had to be readmitted. This is a real problem for all of us. Max Green is demanding that we send them home as soon as possible, but if we do and they have to be readmitted later we create serious financial problems for ourselves."

"What's the answer?" asked Emily Craven.

"Don't fuck up?" suggested Andrew.

Lori snorted, trying to suppress a laugh.

Milton Weiner scowled at her. "This is not funny, Dr Diesel."

"No," she said. "Sorry." But she snorted again.

Weiner sighed. "Okay. Next. Please present your case, Dr Plummer."

The tall attending nephrologist unhooked his old-fashioned, gold-rimmed spectacles from his ears and rose to his feet. "The patient was extremely underweight. He had quite extensive liver disease, leading to cirrhosis. I performed a liver biopsy. Subsequently, before surgery, there was bile leakage into the abdomen, causing a biliary peritonitis."

Weiner looked at his notes and prompted him. "And there was also bleeding from the kidney, which caused a hemorrhage."

"Yes," Plummer said. "But apart from that, he was fine."

"Fine?" asked Weiner. "How so?"

"Either the leakage or the hemorrhage may have caused the negative patient outcome."

Andrew looked up from his doodle. "Wait a minute! You mean, he *died*? From a biopsy?"

Weiner frowned. "Dr Sharp, we prefer the term 'negative patient outcome'."

"Of course we do," said Andrew. "But he died, right?"

Weiner nodded and looked at Dr Embers. "Pathology? The slide, please?"

Embers wheezed "yes" like an old squeezebox, and turned out the lights. She clicked around on the computer with nicotine-yellow fingers until a picture appeared on the screen. "There you go," she croaked and with a wet cough waved a laser pointer at the offending image. "What we have here is fat, followed by liver, followed by more fat, followed by kidney, followed by fibres that are probably muscle."

Andrew asked, "Is this by any chance a kebab?" Everyone sniggered and there was a particularly appreciative guffaw from Emily.

"It's not funny," said Dr Plummer, looking sweaty and hunted. Immediately, everyone pretended to agree with him.

"But what I don't understand," said Emily, "is what exactly happened."

"What happened, honey," explained Lori, "is that he stuck the needle right through him!"

"He was very thin! And there's no evidence that the biopsy caused the negative outcome."

Weiner said. "Yes, yes, that's what we'll have to tell the lawyers."

"Fine," agreed Andrew, "but what we should say here, in this room, is that it's neither acceptable nor appropriate to stab the patients to death."

Plummer said, "I was hurrying. He didn't have insurance."

"Even if they don't have insurance!" Andrew's words were greeted by an uneasy silence. Their new CEO's directive had been clear: they were to hurry all low-revenue procedures. "Can we at least agree on that?" Andrew continued.

"Absolutely!" said Emily.

Andrew wasn't interested in her support. She was such a suck-up. If ass-kissing were an Olympic sport, he thought, Emily Craven would spend her entire life on the podium. He found himself wondering if she'd be any good in bed. He was sure she'd win a gold for effort.

10

Max set up an urgent meeting with Blanche to discuss how they could extract more money from Medicare. "The problem," Blanche explained, "is that the government's priorities were completely wrong: Medicare was set up to help patients, not profits. It sucks!"

"What can we do about that?"

"Well… there are some possible steps that your predecessor was unwilling to take."

"Like what?"

"Medicare sets its own prices. We can charge an uninsured patient $108 for a tube of bacitracin that costs $5 at a main street pharmacy but we can't charge an insured patient that kind of price."

"Why not?"

"Because the insurance companies negotiate discounts which we have to agree to or we don't get their business."

"Wait a minute. I thought we didn't want uninsured patients,"

"That depends. We don't want them if nobody else pays for them, because then *we* have to pay. But if we can get the government or the city or anybody else to pay for them, then we *love* uninsured patients because they don't get discounts. That's why the biggest bills go to the uninsured patients."

"Oh… I didn't get that till now."

"What you need to understand is that list price may be highly inflated and it's really just the opening gambit in a negotiation. The list price is paid by very few people – not by Medicare, and not by the private insurers who negotiate their discounts. The *only* people who are charged the full price are the uninsured. So they can be valuable."

Max thought about all that for a moment. "Okay," he said. "That makes sense. But let's get back to Medicare. What are the possible steps that would make it work better for us?"

"There's only one. And we'd have to get the co-operation of our senior doctors. Most of them are attending physicians, which means they have rights here and beds available, but they work for their own corporations. We'd have to buy up their businesses."

"Are you kidding? Wouldn't that cost a fortune?"

"A lot of money, yes. A fortune, no. And the savings and profits for Samaritans would be immense. Best of all, it's safer for the patient."

"That's not our problem."

"Yes it is, Max."

"Well, yes, it is, I guess, but it's not the problem we're discussing right now."

"Yes it *is*. Many doctors would like my plan if, say, the primary care physician shared records with the hospital cardiologist. They would each know what the other is doing because they'd have the same database. They'd have the same notes. That's good for the patient, it avoids mistakes that cost us money and it avoids overlaps and repeated, unnecessary tests. Which means the doctors' time and our money isn't wasted. Increased productivity."

"Okay…?" Max was guarded. He couldn't yet see the point.

"That's how we sell it to the physicians. The big advantage to *us* would be the facility fees."

"What are they?"

"Extra revenues from Medicare! More money for us from the government!"

Now he was interested. "That's what I'm looking for. Go on."

"For years Medicare has paid hospitals more than it pays independent physicians for outpatient care, even when they provide exactly the same services. Those extra payments are called facility fees."

Max was puzzled. "Why would they pay us more for the same thing?"

"Theoretically, it's to compensate hospitals for public service. In reality, if Samaritans buys up all the independent practices owned by our attending physicians, all these facility fees will become revenue for us because *we* would now be providing the services. It's great! Our path labs will get the income from blood or pathology tests at the same lab that the doctor now owns, and we'll get a higher rate from Medicare without changing our service in any way. The *only* thing that will change is that all the services those doctors provide will be reclassified as 'internal'."

"Seems too good to be true," said Max. "What's the catch?"

"No catch. Except that we have to buy out the doctors first."

"Will that cost a lot?"

"Yes, but nothing like as much as the extra revenue we'll generate."

Max asked Blanche to show him some numbers. Efficient as always, she had them ready on her iPad. There was a story from the *Charlotte Observer* and the *Raleigh News & Observer* showing that Duke's Hospital had aggressively bought up local cardiology practices, increasing the number of echocardiograms notionally done "in the hospital" by sixty-eight per cent in one year. As a result, the Medicare payment on each EKG went up from $200 to $461. And in Denver, *The Post* reported, a patient's cardiac stress test cost $2000 one year and around $8000 the next, after the cardiologist's practice had been bought by the hospital.

"I love it! It's a kind of bait and switch." Max was gleeful. "That's four times the price. Nice job, Blanche. But will we have to find office space for them all, within the hospital?"

"No," she smiled. "*Nothing* has to change, except ownership."

"So there's no problem? It's just legalities?"

She brought him back down to earth. "Well, there is one problem – you have to persuade the doctors to sell their corporations to you. And a federal commission has reported this facility fee loophole, so the government wants to close it, to save money on Medicare. Look." She showed him the data again. "Their report last June shows that Medicare pays $58 for a fifteen-minute visit to a doctor's office but seventy per cent more – $98.60 – for a consultation in a hospital outpatient department. Patients don't like it any more than the government does, because their co-pay goes up too, from $14 to $24."

Max chewed his lower lip. "So... the bottom line is that we have to buy up our doctor's practices right now, in case this loophole goes away."

"Correct. Because if that happens it would be even worse for us than it is now. Our clinics could lose five per cent of our Medicare revenue."

"Why would the government do that to us? I thought they wanted us to treat Medicare patients?"

"They'd do it because the Medicare program, and the patients, would save $1.8 billion a year between them."

"But if we lost all that money we couldn't afford to treat them at all."

"We're obligated to."

"Not if we close the emergency room. Not if we offer fewer services for chronic patients and patients who can't afford us."

"They still need to get health care from somewhere."

"Fuck 'em!" said Max. "That's not my problem."

11

Shortly after the M&M meeting at which the hernia "pop-out" on the eighty-seven bus was discussed, Weiner complained to Max about the must-go-home-the-same-day rule. So Max took Andrew out to dinner to discuss it and Andrew reassured him over apple martinis that it was normal practice in virtually every hospital to send hernia patients home on the same day.

"So I shouldn't fire Singh?"

"Well, no. Mistakes happen. Every patient is different. Medicine is as much an art as a science. Maybe he didn't do the hernia that well; he's young, and hernias shouldn't just... pop out. But most hospitals have discharge rules and procedures. In my opinion the patient shouldn't have been sent home unaccompanied."

"Maybe she had someone with her," said Max.

"Maybe. But I'm not sure about going home on the bus. And I agree with Milton Weiner that it's a mistake to rush people out of the door."

"It's not just us," said Max, on the defensive. "Medical Centers are making rules everywhere that patientsshould to be discharged by 10 a.m. That seems a pretty good idea to me. I'm looking into the cost benefits."

Andrew didn't want to get involved in debates about administration. "That's your business. All I know about is surgery."

Max changed the subject. "Is your secretary working out okay?"

"Cathy? She's fine."

"Fine. Not great?" 'Great' had been the adjective of minimum praise in Vegas.

"No, she's cool, though I think maybe she has a chip on her shoulder. She asked me what brought me to Samaritans. I told her it was the money that attracted me. Compared with the NHS, I said, it's serious money. She asked me what I meant by serious money."

"You didn't tell her your deal, I hope."

"Of course not. But I told her it's a lot. She said most of the doctors here don't do that well financially. And frankly Max, after listening to Dr Plummer explaining how he skewered a patient with a biopsy needle and killed him, that doesn't surprise me. But I told Cathy I was sure the good doctors make a lot."

"What did she say?"

"She said, 'That depends on your definition of a good doctor.' So I said, 'You think there's something wrong with making money?' She didn't answer, exactly. She asked me if that's why I became a doctor."

"Is it?" Max was curious.

"I told her it's in my genes. My dad was a plumber and my mum was a seamstress." Max laughed, as he had done when Andrew told him the story of the fatal biopsy kebab. He prided himself on being good audience. Then he thought for a while and said, "Andrew, tell me, when Samaritans really screws up and the patient dies, how does anyone know?"

"The autopsy reveals it."

"That's what I thought. But by then it's too late to help the patient, right?"

"If he's dead? I would say so. But it could show us where we went wrong."

"By then, who cares?" Max said. "It's over. Why bother?"

"It's better to know what killed the patient."

"Why?"

"For the family. The bereaved."

"Any other reason?"

"Yes. It increases the sum of our medical knowledge."

"Fuck that!"

"That would be the other point of view," said Andrew.

"You say it's better to know what killed him," Max argued. "I say it's better *not* to."

Andrew was surprised. "Why?"

"Because then nobody can sue us."

"But—"

"We have to increase the return on the capital employed ratio."

"What the fuck does that mean?"

"You doctors don't live in the real world. That's what you do whenever you rationalize a business."

"What are you trying to say, Max? Put it in English."

"Insurers don't pay for autopsies. We do. Why waste the money? All the surgeons would be happier without them anyway, because they sometimes reveal malpractice." Max had been online again and researched the statistics. "According to the Centers for Disease Control and Prevention, there are autopsies nowadays on only about five per cent of sudden, unexpected deaths. Hospitals are no longer required to offer or perform them."

"That's true," Sharp said. "But it means many diagnostic errors go undiscovered. Opportunities would be lost, to learn about the effectiveness of medical treatments and the progression of diseases. And inaccurate information would wind up on death certificates, which undermines the reliability of health statistics."

"YP."

"YP?"

"Your problem. My problem is that an autopsy costs about twelve hundred dollars – actual cost. Medicare and private insurers don't pay for them. They only pay us for procedures used to diagnose and treat the living. Insurers don't treat the dead. An autopsy is just a hospital expense. An unnecessary hospital expense."

"Yes but—"

"You're right about the medical knowledge," he said. "But I'm righter! Because we have to spend our limited resources on live patients, not dead ones. *That's* what's obvious! So this will be my first major cut: the autopsy is history."

In view of the hospital's financial situation, Andrew didn't want to argue. Instead he phoned Emily. She was available late that night after his dinner with Max so he asked her if she'd like to drop in at his place for a drink when she got off work.

When she arrived at his apartment they had brief martinis, during which she produced her toothbrush and a nightie from her purse. She was planning on staying until morning. This gave Andrew a moment of buyer's remorse. He regretted having sex with her before they'd even had it, but there was no going back now. And, on balance, he felt that sex with Emily would still be better than sex with nobody. He was right. They had an energetic night, Emily did her utmost to please him and he regarded the experience as sort of okay though somehow not quite satisfying.

She, on the other hand, regarded it as highly successful. Dr Emily Craven wanted, needed, to reach Andrew Sharp's position of eminence as soon as she could. She carried the burden of a student loan of three hundred and nineteen thousand dollars, plus interest. She needed the highest recommendations from her superiors if she was to pay it off before her mid-to-late forties. This looked like the best route and anyway he was a real hunk.

Currently she was working at a hospital that was not highly regarded, but the opportunity to work with – and sleep with – a rising star like Andrew Sharp had raised hopes in her breast that she might get an appointment at a major hospital with a concomitant increase in her status and income.

At this point in her life a mortgage was out of the question and marriage did not present a potential answer to her money problems. Marrying a rich man was beyond her, partly because she had never met one and partly because if she had a date with one she would probably fall asleep anyway. She worked such long hours that she hardly had enough time to date anyone outside the hospital. Her off-duty time was mostly spent, to her considerable frustration, alone in her bed.

12

Emily dropped Andrew off at the hospital early the next morning but they agreed to go in by different doors – he through the main entrance and she from the parking lot at the back.

Max wanted to see his star surgeon at work, so he too rose early and arrived at the operating suite at 6.30 a.m. He told one of the nurses to help him into a gown and point him in the direction of the scrub room. Weiner was there, washing his hands in the almost scalding water, and so was some other young woman.

They both turned, surprised to see him. Weiner looked stunned when he saw what he was wearing. "Max? What are you doing here?" The M&M meeting had been bad enough. This man was everywhere.

"You can't come in here," added the other young woman. "Surgical staff only – right, Dr Weiner?"

"What are you?" Max said. "A nurse?"

"A doctor. Emily Craven, MD. Surgical resident." Max waved her away.

"Dr Craven's right, Max," said Weiner. "Surgical staff only. That's the rule."

"Milton," he said, "I don't think you understand something. I run this hospital. I go wherever I like."

Weiner drew himself up to his full five foot four-and-a-half inches. "I'm still Chief of Surgery, I think?"

"Sure," Max agreed. "Surgically you're in charge. For the time being. Within certain economic guidelines, of course."

At once Emily saw which way the wind was blowing. "I'm sure there's no real problem in your being here in the OR, Mr Green."

"Hey! Smart chick!" Max smiled at her, ignored Weiner's dirty look and made a play of consulting his files. "So, Milty, I thought we'd have a word about your first surgical case this morning. The patient may not be good for the co-pay."

"I can't help that. She's sick."

"HP," Max said.

"HP?"

"Her problem. Not mine. There's a limited budget here. I've been told second generation penicillins are five times cheaper than fifth generation cephalosporins."

Emily Craven said, "That's right, sir."

"A drug company rep gave you a fact sheet?" Weiner sneered. "I hope you got the free pen."

He still doesn't get it, thought Max. *How the fuck can you be so dumb and still be a surgeon?* "Dr Weiner," he said. "Listen carefully. You may continue to work at Samaritans only if you abide by the new rules."

"What new rules?"

"I'm making one right now: this patient gets minimal nursing. No more. Then you are going to send her home. Is that clear?"

Before Weiner could respond, Andrew Sharp strolled in. "Hey Max! Thanks for dinner. Good morning Emily. How are you?"

"Good morning Andrew," she replied with what looked suspiciously like a smirk. "Fine, thank you."

"Sleep well?"

"Hardly at all," she said. "But I'm really energized this morning."

"I can give you something for that, if you like. I'm a doctor."

"You gave it to me already, thank you." A conspiratorial smile.

"And what the hell are you doing in here, Max?" Andrew asked.

"Precisely!" Weiner pouted. "He should not be in here."

"Right," agreed Andrew. "You ought to be out shopping for my Porsche." Emily's eyes widened and Weiner looked bewildered.

"But," continued Andrew, "if you want to learn about cardiothoracic surgery, Max, go ahead and scrub up!"

"No thanks," Max said. The thought of being up close and personal with actual bloodshed had made him change his mind. "Okay, everyone, let's get this moving. Time is money. Chop-chop." He strode out, looking busy.

*

Five hours later, Andrew returned to his office. "I'm celebrating," he told Cathy.

"Celebrating what?"

"I did it! I broke this hospital's record for the fastest ever heart transplant."

"Fantastic!" said Cathy. "How's the patient?"

"Alive and well, surprisingly." Andrew grinned and made himself an espresso from the big shiny machine Max had installed for him. "Any messages?"

"There's one from the CEO. He wants to know if you like green?"

"What's that about? Environmentalism isn't his thing, surely?"

"Perhaps it's some odd way of asking if you like him, since that's his name."

Andrew shook his head. "He's a narcissist, he assumes I like him. What did you tell him?"

"I said I thought you'd like green as it's the color of money."

Andrew was pleased that she was cheeky. That was usually a flirtatious sign. "Do you think money is that important to me?"

"Since you ask, yes."

He took a sip of coffee. "Hmm. Do you have dinner plans?"

"Yes I do," she said.

"How about tomorrow?"

"I have dinner plans every night."

"Oh. You have a boyfriend?"

"There is a boy I see every night, yes." She hesitated. "Can I ask you something?"

"Go ahead."

"Is it okay with you if I don't wear this miniskirt to work now?"

"What's it got to do with me?"

"Mr Green told me to wear one for your arrival. He also told me to keep the top buttons of my blouse unbuttoned."

"Are you kidding me?"

"No. He said it was until you signed your contract."

"Wear whatever you like. Though, I must say, you do look hot."

"You're not allowed to say that. You're not allowed to tell me I'm attractive, good-looking, sexy, easy on the eye, or that my legs look great."

"Nice rack?"

"No." She was cool. "The only compliment you're allowed to give me is that I look healthy."

"Since you know the harassment laws so well, why did you agree to wear these…

healthy clothes if you don't want to?"

"Jobs aren't so easy to find right now. I don't want to lose this one."

"I see." Andrew brooded for a moment. "You know what you said about me liking green because it's the color of money?"

She nodded.

"I had a big financial struggle to go to college and medical school, you know. I had to get scholarships and I still have loans to repay. It's going to take until I'm nearly forty."

"Poor you," she said.

"I'm just explaining why I want to make serious money, that's all."

"You don't have to explain yourself to me."

He knew that. Why was he doing it? "Can you give me a lift home tonight?"

"Sure," she said. "But I have to leave punctually at six."

"Um… okay." Andrew felt that he wasn't in control of this relationship. But oddly, he didn't mind.

*

After Cathy dropped him at his apartment building she collected her five-year-old son from his play date and drove to their one bedroom in Anacostia. She asked Ben about his day. About school. About how his history class went. He was tired and not interested in talking much. When she got home she made him a burger and fries. He poured ketchup all over it and ate with enthusiasm. She sat and watched him, full of love.

"Good?"

"Yeah."

"Ice cream to follow?"

"Ye-eah!"

"Yeah what?"

"Yeah please."

She stood and headed for the fridge. She felt her son's eyes on her. She was still in the miniskirt, five-inch heels and low-buttoned blouse.

"Mom?"

"Yes?"

"You look really cool today."

She sighed. "Men!"

13

Mrs May Jefferson leaned against the wall of the emergency room, still waiting to see a doctor.

Jordan Waters, still on duty, wondered why she didn't sit down. But she knew how Mrs Jefferson felt. Jordan's own mom had traveled the same road from South Carolina in the late sixties and had told her the stories many times. Her mom had waited for space at the crowded "colored" section of lunch counters. She had waited for the National Guard so that she could go to school, and waited for her father to come home after he looked the wrong way at a white woman.

He never did.

Jordan felt guilty that she had never expressed enough sympathy for what her mom went through when she was alive. Now she was dead and it was too late. Mrs Jefferson brought all those uncomfortable regrets to mind, but Jordan was determined to look forward, not back. She had pulled herself up from poverty, she had a decent job and, though she would help the homeless, the poor and the uninsured patients all she could, her first commitment was to running the ER with efficiency. She saw no contradiction in this and she would not put herself at risk, but she knew May Jefferson was distressed.

The ER was filling up again. Many others had been seen by doctors and she was still waiting. "Excuse me, ma'am," she began.

Like a bartender at a crowded bar, Jordan had tried not to catch her eye, but eventually there was no avoiding it. "Yes, Mrs Jefferson?"

"I've been here for hours, and I'm in pain. Nobody has seen me yet."

"I told you it would take a while."

"How much longer?"

Jordan looked around the ER. "It should be only another… uh… five or six hours." There were tears in Mrs Jefferson's eyes. "Just sit there, okay?"

"I can't sit any longer. I have a hip problem and my back's in a spasm. That's why I'm here!"

"Can you lie down?"

"Yes, I could."

"Okay, we'll find you something." She sighed, and looked around to see if there was a spare gurney somewhere as, amidst much commotion and hurly-burly, some paramedics rushed in the latest patient on one and skidded to a halt right in front of her.

"Heart attack," they shouted.

A team of doctors and nurses appeared from nowhere and immediately started pounding the patient's chest.

"Stop!" shouted the paramedics. "We did all that. His heart's beating now!"

Jordan noticed Blanche Nunn watching everything from a distance, making notes on her tablet, sidling over to listen as the other paramedic asked, "Any available beds?"

"I'm sorry," said Jordan. "We have hotel rules now. No check-in before four p.m. Checkout before ten a.m. No late checkout without paying for the next night."

Blanche nodded her silent approval.

The stricken patient lifted his head from the gurney and asked in a weak voice, "Are you kidding me?"

"No sir," said Jordan.

"Isn't it after four p.m.?"

"It's three thirty-seven."

"Do you know who I am?"

"No sir. Who are you?"

"Victor Stone. *Now* do you know who I am?"

"Yes. Victor Stone. You just told me."

"But do you know who I *am*?"

Jordan looked around for help. "Is this some kind of riddle?"

Victor Stone lay back on the gurney, stunned. "She doesn't know who the fuck I am."

"Who the fuck are you?" said a nearby patient, avidly following the conversation.

Jordan said, "Mr Stone, as it's after three, I'll do my best to check you in." She picked up a form. "But before we go any further, do you have insurance?"

"The real question," said Victor, "is does this hospital have any insurance?"

71

"Occupation: Lawyer," Jordan murmured as she wrote it on the admission form.

"You'll sure as hell know who I am by the time I'm finished with you."

Blanche appeared at her shoulder. "Jordan, haven't you seen Mr Stone's reality show?"

"A TV program?"

Jordan felt Blanche's hand on her elbow and she eased her to one side.

"This gentleman's a celebrity lawyer," Blanche whispered, "with his *own show*. He could sue the shit out of us. The cost would be enormous and the publicity would be catastrophic."

"I'm just following the new rules."

"I know. I'm going to go find Max. Just… don't upset this patient more than you already have, okay?"

As Blanche hurried away from the counter, Mrs Jefferson grabbed her arm. "Excuse me… you look like you're in charge here. Can you help me?"

"I'm not medical. Nurse!"

A nurse hurried over. "Yes, Ms Nunn?"

"This woman wants to talk to you." Blanche pried May's fingers off her arm and hurried away.

"What do you want?" asked the nurse, not unkindly.

"Please…" begged Mrs Jefferson. "Can't you find me a doctor?"

"I'll try. But several emergencies have come in in the last little while."

"I'm in a lot of pain."

"I understand, but that's not the same as life or death. We'll get help for you as soon as we can."

14

Blanche found Max in his office, and told him about Victor Stone's arrival in the ER. "He was really angry."

"Where's Andrew Sharp?"

She didn't know so they called his office. Cathy picked up. "He's operating."

Max said, "Get him out of there. We need him in the ER."

"I don't think I can, Mr Green, he's in the middle of major heart surgery."

"I don't want your opinion, I want you to do as you're told." Max hung up and looked at Blanche. "She wasn't helpful. We'd better get over to the operating suite ourselves."

They hurried along the wide corridors with the faint, familiar odor of recently sprayed air freshener. "This incident," he said, "demonstrates that the ER automatically opens us up to lawsuits. We have to look at the big picture – the ER is not only a luxury we can't afford, it's a bag of snakes. I checked, and do you realize we have more lawsuits stemming from emergency care than anything else?"

"I do," said Blanche. "But Max, you have to look at the bigger picture. Closing it would cause an uproar in the community, and we need all the donations and grants and tax breaks we can get. There are so many other departments we could close down that DC and the media wouldn't even notice."

"Write me a paper on that. We may have to close them too."

"Wait," Blanche persisted. "There are other ways to make the ER a better business proposition. For example, right now we lose a whole lot of money on trauma patients, but we could just add a trauma activation fee to all those bills."

"For how much?"

"Say… ten thousand dollars?"

"Can we get away with that?"

"Easy."

"With Medicare?"

"With Medicare, not sure. With insurance companies, no problem."

"Fine. Do that, until we find a better long-term solution."

When they reached the operating suite, Max and Blanche were surprised to find Cathy there already. "I want to talk to Dr Sharp," said Max. "Not you."

"They won't let you."

"The duty nurse buzzed me in earlier today."

Sheila intervened. "That's why I'm here now, Mr Green. I'm the head nurse. I'm sorry, but I can't let you in the OR right now."

"I warned your nurse earlier today that if she didn't let me in, she'd be fired."

"Dr Weiner fired her because she *did* let you in."

"Are you kidding me?"

"No sir. I would not joke about a thing like that. She shouldn't have done it."

"Look," said Max, trying to control his impatience, "I appreciate you're following the rules. Gold star. But listen carefully: I'm the boss here."

"Dr Weiner is my boss, sir."

"Wrong. I'm the CEO, the captain of the ship. I'm the boss of the whole schmeer, so I'm your boss too, okay? Get it? Now, Victor Stone, the celebrity attorney – you've heard of him, right? – is in the ER with a suspected heart attack. He may need a quadruple bypass, for all I know. Dr Sharp is the Head of Cardiothoracic Surgery and I need to speak with him *right now*."

"I'm sorry, sir, but they're at a critical moment in the surgery he's performing."

"But there's an *emergency* in the emergency room."

"Sounds like the right place for it," Cathy said.

"You, shut the fuck up!" Max snarled.

"Please drop this, Mr Green," said Sheila. "I can't let you in. It's impossible."

"It's not impossible. You just won't do it."

"Why is it so urgent?" said Cathy, apparently refusing to shut the fuck up. "Is it because Victor Stone is rich?"

"Not just rich. Everything that goes with it: famous, influential, important. He's a big enchilada!"

"I'll bet," Cathy said, "that whoever's on the operating table thinks *his* surgery is pretty important too."

Max scowled at her. "I don't like your attitude," he said.

She shrugged.

Now he liked her attitude even less. He turned to Sheila and told her that if she wanted to be head nurse for much longer, she'd better open the fucking doors.

She shrugged too.

"This is a formal warning," he told her.

Sheila stuck out a truculent chin. "Let me get this straight," she said. "My choice is that I let you in and Dr Weiner fires me – or I *don't* let you in and *you* fire me?"

"I'll see that Weiner doesn't fire you. Just let me in."

"I can't do that. A patient's life is at stake."

"And downstairs too. A VIP patient. Let someone else take over in there."

"Who?"

"We have other cardiothoracic surgeons."

"Not like Dr Sharp. And not available instantly."

"This is a business decision. In business you have to prioritize."

He pushed Sheila out of the way and pulled the door handle. The door didn't move. He pushed, then pulled, then pushed again.

Sheila failed to suppress a smile. This enraged him. "What's your name?" he snarled.

"Sheila."

"Your full name."

"Sheila McIntyre."

"Open this door immediately, Sheila McIntyre, or you will be downsized!"

"If you downsize me for doing my job, you'll have a nurses' strike on your hands!"

A couple of janitors were passing by, pushing a large biological waste bin. They hesitated. It was clear that they had heard her. "You hear that? You hear what she just said?" Max asked them. "Threatening a strike?".

They nodded.

"Perfect! I have witnesses. Gimme your names." As he wrote down their names he said to Shelia, "You are *so* fired!"

Inside the OR, the shouting and thudding against the outer door, though muted, had been heard. "What was all that noise?" asked Andrew, working fast. "Clamp."

"Clamp," repeated the circulating nurse as she handed one to him. "I think it's the new CEO, trying to break in."

"You serious?"

"Yes sir," said the nurse.

"Ignore it," said Andrew.

"What I respect about you, Dr Sharp," said Emily Craven, "is your sense of what's really important."

Lori Diesel gazed at the Styrofoam ceiling tiles that lay between her and the heavens.

"I deeply respect your strength, your confidence," Emily continued.

She makes me feel tired, thought Andrew. "Emily, would you like to close today?" he said. "I think it might be good practice for you."

"Anything, Andrew. Just tell me what you want and I'm there for you."

"Suction!" said Lori.

Andrew's eyes twinkled at her over his mask.

15

Mrs Jefferson was lying down, not yet in a cubicle but in the crowded corridor that led back to the main hospital, which her gurney slightly blocked. A young nurse with a needle and swab on a tray arrived to give her an injection. She asked the old lady to roll over onto her side, and pull up her skirt.

"Please explain, dear. Who are you?"

"I'm a nurse."

She had a soft voice and Mrs Jefferson was a little hard of hearing. "Not a doctor?"

"No. Please do as I ask."

"What are your qualifications? You a nurse practitioner, at least?" Mrs Jefferson had been in the hospital before.

"No, I'm a nurse nurse."

"Get me a doctor, dear, please?"

"I've been told to give you this shot."

"Who by?"

Max, hurrying into the ER, tried to get past them. "What's this? You got a problem? Because I'm in a hurry."

"This patient won't let me give her this injection."

"Why not?"

"I don't know."

"What is it?"

"A painkiller."

Max turned to Mrs Jefferson, "You in pain?"

"Yes. I've been waiting here for hours and—"

Max turned back to the nurse. "Give me that." He took the syringe. "In the buttock?" The nurse nodded.

"Who are you?" asked Mrs Jefferson. "A doctor?"

"Better than that. I'm the boss."

He rolled Mrs Jefferson over onto her side.

She cried out, "Ow. *Ow!*"

"Gimme a hand," Max told the nurse. He yanked up Mrs Jefferson's skirt. The young nurse pulled her underwear down a few inches and Max stuck the needle into her. He turned to the nurse. "What's so difficult?"

Handing the syringe back, he looked down at Mrs Jefferson. "Okay, dear?" He spoke loudly because he could see she was old. "See?" he said to the nurse. "She's so grateful, she's weeping." He raised his voice to her a little. "It was nothing. You'll feel better soon, dear."

He pushed the nurse aside and went in search of Victor Stone. Looking around the packed ER, he could see no sign of him. He asked Jordan Waters, who pointed to a cubicle and told Max there was no panic now as the ER resident had taken a look at him and didn't think it was a heart attack after all.

This was good news. Nevertheless, Max was pretty sure that some good PR was needed. He hurried to the cubicle where Stone lay, curtained off. At least, Max thought when he saw him, he's hooked up to all the appropriate machinery, plastic tubing inserted in the veins in his hands and electrodes stuck on all over his chest.

Victor was a bigger man than he expected from seeing him on the screen. He sported a pompadour haircut and had a large stubby nose with open pores. "Who the fuck are you?" he asked in an incongruous, high-pitched voice. "You a doctor?"

"Mr Stone, I'm Max Green, CEO of Samaritans. It's a pleasure to meet you."

"Oh yeah?"

"And I mean that most sincerely."

"Ow," Victor replied, as Max clasped the cannula embedded in the back of the legendary advocate's surprisingly dainty hand, in one of his most heartfelt and prolonged two-fisted shakes. "Careful...!"

"Sorry," said Max. "We are just so honored to welcome you to the Samaritans Medical Center. We'll admit you right away, of course, if any tests are necessary."

"About fucking time. I've been here an hour."

"But I gather," Max continued, undeterred, "that it's probably not a heart attack. Great news."

Stone looked embarrassed. "I ate too much cheese last night. Gave me palpitations. Happens."

"A cheese attack?" said Max with a big smile. "That's a new one! *Much* better than a heart attack."

"I got allergies. That's not unusual." Victor Stone, in defensive mode, explained that he couldn't eat shellfish, eggs, eggplant, peanuts and many other things, but his hosts at the previous night's dinner party had forgotten; bread and cheese was the only food on offer that he could eat. And since he was hungry, and bored by the company, he ate a great deal of it: Brie and Camembert, Stilton and Double Gloucester, Gouda and Gorgonzola. He woke up with every known symptom of a heart attack: chest pain, a pain in the middle of his back, a pain his left arm, palpitations and tachycardia.

Max knew Victor wouldn't stay on the defensive for long. It wasn't his style. And he was right. "Samaritans will be hearing from me about your ridiculous new check-in rules."

"But I understand you were examined the minute you got here."

"I had all the symptoms of a heart attack. Who knew it was the cheese?"

"Fortunately, our doctor knew. But we'll make a special deal on your charges."

"You bet you fuckin' will."

"And Mr Stone, I have an additional proposition for you – one that could benefit both of us greatly."

Stone raised a skeptical eyebrow.

Max smiled. "You have a number of outstanding lawsuits against this hospital. But may I ask you a question? Why would you ever want to sue us?"

"Why wouldn't I? On behalf of all the malpractice patients who deserve compensation, that's why."

"But you know we don't have any money. And you sue Samaritans even when there hasn't been even a hint of malpractice. You sue us whenever you can possibly find an excuse."

"What's it to you? Your insurance pays."

"Not for much longer. We have so many lawsuits, our insurance is through the roof. It's so high that we can't afford the same level of coverage. If patients keep suing us we'll have to find the extra money by shutting down the trauma center and the ER."

"That's your problem."

"No," Max said. "That would be *your* problem. Because no emergency care and fewer patients will mean fewer lawsuits for you. You're killing the goose that lays the golden egg."

Max could see Victor hadn't thought about it like that.

"What are you suggesting?"

"Don't sue us. Sue the doctors instead. Doctors have access to money through their insurance, and there are so many of them that the load is spread. Amortized."

"Why would I agree not to sue you too?"

"Because in return for not suing Samaritans, I could refer all patients with a grievance against their doctors to you. That way we both do well. We could even give each other referral fees."

For the first time that day, Stone was amused. "You know what? You're the first hospital administrator I ever met who's also an ambulance chaser."

"That's not me," said Max. "Wrong. Totally wrong. That's not who I am. You'd be suing anyway. I'm simply aiming you at a more lucrative target. Plus, I can give your office all our debt collection suits if you like. Interested or not?"

Victor Stone licked his lips. In Max's book, that meant he was very interested indeed. After he left the cubicle he beckoned Jordan Waters. "Mr Stone in there, he's a VIP attorney. Get him anything he wants, high-speed internet connection, drinks, girls—"

"Girls?"

"Uh – you know, nurses. Female nurses. Nice ones. With, uh, open minds, get it?"

Jordan didn't get it. "You mean, nurses who don't mind lawyers?"

Max sighed. "Yeah, okay, find a couple of pretty ones for now, okay?"

16

Andrew Sharp sat at his computer late that afternoon, reading reports from radiology and the path lab. Cathy was across the room, printing out the paperwork when Max popped his head round the office door.

"You busy?"

"Yes," said Andrew. "But come in and sit down."

Max brandished a bottle of Dom in one hand and threw Andrew a key fob with his other. "We are celebrating! Your Porsche is parked out front."

Andrew was completely surprised. "Max… I was joking about the Porsche."

"You don't want it now?" Max's mood changed. There was suddenly something intimidating about him. "I went to a lot of trouble to get this, buddy."

Andrew's incredulity turned briefly to delight, then, under Cathy's cold stare, embarrassment. "Well… uh… thanks…"

"My word is my bond," said Max. "Never forget that, Andrew. Ever."

Andrew felt Cathy's blue eyes turn a couple of shades more icy as Max popped open the Dom with a practiced flourish. Perfectly chilled champagne filled two of the four flutes on Andrew's bar.

Max handed a glass to him, clinked it against his own, and sat back in one of the overstuffed armchairs. "This is good," he said. "This is just how a hospital ought to be. A place where you feel better. Nice and relaxed, know what I mean?"

Cathy shook her head slowly in wonderment, but Max didn't appear to notice. "So, tell me about Victor Stone's condition. It's not serious, right?"

"I don't know yet," said Andrew. "I haven't examined him."

"He told me it's a false alarm. A cheese attack." He laughed.

"Could be," said Andrew, but he had a bad feeling about the ER resident's diagnosis. "The heartburn explanation doesn't quite add up. We need to do some tests to make sure."

Max wasn't worried. "Fine. In the meantime I gave Victor Stone the VIP check-in: pretty nurses, frequent flyer miles, flowers, fruit, the works. I told him I'd find him a host. A hostess might be even better."

"A hostess?" Andrew asked.

"Yeah, you know, a nice chick. Easy to find, they have websites now."

Cathy's mouth fell open in horror.

Andrew was painfully aware of her. He said, "We'd better make sure there's nothing wrong with his heart first…"

"Okay," Max said. "Now, moving right along, there's something important I want to share with you. And celebrate. I made a major bet with Bill More at our biggest big insurance company, American Health. We now have a plan, a rock-solid financial guarantee, to take care of five hundred thousand people for two years for a set amount of money, whether they're sick or not. Here's what's great about the deal: if we do it for less, we win."

"What if we don't?"

"Don't what?"

"Do it for less."

"They win."

"What are the odds?"

"The odds are on our side or I wouldn't have made the bet. The point is, if we do it for less, on average, *we keep the difference*. 'Course, I had to pitch it low, so the downside is we may lose if we order unnecessary tests."

"What if they're necessary?" said Cathy.

"What?" He looked at her, then back at Andrew, raising his eyebrows to indicate he couldn't quite grasp why an assistant was joining in the conversation.

"I said," repeated Cathy quietly, "what if tests are necessary?"

"What do you think, I'm some kind of monster? If tests are necessary, we do them." Max sipped his champagne. "So long as we can afford them, of course."

Cathy stared at him with withering, undisguised contempt. He turned to Andrew. "May I have a word with you?"

"Aren't you doing that already?"

"Just you."

"Sure. Cathy, would you mind?"

"Happy to go." She stood up and headed for her cubicle outside the office.

"Leave the door open," said Andrew, who liked the breeze.

"No, shut it," said Max. As soon as she did so, he could no longer contain his rage. "That young lady is highly disrespectful to me. I want her fired."

"Who? Cathy? You chose her."

"I know. I gave her this plum job. I made a mistake. My fault. She's history, okay?"

"What's she done wrong?"

"She refused to follow my instructions. She was insolent and disrespectful."

"Really? I've never experienced that. When? What about?"

"That's not the point."

Andrew thought for a moment, then stood up, went to the door and opened it. "Cathy, come in please."

She stood and followed him into the room.

"Max tells me you refused to follow some instructions he gave you."

"That's true," Cathy agreed.

"Why?"

"He ordered me to get him into your operating room while you were in the middle of mitral valve surgery. I refused."

Andrew looked at Max for his response. "It was urgent," Max said. "It was for the good of the hospital. I needed to tell you about Victor Stone."

Andrew looked back at Cathy, inviting her to respond.

She obliged. "I asked Mr Green if he wanted you to abandon the surgery you were in the middle of, to attend to another patient, Victor Stone, just because he's rich. Mr Green said yes, that was the reason. And then he said he didn't like my attitude."

"Thank you, Cathy," said Andrew. "You can wait outside."

She left the room, this time leaving the door ajar so she could hear the rest of the conversation from her desk.

"I guess there's nothing more to say," said Andrew.

"She doesn't get it," agreed Max. "She doesn't understand economic and business priorities. She's got to go."

"No Max, *you* don't get it. She stays. Or I go too."

Max stared at him. "Are you kidding me?"

83

"No."

"Wait a minute! There must be something else going on here that I don't know about. Are you fucking her?"

"I am not. I suggest you talk to her yourself if you have a problem." He put down his champagne. "I'm going home."

Max looked bewildered. "Wait a minute! What's this about, Andrew?"

"I guess I just don't like unfairness." Andrew put on his coat and walked out.

"You didn't have to do that for me," Cathy said as he passed her desk.

He stopped.

"I didn't," he said. "I did it for myself."

"Well – thank you, anyway."

"And I did it for your kid."

Cathy was surprised, "How d'you know I have a kid?"

"It's kind of obvious. That's the boy in your life who you have dinner with every night. Right? He's the one you need the health insurance for?"

"Yes."

"Good night, Cathy."

*

Max, standing alone in Andrew's office, still holding his champagne, overheard their conversation. He didn't know what to make of Andrew's gross ingratitude. And right after he gave him a Porsche!

There was only one possible explanation. Andrew must think this was a way to her heart. From there, it would be a short journey into her panties. He understood that. Cathy's cute, he thought. But whatever it was, Max felt that Andrew was going to be an important ally in the struggles that lay ahead so he needed to fix the situation right away.

He went to the door. Cathy was at her desk, but Andrew was gone.

"Cathy." He smiled at her. She eyed him with suspicion. "Come in here. I'd like to talk to you." He went back into Andrew's office, picked up the Dom and poured some for her. "Champagne?"

"No thanks." She stood in the doorway, deadpan.

"Come in. Close the door. Sit down," he said. "Please?"

She was reluctant, but she did so.

He offered champagne once more. She didn't take it. "I can see," Max began, "that I have been insensitive."

She said nothing.

"I'd like to apologize. I didn't know that you have a child. Tell me about him."

"Nothing to tell."

"There must be something. What's his name?"

"Ben."

"Ben? That's a nice name." She still said nothing. "Does he need health insurance for anything in particular?"

"He needs eye surgery. The insurance companies won't take him on at a price I can afford. They find one excuse after another. I guess that's why it's called health insurance – you can only afford it when you're healthy."

"Cathy," Max said, sincerity at full blast, "I'm going to make you a promise: so long as you work at Samaritans, Ben will always have full health cover. No matter what it costs."

"Thank you. I have that now. That's why I haven't left."

"All I ask in return is that you keep an open mind about me and what I'm trying to do here. I'm not such a bad person really."

Once again she said nothing.

"But remember," he added. "Now you owe me."

She was cool. "I won't sleep with you, if that's what you mean."

Max was affronted. "That's not what I meant. I would never dream of having sexual relations with an employee of the hospital."

17

Still concerned about Victor Stone, Max returned to the crowded ER, pushing through the jostling patients and the nurses. He glanced around seeing only a disaster area, a minefield of accidents and future lawsuits.

Paramedics wheeled in the latest strokes, gunshot wounds and stabbings. Max passed old Mrs Jefferson, still lying on her gurney, still asking anyone in scrubs to find her a doctor. Max didn't notice her this time. "I'm busy at the moment, dear. But I'll find you someone as soon as I can," a helpful nurse told her as he hurried by.

Blanche was at reception. "Oh, hi," she said. "I dropped in to check up on Victor Stone."

"Me too," said Max.

"He's in that cubicle – but don't go in. I had a good conversation with him. He's interested in your idea."

Pleased and relieved, Max followed her advice and took her for dinner instead. He told her about the commercial he was shooting the next day. He had always admired the old ads for the Tropicana, one of his rival casino hotels in Vegas. They showed blue skies, men in tropical suits and women in revealing costumes hanging out to the sound of a Caribbean steel drum band, and Max decided this would be the perfect way to market Samaritans. Make the place look more like a fun resort.

He would dress in a white linen suit and be the pitch man. The ad agency had liked the idea, and the time had arrived to film the first one.

Early in the morning the crew met outside the front of the hospital. A couple of attractive models were dressed like nurses – not like real nurses in ugly, shapeless green scrubs, but fantasy, naughty nurses in white uniforms with red crosses on the front, and short skirts.

The director chose the angle, picking the side of the crumbling building that was the least dilapidated. It had a view of the massive SAMARITANS sign, high on the roof in the distance above Max's head. Unfortunately the director was oblivious to the hospital's ongoing needs and the chosen location was right outside the arrival doors of the ER.

Max thought it would be good to shoot in the sunshine, but the director of photography refused. There would be nasty black shadows over the eyes, he said. Instead he erected a huge, white silk shade, suspended from four poles at the corners, so that Max wouldn't have to squint when he looked into the lens. They would keep the very wide shot, which would be done without the big silk, for late in the day when the sun wouldn't be directly overhead. The light would be warmer and the shadows soft.

Max's lines were on cue cards. The director assured him that no one would be able to tell he was reading. They rehearsed a couple of times, then everyone got ready for the shot. His face was powdered to neutralize the shine from the heat, and he stood on his mark.

"Action," commanded the director.

At that moment a distant siren began to wail. "Cut," said the sound man.

"What's the problem?" asked Max.

"Sound," said the sound man.

Max was so used to sirens that he hadn't even noticed. It got louder and louder. The crew waited. Finally the ambulance raced around the corner but was forced to slow down as the driver saw that the driveway to the ER entrance was blocked.

"Tell them to turn off that thing so we can get this show on the road," ordered Max. A skinny young PA with a ponytail hurried over and had a word with the paramedic driver. Then she ran back. "He says he must get to the ER, he has an urgent case on board."

"Who?" asked Max. "Anyone important?"

"He didn't say."

"Tell him we'll just do this shot first. Won't take long." Max nodded at the director.

"Roll it," said the assistant director.

"Action."

Max was a natural. He read the cards like a news anchor. "Nobody wants to be in the hospital longer than necessary. If you need surgery, it's easy: arrive in the morning, head home by five. But if you do have to stay longer, why not enjoy it? We have a business center for patients. And a spa."

At this point the models dressed as nurses joined him in the shot. One blonde, one brunette. Perfect teeth. Perfect smiles. Long legs. They put their arms around him and giggled at the camera.

"Delightful nurses to attend to your every need," he continued.

"Hi," they chirped. "Your every need."

"And don't forget our special offers: a discount for every fiftieth surgical patient!"

"Cut," said the director. "Do you think we'd better let the sick people through?"

The giant silk was hastily dismantled and moved out of the way and the ambulance nosed past the film crew to the doors. Max buttonholed the director. "Was that okay?"

"Great," said the director.

"Do we have to put up this shade again?"

"We had to shift it anyway, because the sun has moved. But we won't need anything so big now, because we move into a mid shot of you and the two girls. You know, waist up. Then we do it all again in close-up. Then we cut to the Happy Patient, with a cute nurse sitting on a hospital bed beside him. He'll be holding up a large piece of cardboard with 'Gift Certificate' written on it."

"I know," said Max. "I approved the script, remember?"

The shade was reassembled and they went on filming. Max did the mid shots a couple of times and then the last words in close-up. It was the logline, to which he had given much thought: *Samaritans Hospital: Making health care more responsive to patient choice.*

The director was delighted with Max's performance. "You know, you're genuinely good at this. You have a lot of charm. You could host a game show."

Not a bad idea, thought Max. *Maybe we can create a game show in Samaritans. Or better still, a reality show.* The director showed him the playback and Max was pleased. "I do have a lot of charm," he agreed. "Tell me, where did you find those chicks who played the nurses?"

"Modeling agencies."

Max asked a PA to find one of them, preferably the blonde, and bring her to talk to him before she left.

"Hi, Sugar," he said when she'd been found and delivered.

"Hi."

"Ever wanted to be a nurse?"

She giggled. "You mean, like, role-play?"

He was hooked. "Not quite what I meant, but I sure like that idea," he said.

She gave him her number.

As she left, Max saw Blanche near the Stephen P Murphy Revolving Door, named that week for a grateful and wealthy patient whose life Andrew had saved. Blanche was watching him with her most penetrating stare. He strolled over to her.

"Hey, Blanche?" he said. "What did you think?"

"I was spellbound," she said. "Blown away. It was so great!"

"What was?"

"Your performance. You! You were great!" She hugged him. "You're a genius, Max."

"Thank you, Blanche." Max was happy to be recognized as such. He actually felt it should happen more often.

"You're doing such a great job here," She seemed embarrassed. She hesitated, and backed away. "Your wife must be so proud of you."

"I'm not married, Blanche."

"Oh!" she said, "*Oh!*" flustered, but visibly delighted.

He realized she was flirting with him, which was a big surprise after all the Jesus stuff, but he figured that evangelicals have hormones too. Maybe more of them because they're so repressed. "Why did you think I was married?" he asked.

"I just assumed. How come no woman was ever able to land you? You must be quite a challenge."

"No challenge at all," he said. "I love smart women."

"Do you think I'm smart?"

"Very smart."

She kissed him on the mouth, tongue and everything. He thought, *she's serious about this*. "And you're very kissable as well," he told her, when he caught his breath.

18

Blanche went back to Max's apartment with him. He had found a spacious, open-plan penthouse well away from the hospital, just around the corner from Union Station in something they called the H corridor. Washingtonians considered it a classy neighborhood. Sidewalk cafés, bars, nightlife. He didn't have much time for that kind of thing, but a cool apartment with a great view impressed the babes and this one had huge windows with views of the Capitol and the Washington Monument. It also had a pool on the roof, although that was only good for a few weeks in spring and autumn. The winters were freezing and the summers hot and sticky, nothing like the dry heat in Vegas which Max much preferred.

"Washington," he confided to Andrew Sharp over a drink the next evening, "has typical east coast weather, hot and wet, which I like in a woman but not in a climate." He laughed at his own joke. Andrew smiled weakly.

The lobby of Max's apartment building was clad in wall-to-wall beige marble. He instructed the Samaritans Buildings Department to redecorate his apartment monochrome: black and white carpets, white leather sofas, black curtains, black and white towels in the master bathroom, and – in the bedroom – black satin sheets with white pillowcases. "Women think black and white is a cool design choice," he told his decorator from Vegas.

"That's interesting," said the decorator, thinking of all the women he knew who liked color.

Max said, "I have no interest in color at all except I like black chicks sometimes." He sniggered.

"Really?" The decorator was not that interested in Max's theories about women and Max found him uncongenial company. He sent him back to Vegas as soon as he could.

*

That evening, Max gave Blanche a warm welcome, turned the lights low and put Tony Bennett on the stereo iPod. She joined him on the sofa, nuzzling and kissing, and it wasn't long before they needed to loosen their clothes.

"Listen baby," murmured Max, "there's something I want to ask you."

"Mmm... yes...?"

"Besides the ER, what other departments could we close?"

Strangely, that broke the mood for Blanche. "Oh." She sat up. "Oh. Well, you know, there is one department where we can definitely economize."

Max was kissing her nipple. "What's that, baby?" he said in his sexiest whisper.

"O.B.G.Y.N. Forbid all abortions."

He was irritated, though he realised he should have seen it coming. "No way. Abortions are great, rapid turnover. It's a profitable segment."

She pushed him away. "The right to life! The right to life is paramount." Blanche had become suddenly emphatic and strident. "A hospital's duty is to protect life. There can be no exceptions."

Max saw that he was not going to get laid if he disagreed. "Okay, Blanche, if you feel that strongly."

"I do."

"Fine. Okay, I can live with that." He stroked her arm and soon she started kissing him again, unbuttoning the front of his shirt, all the way down his chest and belly. He lay back, relaxed. Her hand slowly unzipped his fly and slipped inside his pants.

"Giving birth, abortion," he mused, "there's no real difference."

"*What?*" She sat up. The mood evaporated again.

"From a financial standpoint, I mean," he said.

"Max, there *is* a difference. Whatever you believe personally, if we are solidly pro-life here it'll attract all the Republican money and conservative Christian donations. They have a lot to give."

"You're right. But I need some divestment."

"How about this?" Blanche smiled and slipped off her panties and waved them gently across his face.

"That's my kind of divestment," he said.

She sat carefully astride him.

"Mm. That's even better!" he murmured.

"Yes... oh yes! Max?"

"Yes baby?"

"You wanted to know about doctors who are not – *aahhhh!* – I've been through all the numbers – *ahh!* That's so great—"

"I love numbers too, baby—"

"Yes... yes... *ye-e-e-es!*" Blanche replied.

*

She stayed all night. It was a big success. In the morning, both of them wrapped in big, soft towelling bathrobes he had brought from The Lions' Den, Blanche watched Max make coffee in the kitchen while she sat on a dark gray stool and leaned her elbows on the light gray granite counter.

"Max? How did you get into health care?" She couldn't put it together. What sort of man was he? "It doesn't seem like your thing."

He smiled at her. "It started in Vegas. Well, really it started at Wharton, when I got a place at the business school. I had gotten straight As in college."

"Yay!"

"Then I worked at a bank – Goldman, actually – in those great, easy-money days before everybody began to suspect their motives."

"Those days are back now," she said. "At least, some people still suspect their motives but nobody cares anymore."

"Right," he said. "But I made a mistake: I went into private wealth management. I would have been good at it but I didn't know any wealthy people. I came from nothing. I thought Goldman would give me the clients, I'd be their investment advisor, and make a big commission. Plus the fat bonuses I always used to read about. But no, it turned out that I was just a junior salesman making cold calls to individuals and private corporations with such a high net worth that they had at least twenty-five mill in cash available to invest."

"And?"

"It was a tall order. I'm a good salesman – I'm a great salesman – but were those people going to respond to a cold call from me? No fuckin' way. If you have twenty-five mill in cash you already have your own people. Why would you give a shit about a kid straight from business school? You wouldn't, I wouldn't, and they didn't! So after a couple of years of schlepping and making jack shit, I moved on."

"To Vegas?"

"I saw an ad. The job was at a major casino, The Lions' Den, on the hotel operations side. I had always liked Vegas. I'd been there a million times. Slight exaggeration. But I'm a great poker player, I'm real quick at figuring out the odds in craps and I like blackjack too. When I went there as a civilian for the weekend, I usually won more than I lost."

"How?"

"Because I'm smart, that's how. I knew when to walk away. Anyhow, I applied for the job and I got it. I wasn't surprised. I've always gotten anything I applied for. Why not? I'm okay looking, I dress well, I'm six-one and a hundred and sixty pounds, I'm in good shape, good six-pack, I don't have male pattern baldness. Plus the bank gave me great references. I was honest, reliable, pleasant, hardworking and although I hadn't been much of a success finding individuals and corporations with high net worth and twenty-five mill in liquid cash to invest, I had also learned that *nobody* managed to do that unless they came from money. Or married it.

"Besides, the Vegas job was in management, not in sales. Well, everything is sales but it was called management. I started as a host. That means I took care of regular guests who gambled a lot. You know, there's some sort of myth that in Vegas they don't want people to win. That's a lie."

"Really?"

"You want them to win because then they keep coming back. Winning is the bait that hooks the fish. The odds favor the house so the casino makes plenty in the end."

"Winning is the loss leader?"

"Right. It gets you market penetration."

"I love penetration."

"I know you do, baby." He kissed her, long and slow.

"What does a host do?"

"Keep the guests happy." He nibbled her ear. "You send them a limo to meet them at the airport, you comp them a room or a suite if they play enough, you get them drinks, meals, women…"

"Women?"

"You think it's a sin?"

Blanche did think so, but she wasn't sure how to reply.

He looked her in the eye. "You think what we did last night was sinful?"

"Well, yes, I… I think I do…"

"Do you regret it?"

"No. But... maybe I should."

"Honestly?"

"I think..." *Time to confess.* "I think maybe it was really just lust."

"Certainly was," said Max with a smile. "I don't mind admitting it. Is that so terrible?"

"The Bible says—"

"Never mind that. Christians believe in love. I was expressing love for you. And you were expressing love for me, right?"

He seemed to be saying he loved her. "Yes. I was." She felt something like joy.

"I think God will forgive us for that, don't you?"

"I hope so. I think He will."

The coffee was ready. Max poured it for her. "I was telling you what a host does. You get your guests whatever they want. Within the law, of course."

"Is getting them women within the law?"

"In Nevada, more or less."

"What about drugs?"

"No hard drugs. I never touched that. And you never take a tip, it's against the rules and you can't do it on the sly because the CCTV cameras are everywhere and nothing goes unseen, believe me. But you can make a little arrangement with a guest so that they mail you some cash in an envelope a week or so after they leave. Nobody would ever know."

"You're so smart." She hesitated. "Did you have a girlfriend in New York?"

"Of course."

"Did you take her to Vegas?"

"No." He put down his mug of coffee. "I never took girlfriends there. The place is full of great-looking chicks with wet pussies interested in partying with rich guys. Why take a grain of sand to the beach?"

Blanche giggled. "That's a terrible thing to say." But somehow she didn't mind. In fact, it aroused her a little.

"I enjoyed Vegas. I rose pretty high. In a few years, maybe ten, I had become the general manager of hotel operations. I was on a big salary. But it didn't satisfy me. I'm an entrepreneur at heart. I don't want a ceiling on my income, I don't want to be an employee, a million two a year was good and Vegas was not an expensive place to live but I want the American Dream. All of it. And when I saw the ad for this job I realized Samaritans could be my route to the big bucks."

"How?"

"Stick with me, baby. You'll see. I think we'll make a good partnership."

"So do I, Max," said Blanche. "So do I!"

She was talking about the life partnership that she longed for. She didn't realize that he was just talking business.

19

Max explained his deal with Victor Stone to Blanche as he drove them to work. "We worked out an arrangement that could substantially reduce the number of lawsuits against this hospital. When patients check in, we simply add an extra form for them to sign."

Only an hour later he watched the plan being tested on May Jefferson when she was finally admitted. Dr Duff, the orthopedic surgeon, got around to seeing her late the night before and decided that she needed an immediate hip replacement, followed by lower back surgery if necessary. Although surgery is generally profitable there was a risk that her condition could become chronic and Samaritans didn't want consumers with chronic conditions. Max was happy because he had found a way to mitigate the problem, and he saw Jordan sign her in, watched by some new nurses-in-training.

*

"Mrs May Jefferson?"

"Yes?"

"I remember you," Jordan said. Nevertheless she checked the birthdate, according to the rules, to be sure she was the right Mrs May Jefferson. "Okay," she said. "Let's get the paperwork over first. Here are some forms you have to sign before they do the surgery."

"Just give me the pen."

"Not yet," the nurse said. "This form is called *Consent to Surgery*. This page informs you of the risks. And this one asks you to nominate your lawyer."

"Lawyer?" Mrs Jefferson was confused. "Why do I need a lawyer?"

"You don't, not right now. But if you do at any point in the future, the hospital recommends Victor Stone, and he will give you a twenty per cent discount if referred by us. That's huge. You should sign."

"But nothing's gone wrong. Or has it?"

"No, you're fine, this is just a formality, a helpful service we provide, to anticipate any patients' legal needs, if necessary. Do you want to read it?"

Mrs Jefferson lay back on the gurney. "Oh my God... how many pages?"

"Only nine. Just boilerplate."

"Boilerplate?"

"Means it's just routine. Everybody signs it." Jordan was encouraging. "I'll read you the important stuff. '*Possible surgical complications which could lead to lawsuits include infected wound, blockage of bowel, stroke, heart attack, blood clot to leg or lung, infiltrated IV*', and so on. All you have to do is check this box now, while you're still healthy, then everything's ready to sue the doctor later if you want to."

"What if I wanted to sue the hospital as well?"

May Jefferson was no fool. Jordan couldn't help admiring her. "You'll find Victor Stone doesn't recommend that."

"Why not?"

"The hospital doesn't practice medicine, the doctors do. We just give them the facilities."

"I see." Too weak for any further argument, Mrs Jefferson checked the box, and signed. Now she was ready for surgery.

*

Max threaded his way through the crush of waiting patients to Victor Stone's cubicle. The VIP lawyer was still wired up to heart monitors and connected to IVs. He looked pale, Max thought. His face was a sort of dirty white.

"Hi Victor. Just popped in to tell you our new little deal is working already. Everything okay with you?"

"Yes thanks," Stone said. "You can go now."

"Do you have everything you need?" Max asked. Stone held up his hand to silence him. "Well, let me know if there's anything I can do."

"There is one thing."

"What's that?"

"Go away!"

"Certainly."

Max backed out of the cubicle as if leaving the presence of royalty, and almost collided with a tall, skinny young man in a gray suit that hung off him.

*

Leo Pfiffig, energetic and determined, a recent graduate of Brooklyn Law School, found the gap in the curtains and peered through it. "How are you today, Victor?"

"Not so good. Don't know why. How's things at the office?"

"No problems. You're suing Samaritans, I suppose?"

"No Leo, I'm not."

Pfiffig was surprised. "You couldn't find anything they did wrong?"

Stone smiled his crocodile smile. "I couldn't find anything they did right! But this abattoir is run by an obliging fellow called Max Green and he likes to make deals."

"You scared him?"

"Shitless!" Victor sniggered. "Mind, it wasn't hard. We've cornered the market as far as this hospital's concerned."

"You'd rather make a deal than sue for malpractice?"

"If it's a better deal? Sure."

"Tell me about it," Pfiffig said.

20

Blanche Nunn felt alone and unloved. It was a chronic condition.

She had grown up without affection on a remote farm about fifty miles from Brownsville, Texas, on the Gulf Coast in a God-fearing family, fear being the operative word. The nearby town had been almost wiped off the face of the earth by a hurricane in the sixties and, although the sixties were over long before she was born and she had never experienced God's wrath directly, the threat that it might happen again hung over them all as the ultimate punishment for sin.

Her mom spoke maybe four or five brief sentences to her in a day, no more. Blanche understood now, after many years of working in hospitals, that she had been brought up by an autistic woman, but she as a child believed that her mom had no love for her. Her two older sisters, who had suffered the same lack of attention, were cold and hostile and gave her no support when, as a teenager, she had her first breakdown. She lay in bed and wept. Nobody really knew how to help her. Nobody understood her depression, least of all herself.

After some weeks she had dragged herself to a doctor, who gave her Prozac and told her to think positive. Her dad, whom she loved and who was the only person she could talk to, developed premature Alzheimer's around that time. Senility, they'd called it. He had stopped communicating with her, or anyone else.

She did her best to think positive and, desperately aware that if her life was ever going to get any better she had to excel academically, she found a new and focused energy. She graduated high school and went north to college in Amarillo, the hot, dry, meat-packing city in the Texas panhandle nicknamed "Bomb City" because it was where they assembled nuclear weapons.

She was not equipped to deal with life on her own. Fear of God and suspicion of other people had been so instilled in her that she shunned all boyfriends and remained isolated. But her combination of Nordic beauty and seemingly impenetrable loneliness proved irresistible to an amiable college athlete with freckles and an open honest face named Jim.

Succumbing to his persistence, his charming southern manners and her raging hormones, she endured her first sexual encounter.

It was painful, awkward and not in any way enjoyable, but the worse thing was the profound sense of guilt that enveloped her when Jim pulled on his jeans and T-shirt and went home immediately he was satisfied. Lying alone in her bed, with only her despair for company, she knew God would punish her.

And He duly did. She fell pregnant.

She had always been taught that the only form of acceptable birth control was abstinence, and she had not abstained. Legal abortions were hard to come by in Texas so, unable to face the disgrace of unmarried motherhood, she had one illegally.

This caused a septic infection which she ignored for as long as she could, but which, when the pain was too great to bear, sent her to the hospital.

Overwhelmed by shame, and by the dreadful feeling that she had murdered an innocent child, she lay alone in bed once more, this time for weeks. Jim the charming athlete never came to visit her. Nor did her mother, or her sisters.

She didn't want to go back to college when the hospital discharged her, and she couldn't go home. She lay down on the railroad track one evening in the twilight as darkness shrouded the desert landscape, but the 7.40 train was late and before it came along she was spotted by a pair of passing hikers who picked her up and took her along to their evangelical church. There she was introduced to a new and different sort of God.

"Man was made in the image of God, as the supreme object of God's creation," the Reverend Derwent Spittle told her. "But Adam and Eve became alienated from God through disobedience, and as a punishment we are all are born with a sinful nature and choose to sin against Him."

Blanche knew all that. It had been drummed into her that she had been born with a sinful nature. But Spittle helped her to understand that she was not responsible for her own bad ways. "Sin results in physical and spiritual death which cannot be overcome by human effort."

Hopelessly she replied, "If it can't be overcome by human effort, there's nothing I can do about it."

"But there is." Struck by her beautiful deep blue eyes, Spittle was determined to save her.

"You mean, by self-improvement or good works?"

"No, that won't do it. Salvation is God's only provision for the penalty of sin. Only by turning from sin and trusting in Jesus Christ alone for forgiveness can you be born again and have your relationship with God restored. And when you do that, since this restoration is based on God's grace and not on your effort, salvation – once gained – cannot be lost."

Salvation that could not be lost sounded right up Blanche's alley. She started attending his church every Sunday. And when he proclaimed to the congregation, "Among other things, the Christian should demonstrate a lifestyle of selfless service to others, influence those who have not yet trusted Christ to believe in Him, and seek to worship God both individually and corporately," her future course was clear.

Corporately. The word inspired her. It was the word of God, and from that moment on she knew that corporate life was to be her path. She studied hard at college, graduated *cum laude* and won a scholarship to business school where, like Max, she excelled. But how could she use her skills to help others? The Reverend Spittle confirmed that God had prescribed the answer: unregulated, free-market, corporate health care. She embraced it.

Now a successful business executive, her outward confidence had an electric effect on men. Imbued with strength by the Holy Spirit and by regular conversations in bed with the Reverend Derwent Spittle whenever he could get away from his wife and five kids to the local Motel 6, she discovered that the guilt she could never put behind her was greatly preferable to her previous helplessness. Though she didn't realize it, her guilt made her more powerful and more important. You can't feel irrelevant if you feel guilty.

She had learned for herself at last the truth that her doctor had told her when she'd had her teenage breakdown: if you can't change something, you can change the way you think about it. She felt gloriously free to experiment with sex now she understood that her salvation, once gained, could not be lost, and the Reverend Spittle was happy to aid her in all her sexual experiments.

Christianity was about care for others and she knew from experience that care was so much better if it was provided in a faith context. Social services made people fill in forms and give up their privacy to the government, but help from your church meant you were talking to another human being who cared about you. She read extensively about the world and learned about weak welfare states that provided for some but failed many. They would, she knew, be increasingly unable to provide for everyone in the future.

When she moved east she saw so many lost souls in big cities, people with no real hope, echoes of her former self, welfare dependent, not only because they lacked opportunity but also because they also lacked self-worth or a sense of purpose. She had pulled herself up by her bootstraps – they must too. No welfare system could teach people that.

Her life was good now. And yet, although she could say with honesty that she no longer felt guilty, and although her decision to be to be born again had improved her life, it had not quite done the trick. The feeling of being unloved still followed her around like a lame puppy. Sometimes, at night, she still felt alone and empty. Derwent Spittle was in Texas and still married with five children so that relationship was long gone. Her need for attachment, for love, for appreciation, was not fully satisfied by her love for Jesus or His love for her. She still felt the same desperate need to be wanted, nurtured and appreciated, to belong to a family or a man, maybe with a family of her own.

Many relationships and a couple of marriages had already failed because of her neediness. Only a man could help assuage that need, and it had to be the right man, someone who was a match for her intelligence, strong and totally sure of himself, a man without doubts, a confident man who knew who he was and what he wanted. For the first time in years she was within sight of happiness.

Maybe Max had been sent by God.

That Saturday night, after she had been particularly inventive sexually, Blanche asked him if he would go to her church with her the following morning.

*

Max, though enjoying his relationship with her both in bed and out of it, wondered if this was too high a price to pay.

He shook his head. "Church isn't really my scene, baby."

"I think you'd be surprised," she said, gently stroking his balls. "Don't you think I know what you like?"

"Uh… yes, I *know* you know what I like. In one department, anyway."

"You can't divide your life up into departments."

He considered that. "I can, you know."

"Just try it. What can you lose? An hour? You can afford that."

Max had to agree. And he had always been up for new experiences. So the next morning they set off together.

Max estimated there were two or three thousand people in the hall. He looked around. No crosses, no altar, no pulpit, just a stage where a band from Nashville (or so they said) was playing country music to warm up the crowd. A couple of hymns were sung, everybody applauded and then it was time for the main event: bursting with energy, the Reverend Barry Swallow bounced on to give the sermon.

Barry was short but handsome with thick salt-and-pepper hair and seemingly limitless energy, wearing a glistening light-gray suit, the sort that Max had worn in Vegas. A tiny microphone was hooked around his ear so that he could pace around the huge platform as he spoke like a TED talker. He was well amplified. "We are living in the church age," he began. "And we are moving inevitably towards the Rapture. When Jesus comes again, he will Rapture all true believers out of this world."

Not recognizing "rapture" as verb, Max wondered for a moment what that meant. An explanation was soon forthcoming.

"They'll just disappear, they'll go *up* to heaven with Jesus. And then—" the voice became dark and sombre, "—with the loss of Christian influence in the world, Satan will have free rein to take power. He will do it through a political leader called the Antichrist, who is then going to rule over the world for seven years. This period is called the Tribulation. This will happen." His voice rang with certainty. "Antichrist rule will lead to a series of wars which will culminate with Jesus coming with an army of saints and fighting the battle of Armageddon in the land of Palestine. Jesus will defeat the Antichrist, vanquish evil and establish a new kingdom. All of this has been prophesied in the Bible and *will* come to pass, and we are getting closer – and closer – and closer – to the Second Coming of Christ."

Blanche looked at Max to check that he was listening. He was trying to, but his eyelids were getting heavy. He was also wondering how long Blanche would want him to listen to this crap. It looked like the preacher was only just getting going. Some people, they puff themselves up like little frogs.

"All nations – yea, even America! – *all* nations are going to concede their power in the End Times to a totalitarian political leader who is the Antichrist. We are living in the last days; you're moving towards the End Times, and you must be suspicious and skeptical of *anything* that seems to undermine individual rights and individual liberties, anything that is going to give more power to the state.

"Why? Because in spite of the trials and tribulations to come, there is hope! There is joy! Jesus Christ will return soon to gather the Church to Himself and He will then establish a thousand-year reign on the earth. Everyone who has died will come back to life and those who have trusted Christ will be judged and rewarded. But—" and here he adopted a more threatening tone, "—those who have not believed will be judged and condemned: 1 Thessalonians, 4:13 to 5:11, and Revelations 20:1-6. We must save those souls."

Cries of "Amen" and "Hallelujah" echoed all around him.

"Am I supposed to be one of those souls?" whispered Max. Blanche nodded.

He tried not to laugh. "Oka-a-ay!"

Mr Swallow was now in full swing. "The Book of Revelations speaks of '*the mark of the beast*'. This mark was given to those who bowed and worshiped the image of Caesar, and those who received it are judged by God – Revelations, 14, 11."

Max looked around. The audience – perhaps he should call it the congregation – was rapt at the thought of the Rapture.

"I would not say," the Reverend Swallow continued, "that the Affordable Care Act was the mark of the beast, nor that our government leaders were *intending* to serve the Antichrist. Yet there is a principle here: Christians must not obey civil leaders who command us to disobey Christ, whether they intend this or not. I tell you that we must obey God, not man."

Max yawned. He'd got the point. Giving more power to the government was a bad idea. Especially Obamacare. No great insight there, but as Max looked around at the huge crowd that filled the purple plush seats, he couldn't help admiring the man's skill in monetizing his sales pitch even if his arrogance was a little off-putting. He yawned again.

Blanche was embarrassed by his obvious boredom. "He's talking about health care," she whispered. "This is about us."

"Sorry, but you exhausted me last night. You were fantastic, babe."

"*Ssshhh!* This is important. Look at him, not me. Didn't you hear what he just said about repealing Obamacare?"

"Babe, I didn't much like the Affordable Care Act either. But the Antichrist? Gimme a break!"

"You haven't been listening." She looked stern.

"I think I have. I got it all, believe me."

When they finally left the church they stopped in a café. Max ordered a latte for Blanche and a black coffee and a cheese Danish for himself.

"Blanche," he said. "If that stuff makes you happy, that's fine, but why did you think it would interest me?"

"Because it's really important—" she fixed a severe and intense gaze upon him, "—that you understand it."

"I understand it, babe. I just don't buy it."

"That means you don't get it. Don't you see? We must help the sick through Christian charity, not government programs. In Eastern Europe, in Poland, Christianity was the battering ram that tore down the walls of the Soviet Union. The defeat of communism."

"I thought it was Reagan."

"God, acting though Reagan! But the modern welfare state sees itself in the place of God, trying to meet people's cradle-to-the-grave needs. It has the opposite result: there's a mass of data showing that the decline of Christianity in the West can be correlated with the expansion of government."

"No kidding!"

"That's right. Satan inspired the utopian vision of Marxism, the scientific facade of secular humanism and the religious fanaticism of jihad. America must defend the Christian heritage with a strong military, gun rights, traditional values, unqualified support of Israel and small government. Charity depends on trusting the free market, which is divinely inspired."

"Wait! I'm lost. What's divinely inspired – charity, or the free market?"

"Both, obviously. The United States is one of the most modern *and* one of the most religious countries in the world. We have demonstrated how religion plus capitalism can provide a superb array of social services in the absence of an effective welfare state."

"Is there such a thing as an effective welfare state?" asked Max.

"That's the point! You know there isn't."

Max thought for a moment, "Free enterprise is the only way to financial success," he agreed.

"Right. And the secret to America's financial success," continued Blanche, "is its churches. Capitalism is God's ordained economic system. Capitalism is morally neutral, it's simply an efficient way of ordering economic production and exchange in a world of scarcity."

"I agree with that," said Max, surprised. "Is that what you've been trying to say?"

"Of course," she said. "Inequalities do exist, but they are divinely ordained. The Bible forbids any welfare program."

"It does?" Max was even more surprised.

"Yes. Because although cut-throat competition harms some people, it works out best for our society as a whole. Our whole system of government is based on the pursuit of self-interest. You've read Adam Smith? And Friedman? Hayek? We rely on a system of checks and balances to compensate for human depravity."

"True," said Max, struggling to keep track of her argument.

"As Jerry Falwell said, 'The free enterprise system is outlined in the Book of Proverbs.'"

That stopped Max short. He'd been to Bible class in his trailer park and he was pretty confident there was no mention of free enterprise in Proverbs. He concluded that she was back in cloud cuckoo land and decided to drop the subject. "Let's go, babe." He waved at the waitress and mimed signing the bill.

"Aren't you glad to know there's a moral, Christian basis for what we're doing at Samaritans?"

"Sure," he said, though to him it was a whole lot simpler. You have to make money. In order for there to be winners, there must be losers. That's capitalism. All the rest was bullshit. Max intended to be a winner but he didn't feel like arguing and he didn't care that she had revealed herself as barking mad. He just loved that she was so horny and, he thought, if this is the price for her continuing to have such great, uninhibited sex with me, okay, I'm quite happy to listen to ten minutes of Biblical yakkety-yak every now and then.

21

Warmed by the feeling that Max understood her and thought she was smart, Blanche phoned him first thing Monday morning. "I have new and useful information."

"Come on over and brain-dump," he said.

Happily she hurried along the admin corridor to his office, sat down and told him to switch off his phone and listen. "I have a great new idea that can make us a lot of money."

"Go on."

"We should open a hospice unit."

Max was appalled. "Are you *nuts*? A unit full of dying cancer patients? Chronic illnesses, lots of care needed... those are exactly the kind of cases that lose us money." He picked up his phone.

"Did you tell me I'm smart?" said Blanche.

"Yes, but—"

"Then turn off your phone and hear me out."

"Okay." He made a show of turning it off and slid it off the desk onto his knee. When it was out of sight he turned it back on.

"Turn off that phone, or I'm leaving. I want your full attention."

Like a naughty schoolboy, Max produced the phone from below the desktop and ostentatiously switched it off again. "This had better be good," he said. "Opening a unit for dying patients? I think you've lost your fuckin' mind!"

"What if they're not dying?" asked Blanche.

"What?"

"What if they're not dying? At least, not yet – not for quite a while? All they would need, to satisfy Medicare, would be a cancer *diagnosis*."

"I don't get it."

Blanche made her pitch. "Hospice care is a seventeen-billion-dollar industry, and it's dominated by for-profit companies. Last year, about fifteen billion dollars of hospice revenue came from Medicare."

"Hospices make money?"

"Tons of it. If the patients are really dying there are huge labor costs: pain specialists, counseling, round-the-clock nursing. But if they're not dying yet, the real costs boil down to occasional medical visits, basic nursing and accommodation. That's all available here already, in our overhead. It's already paid for. And in return, Medicare will pay us a hundred and fifty dollars per day, per patient."

"Even so... is that enough? We need our inpatients to be treated all the time. They're no use to us if they occupy beds without bringing in extra revenue."

"They will. We start bundling – we charge for the oncologists, the nursing staff and every kind of test you can think of. We can really pile it on."

"Have you run the numbers?"

"Sure. Major profit. But I didn't need to. At AseraCare, one of the biggest for-profit chains, hospice patients just keep on living. About seventy-eight per cent of patients who enroll at their branch in Mobile, Alabama, leave the hospice's care *alive*. That's according to their own stats. Some of them live for years longer."

Max was on his feet, pacing, excited. "Blanche, baby, this is fantastic."

"I knew you'd like it."

He stared out of the window but he didn't see the sycamores or the beeches, or the little thrush standing on the branch in the weak sunshine that was trying to break through the humid haze across the street. Instead, he saw a vision of himself running the largest health care empire in America. Then it vanished, suddenly. "There's a catch," he said, turning away from the window. "If all the patients stay alive, Medicare will figure out there's something wrong."

"You're right. Some of them have to die. We just have to do the numbers, to find the right quota. The right percentage."

"What about the others? How long can they stay before they're discharged, still alive?"

"A year."

"My God!" He smiled from ear to ear. "It's a gold mine."

"Yay, baby!" They high-fived.

"But how do the patients react when they're told they're not dying after all?"

"I should imagine," said Blanche, "that they're delighted. Wouldn't you be? *Huge* customer satisfaction."

"So…" Max was trying to get it all straight in his head. "Who determines which patients are 'dying'? Who decides which ones need hospice care?"

"Two oncologists have to sign off on admission."

"I see. I think I get It."

"What we do is open a big hospice ward and encourage the oncologists here to use it if there's any possible reason. Then we make sure that we have, say, twenty-five or thirty per cent of bucket cases amongst them. The rest are pure profit. They're just hotel guests."

"You're a wiz."

"There is one problem. We'll have to be just a little careful, as Asera has been sued by a few whistle-blowers."

"I can handle whistle-blowers." Max sat next to Blanche on the big soft black sofa. These numbers had really turned him on and she was looking irresistible. He started unbuttoning her blouse.

"Blanche," he murmured, "you are the greatest."

"Thank you," she said, and parted her legs.

22

"Thank you for standing up for me the other day," Cathy said as Andrew arrived for work one morning after a few days away at a conference. She had thought about him a lot since then. Had she misjudged him? Could it be that he was interested in somebody other than himself?

"It was nothing," he said.

"It was. You protected me from Mr Green and you didn't let him fire me."

"Couldn't let that happen. You'd been protecting me. I should thank you. It was the right thing to do so unfortunately I had no choice."

She looked at him with something resembling affection. She saw the vestige of a smile. He did have a choice, she knew that, and the choice he made had surprised her.

"Let's forget it," he said. Clearly he didn't want to pursue the matter. Was this tact, or embarrassment, she wondered, or had his interest in her problems now expired?

"Okay." But she wouldn't forget it.

"Cathy," he said. "Tell me, really, what do you think of Max Green?"

"You're asking me? Isn't he your new best friend?"

"I'm concerned about him pounding on the door of the OR the other day, trying to get in while I was doing a mitral valve surgery. Sounds crazy."

"Why don't you talk to Saul Tarnisch?"

"Who?"

"Head of Psychiatry."

"Can you get me his number?"

"He's always in the doctors' common room around one o'clock."

He'd never bothered to go there.

*

He poured some washed-out hospital coffee into a cardboard mug and poured some for Cathy too. Milton Weiner was there. Andrew called across the room. "Hey, Milton. Mr Chief of Surgery. Max Green tried to force his way into my OR during a mitral repair yesterday. Does he often do that?"

A morose, fat, bearded man was slumped in a nearby stuffed easy chair. "What do you care?" he muttered.

Cathy whispered, "That's Dr Tarnisch."

Andrew eyed him with caution. "You mean, the potential heart attack over there?"

She smiled and nodded.

"Excuse me…" Andrew strolled over to him. "Were you just speaking to me?"

"I guess I was," replied the morbidly obese shrink.

"I'm Andrew Sharp."

"I know who you are." He avoided Andrew's gaze.

"And you're Saul Tarnisch, Chief of Psychiatry?"

"I am."

"Saul, you asked me why I care…" Andrew pulled up a molded orange plastic chair and sat down. "Call me old-fashioned, but I worry about an unhygienic administrator bursting in on a patient with an open thoracic cavity."

"Okay," the sweaty shrink allowed with a judicious air, "I can see that."

"Max Green was pounding on the OR door. I'm wondering if he's a little unstable."

"Unstable?" said Saul. "He's completely whacked out."

"Is there a more precise diagnosis, perhaps?"

"Some kind of psychosis. Narcissistic personality disorder? Borderline personality disorder? Who knows?"

Jim O'Halloran, Samaritans' elderly Roman Catholic chaplain, approached the table with the coffee, picked up a packet of chocolate chip cookies and offered one to Cathy. She smiled at him but shook her head. O'Halloran was an unusual priest, and not just because of his unkempt look, and his long, straggly white hair. He had been an army chaplain in Iraq for some years, had been far too close to some improvised explosive devices and giggled whenever he spoke, revealing an unusually high level of anxiety. He poured a coffee for himself, sniffed it with his pointy whippet nose and wandered over to Andrew and Saul.

112

"We all need be careful of Max Green, Dr Sharp." His little chuckle didn't quite disguise his agitation. "If you sup with the devil, you need a long spoon."

"Thanks, Reverend." Andrew had noted the dog collar. " Never heard that before."

Saul turned on the priest, with undue belligerence. "Why do you hang out here with the doctors? Can't you find an Episcopalian or a Southern Baptist to hang out with? Haven't they got a special room for you lot?"

O'Halloran giggled nervously. "I prefer hanging out with the doctors. The clergy tend to discuss theology but as a Catholic I can safely leave my theological thinking to my superiors." He sipped his coffee again. "Saul, I'd like to talk to you professionally."

"Make an appointment with my office."

"I feel anxious and panicky sometimes," O'Halloran continued, to the surprise of absolutely nobody in the room. "When I find myself with those in need of certainty or religious consolation, like at the bedside of the dying, I find it really hard to do my job."

Saul gave a small, hopeless shrug. "That is hard," he agreed.

"Have you tried confession?" Andrew suggested.

A nervous titter. "Oh yes."

"Doesn't it achieve the same thing?"

"Not exactly, no," said O'Halloran. "Unfortunately."

"Okay, you can make an appointment with my office if you like," said Saul. "But this sounds more like a faith problem than a psychiatric one."

Andrew said, "Reverend, Saul and I were talking about Max Green. I was asking him how you handle a boss with a borderline personality disorder."

The priest was intrigued. "I'd like to know the answer to that. I've got the bishop to deal with." He giggled again.

"Handling a boss with a personality disorder," said Saul, "is quite a challenge. I don't know the answer to that."

"You're Chief of Psychiatry," said Andrew. "If you don't, who does?"

"Nobody. There's no approved method for borderline personality disorders." He sighed and wiped his eyes. "And I certainly can't help, I'm too depressed. Also, I'm very angry with you."

"With me?" Andrew was astonished. "How come? We only just met!"

"I know all about you. You've just been hired, at a huge salary. I haven't had a raise in five years, I suspect psychotherapy's being phased out in this place, I've got two kids in college and I can hardly meet my mortgage payments."

"I'm really sorry," said Andrew. "But none of that's my fault."

"Look at you! Big, glamorous heart surgeon! In and out, kill or cure. Bingo! My patients are long term. Very slow, high cost, the insurance won't always pay for them and they can't pay for themselves. I'm probably head of the least financially productive part of this dump." A tear leaked out of the corner of his eye. "It's so depressing. Everybody's talking about me. Nobody likes me…"

"That's not true," Emily said, walking past with a decaf. "Nobody's talking about you. They're not that interested."

Cathy noticed that Andrew couldn't help smiling. And Emily responded by puckering up her lips and blowing him a kiss. Andrew glanced at Cathy, then quickly looked away. He seemed embarrassed. It suddenly struck Cathy that Andrew might be having sex with Emily. Ever since the incident when he'd refused to fire her, Cathy had felt warmer towards him but now, what with the Porsche and now Emily, Cathy began to wonder if her boss, whom she had begun to like, could sink any lower. She tried to put it out of her mind.

Emboldened by Andrew's laugh, Emily turned back to Saul Tarnisch with some aggression. "You're not the only one here with problems. The interest on my student loan is mounting, my credit cards are maxed out. All of us younger doctors are in the same boat. I'm frankly bored with all your masturbatory narcissism."

An embarrassed silence followed. Some doctors studied the dregs in their coffee cups. Others focused with sudden interest on the blotchy damp patches on the ceiling. If Emily had hoped for support or even applause, she was disappointed. She sat down in a corner.

Cathy viewed the inhabitants of the doctor's common room with detached interest. It reminded her of her high school biology class, observing different strains of bacteria in a Petrie dish. Dr Singh of the failed hernia procedure eventually broke the embarrassed silence. "Maybe Mr Green is obsessive-compulsive…"

"He could well be OCD." Saul wiped his eyes with the back of his hand. "He's some sort of accountant, after all. Look…" He pulled a piece of paper out of his pocket, all scrunched-up. "I've just gotten this memo from him: *All psychologists treating patients with amnesia must insist on advance payment.*"

"Why?" said Andrew.

"In case the patient doesn't remember the treatment."

Weiner looked up from the *Washington Post*. "You know, that's fairly sensible."

"It seems to me," O'Halloran said, "that Mr Max Green is a pure Darwinian,"

Dr Duff nodded. "There's certainly no intelligent design in this dump," he said.

"No, what I mean is, Max Green believes only in the survival of the fittest."

"Survival of the richest," said Saul bitterly.

"That's evolution, American style," said Singh. "He can't see an upside to treating a patient who hasn't got the money."

"If that's true," said Andrew, "I wonder why he chose to work in a hospital."

"*You* did," Saul said.

Andrew stood up and brought his half-empty mug back to Cathy at the coffee stand. The look on his face told her he'd had enough of Saul's hostility.

Saul turned to O'Halloran. "After more than twenty years in psychiatry, I've come to the conclusion that human behavior is inexplicable. That's why psychologists conduct most of their experiments on rats."

Lori Diesel raised her head from the moth-eaten sofa under the window, where she was stretched out flat. "Can't you guys talk more quietly? I really resent being woken when I'm on duty."

23

If Max had heard the conversation in the doctors' common room that day he would have been saddened, though not surprised, that his morality was being questioned by members of the medical profession. He regarded many of them as borderline incompetent and in his opinion none of them were above criticism on moral grounds. He, on the other hand, was confident that what he was striving for was both moral and necessary.

He would have had no problem when O'Halloran badmouthed him. He had no more respect for Rome than he had for Blanche's evangelicals. All of them were as much about making and keeping money as he was. Furthermore, everyone knew that priests lost even the pretense of maintaining their position on the high moral ground years ago in the molesting kids scandal which their bosses tried to cover up. In any case, O'Halloran worked for the Church of Our Lady of Perpetual Purity, not for Samaritans, so the bishop would protect him. He wasn't Max's problem.

Following his discussions with Blanche, Max sent a letter to all the attending physicians in the hospital, outlining her plan to buy their corporations. This caused so much consternation that a mass meeting was convened in the old lecture room.

When all the available attending medical staff were gathered, Max stood up. "I want to explain my plan so that you all understand the financial necessity of it. Samaritans is a safety-net hospital, but we're not earning enough to fulfill that obligation. One of our biggest issues is Medicare, and the very limited sums of money we receive from it. My plan would increase that revenue. If the medical center owned all your corporations we could charge Medicare significantly more, because they pay more for in-hospital treatment than for outpatients. So it makes sense for us to buy you all out. That's what I've decided to do."

Nobody spoke at first, as they tried to work out the implications of this surprising announcement. "Um – what would change, if you do this?" asked Weiner.

"Nothing," said Max. "It's a boondoggle. Your offices can stay where they are, your staff stays the same. The only thing that would be different would be ownership."

"I've invested a lot of money in my practice," said Dr Duff. "I would need to be adequately compensated if you buy it from me."

"Of course," said Max. "But not *if* we buy it from you. *When* we buy it from you."

A low murmur went around the room.

"You mean, you're giving us no choice in the matter?" asked the bellicose Saul Tarnisch. His default position was outrage. Max was not bothered by the chief shrink's tone. Saul was right, Max had already decided that the psych department would soon be shut down.

"Of course you have a choice, all of you," he explained. "Your alternative is that you refuse to sell us your corporations, and you resign your privileges at Samaritans as an attending physician."

Saul looked grim. "Hobson's Choice."

Nobody in the room knew what he meant, but he was a shrink so that wasn't unusual. "How does this help our biggest problem?" asked Dr Rachel Park, a slim, confident Korean dermatologist with perfect creamy skin.

"Which is what?"

"Paperwork. On any given day we may treat twenty or thirty patients with as many insurance plans, all requiring completely unproductive paperwork. Most of us have three or four clerks whose sole job is to seek authorization for necessary procedures."

"I can't help you with that," said Max. "That problem's not caused by the hospital, that's the insurance companies. They're as big a pain in the ass to me as they are to you."

Saul Tarnisch's anger bubbled to the surface and exploded. "Their CEOs make millions of dollars a year while we struggle to meet the payroll, pay the rent, and send our kids to college."

"You're right," said Max. "But I can't help that either. However, there is something else Blanche Nunn and I want to talk to you all about. Blanche, go ahead."

"One word," she said. "Tests."

Andrew put up his hand. "Max, if you are about to tell us to make more cutbacks on tests, I'm afraid we can't do it. We need to be able to diagnose our patients using the best tools available."

There were murmurs of agreement.

"I was going to say something quite different," said Max, aggrieved. It was so disappointing. Why did they always misunderstand and distrust him? Even Andrew. He was trying so hard to make the hospital run more efficiently and to give them all more resources. "I'm not telling you to cut back on tests. Almost the opposite, in fact. I *have* been discouraging you from doing unnecessary tests on patients who are insured with American Health, Inc., for complex financial reasons that I don't need to go into right now. And you have all been co-operative and helpful, I know that, and believe me I appreciate it. Thank you all. But we have many other patients here: some are with other insurance companies who don't have an overall deal with us. Some are on Medicare. And some poor souls are uninsured. I want you to feel free to conduct as many tests as you can think of on all those patients."

"Why?" Dr Singh was surprised and suspicious.

"For their own good." Max caught Andrew's eye. "For instance, wouldn't you feel better about your patients, Andrew, if you conducted an echocardiogram and stress test on them every year instead of every three years? And, if in doubt, wouldn't you rather do more angiograms? And Martin…" he turned to a proctologist. "Wouldn't you feel you were taking better care of your patients if you gave everyone over forty a colonoscopy every two years?"

"Some wouldn't need that."

"Colon cancer can be cured if it's found early enough, right? Why leave it to chance? So, apart from the patients insured with American Health, let's have a general increase in the level of testing."

"But… why?" asked Dr Duff. "Not all the patients need them."

Sometimes, Max thought, *doctors are so stupid. They think the health care industry is only about the patients.* "Why do you think?" he said, trying to suppress his irritation. "Tests are a growing profit center. They offer harmless opportunities to bring in revenue."

"Not always harmless," said Lori Diesel.

"Okay," Max conceded. "Maybe not always, but usually. Echocardiograms, for instance, Andrew, are painless and have no side effects, am I right?"

Andrew nodded.

Max turned to the others. "CT scans, blood draws, colonoscopies, MRIs – they don't involve much radiation or discomfort. Ultrasounds, biopsies, heart rhythm monitors, bladder scopes – come on guys, use your imaginations; the sky's the limit. We even have pocket-size devices now that we can buy for as little as five thousand bucks, which can perform some of these examinations. And the beauty of it is that pricing is uncoupled from the actual cost of business. Prices can be high, expenses low. It's a perfect scenario." As an afterthought he added, "And it may even save lives."

Blanche decided to clarify the proposition, and consulted her iPad. "The seven teaching hospitals in Boston affiliated with Harvard, Tufts and Boston U charge an average of only about $1,300 for an EKG. But the hospitals around here charge an average of about $5,200 for the same test. In Philly it's even better: prices range from $700 to as high as $12,000."

"And there's another thing," added Max. "Other hospitals pursue those patients who are uninsured or underinsured for those payments. We will do that too."

"Wait a minute," Andrew said. "I'm not sure if I get that. You want to increase the charges on the uninsured?"

"Of course. We don't have to argue with the insurance companies or Medicare if they're not insured."

"Let me tell you something," said Andrew. "I looked into the cost of echocardiograms when I was working in Europe. In other countries, regulators set fair charges which include built-in profit. In Belgium, the allowable charge for an echocardiogram is $80, and in Germany it's $115. In Japan, the price ranges from $50 for an older version to $88 for the newest."

"*So* much less!" exclaimed Weiner.

"That's their problem," said Max.

"In Britain," said Andrew, "there's no charge at all."

"More fool them," said Max. "This is America. Land of Opportunity. We can charge what the fuck we like. Echocardiograms are one of the most lucrative revenue streams open to us."

"As long as the patients aren't with American Health Inc," Blanche reminded them. "We have an overall deal with AH."

"So what should the threshold be for ordering an echocardiogram?" said Andrew.

"Owning a heart," said Max.

24

It was time for Max to make his next TV commercial. A neurology ward had been emptied for the morning so that the cameras and lights could be set up. When he arrived they were ready for him.

"And... action," said the director.

Max read off his cue card. "Why spend more than you need on health care? Samaritans offers Bonus Buys for patients having multiple procedures: if you have your gallbladder and appendix removed, two completely unnecessary organs, you get a thirty per cent discount on a prosthetic hip!

"And why not sell a kidney. You have two, and you only need one. We can get you the best price."

"Samaritans Medical Center – *making health care more responsive to patient choice.*"

"And... cut," said the director.

"Thanks," said Max.

He had arranged to meet Blanche across the street for lunch. The food in the hospital cafeteria was greasy and unappetizing and like many of the hospital staff he often went to Merv's Deli.

She had been working hard all morning and arrived with her tablet, a briefcase full of papers and her eyes shining with the love of data. She slid into the booth at the speckled Formica-topped table. The décor hadn't changed in decades. People liked it the way it was.

"You once asked me which doctors are not profit centers?" she began. "I've been through all the numbers and the answer is: essentially it's the ones who treat chronic illnesses. Except for the dermatologists."

"I know. Dermatologists are fast, they can treat one patient every five minutes."

A waiter hurried past holding two glasses of iced tea. Max asked him if Merv was in.

"You're not my table," the waiter snapped at him.

Max turned back to Blanche. "What about all the internists? Could we replace some of them with nurse practitioners? NPs make half the salary and do most of the same work at lower cost."

"That's so smart," she said. "Great idea!" She started to make a calculation on the iPad.

The waiter was hurrying back in the other direction. Max grabbed his arm. "Stop!"

"Ow!" said the waiter. "That hurts. Take your hands off me."

"I know I'm not your table but I want a civil answer. Where's Merv?"

"Let go!"

"Cool it, pal," Max let go. "Just trying to make you listen."

"Merv is behind the counter, carving the pastrami. The bald old guy with the glasses."

The waiter hurried away, rubbing his arm, as Max stood and strolled over to the proprietor, working at a long pine butcher's block behind a low, glassed-in partition. "Merv?"

"Take a number," Merv said. "Stand in line."

"I don't want a number, I want to talk to you."

"Yeah? What can I do for you?" Merv carried on carving the red, steaming meat, making two thick sandwiches with mustard on rye. They looked and smelled good.

"Merv, do you get a lot of business from people at the hospital across the street?"

"Sure. Ever eaten there?"

"Whenever I don't have time to come here."

"You work there?"

Max handed Merv his card. Merv put it down without looking at it, and continued carving. "I'm Max Green," Max said. "CEO of Samaritans."

If the statement was designed to impress it was a miserable failure. "You ought to do something about your kitchen," Merv said, still carving. "I don't want to offend you but your cafeteria is..." He looked up, lost for words. "You know, it's indescribably terrible."

"I know," said Max. "That's why I'm here. I'm thinking you and I might come to some arrangement."

"Yeah? Like what?"

"Can you come over to my office this afternoon? I have a proposition for you."

Merv dropped in mid-afternoon and they talked. Max learned that Merv dreamed of retiring but couldn't afford to. He'd lost all his savings in the crash of 2008 and his house was still underwater. Max had the solution. "We'll buy Merv's Deli from you, if you guarantee to stay for five years to keep the quality up. You'll get cash in hand, pay off your mortgage, and we'll make money too. It's a win-win, all round. Name your price."

Merv did so. Max had done his homework, and after a little negotiation they came to an agreement and shook hands. Legalities would take a little time, but Merv was happy and so was Max. Max liked deals and he enjoyed making people happy. It happened so rarely since he had stopped being a host in Vegas.

Next, he phoned Eric Ratoff, who used to do the catering for FlyJet before the airline went into Chapter 11 bankruptcy, stopped serving food on its airplanes and started charging passengers for using the toilet on board. After the call he descended to the perspiring hellhole of grease, steam and rusty ducts that was the humid underbelly of the hospital.

A puffy, plump overseer was putting on his jacket in a little glassed-in office just behind the huge kitchen. He looked up when Max sauntered in. "Good afternoon, Mr Green."

Max noticed his teeth were yellow and crooked. "Pleased to meet you."

"We've met before," the chubby man said.

"Oh yeah?" Max was untroubled by his mistake.

"I'm Harold Berger, Head of Food Services."

"I know who you are."

"Well... good. Would you like a coffee? Iced tea? Soda? Water?"

"Nothing for me, thanks. Tell me, Mr Berger, did you ever travel on FlyJet?"

"Yes, I believe I did."

"What was the food like?"

"Not bad," Berger said. "As I recall."

If Max had had any qualms about firing him, they vanished at that moment. *The man has no taste buds,* he thought, *he shouldn't be in catering, I'm doing him a favor.* "Was FlyJet's food better than the food here at Samaritans?"

"Well, yes. But I was flying Business."

"I'm glad you liked it. Eric Ratoff, whose company did the catering for FlyJet Airlines, will be providing the food at Samaritans from now on."

Berger was confused. "What?"

"I'm letting you go."

Berger's brow crinkled. "Letting me go? I don't understand."

"Not just you, actually – you and your entire staff. I'm sorry, but I was brought in to rationalize things. It's better financial sense to outsource the catering."

"Why?"

Max felt irritated at being questioned, but he opted for staying nice and giving an explanation. "This hospital, as I'm sure you know, is facing major financial difficulties. We need to downsize. We cannot continue to be responsible for so many employees and their pension plans, their health insurance, their payroll taxes and so on. So we just can't afford you and your... unique... food anymore."

Berger did not seem to notice the irony. "But..."

"I'm truly sorry," said Max. "But hey!"

"Hey?" Berger was aghast. "*Hey*? Is that all you have to say?"

"What else?"

"The board won't let you do this."

Max tilted his head like a dog or a therapist, in an attempt to look sympathetic. It seemed to help people. "The board has given me carte blanche."

"What about the union?"

"The union?" Max laughed out loud. The man seemed to be lost in some pre-Reagan time warp.

Berger said, "What about our wives and families? Our mortgages?"

"Mr Berger, believe me, I've agonized about downsizing like this. And the terrible effect on your wife and family. So you'll get a month's severance."

"A month? That's not enough, I've worked here for decades." YP, thought Max, and congratulated himself for not saying it. "So – you're telling me – that's it?" Berger said.

Max nodded. "Yup. That's it."

Berger slowly sat down. Max left him in his little glassed-in basement room to contemplate his future.

*

Ratoff came to his office a couple of days later. He had lost weight since Max knew him in Vegas, and he was now almost as slim as his profits.

"How are things in airline catering?" Max asked him. He already knew the answer.

"Truthfully, we've been hit pretty hard. There's no more catering in coach on any of the airlines we service. We sell some snacks, that's all."

"That's what I thought. Eric, I have an opportunity – and a challenge – for you. We're planning to outsource the kitchens here at Samaritans. I've been reading your literature. You say you have five levels of food quality?"

"We have."

"That's good. But for us you'd need to create a whole new level."

Ratoff smiled. He had big gums but small, rodent-like teeth. "I'm happy to hear that, Max. The new level of quality could be our highest yet."

"No. I want your lowest. I need cheaper food than you've ever served even on the cheapest coach flight. You want to give me a quote?"

"Sure. But – let me just ask you – I mean, this is a hospital – there has to be some nutritional value, right?"

"Fine," shrugged Max. "If you can do it for the price."

"You don't care about nutrition?"

"No harm in it."

"Max, anything lower quality than our economy class catering would be uneatable."

"People expect hospital food to be uneatable," said Max. "And if they don't eat it, so what? Most Americans are obese anyway."

After the deal was done with Ratoff, Max asked Blanche to distribute some rapidly printed flyers to every department, to every nurses' station, every ward, every office and to the ER. *"Fed up with hospital food? Try Merv's Deli (opposite the hospital). Free Delivery!"*

25

There were several neighborhood businesses that were largely dependent on the hospital for their survival. The deal he made with Merv's Deli was a template. The next most obvious possibility was the Heavenly Peace Memorial Chapel & Memory Gardens, a couple of blocks down the street.

He dropped in one morning unannounced and spoke to the boss. Mort Baggitt was trying out mournful organ music on the stereo system but he gave Max a cheery smile. "Samaritans has been a lifesaver for us," he said. "So many of your patients pass away."

"Glad to be of service," said Max, who had figured out that the funeral business was perennially profitable – and especially right here, he thought, so long as our doctors continue to screw up the way they've been doing. He offered to buy out Mr Baggitt as long as he stayed five years, and assured him that Samaritans could make sure that all the bereaved with no other plans were referred to Heavenly Peace. They shook hands on it. Paperwork would follow.

A few blocks along, in the opposite direction, was Temp-o, the temp nurses agency, nestling in a shabby little office on the second floor of a run-down office building at the back of the Burger King drive-thru', right under the gigantic neon sign. Blanche had briefed Max fully; Samaritans relied on Temp-o when extra nurses were needed. He saw it differently: in his view, the temp agency relied on Samaritans.

He met Julia Morris, the ex-nurse practitioner who ran the place. Her lank brown hair, the dark circles under her eyes and her bitten-down fingernails told their own story.

"Would you like us to hire more nurses from you?" he began.

"Well – sure!"

He wasn't impressed with her look but he offered her a similar deal: a generous cash infusion to Temp-o in return for a controlling interest. When small business owners are worried about their future and they can't get a loan from the bank, cash is king. She knew it would help the agency grow during the endless economic downturn.

Max had a bunch of successes to report to the board and before the quarterly meeting he invited Soper for a quiet coffee in the cafeteria. He started with his plan to outsource the catering and, after a taste of the cafeteria's Samaritans Special Colombian Roast, Soper embraced it.

"You know that Victor Stone has been a thorn in our side since way back when?"

"I do."

"He and I have a potential deal that could substantially reduce the number of lawsuits against this hospital."

"A deal with Victor Stone? Sounds promising."

"When patients check in, we'll give them an extra form to fill. If they sign it they are agreeing in advance that if anything goes wrong they won't sue the hospital, because we only provide facilities. They will sue the doctors instead. That means the doctors' insurance foots the bill, not ours."

The chairman beamed. "Genius!"

"So everybody's happy," said Max.

"Except the doctors' insurance companies," said the chairman.

"They're happy too. They can put up the doctors' premiums to cover it. And it won't cost the doctors anything either, they can pass on the higher premiums to the patients. Money circulates. The economy grows. Everybody benefits. The hospital, the doctors, the insurance companies…"

"Everybody except the patients," said Soper. "The patients will be paying more for their insurance."

"You can't please everyone," said Max. "But this is how trickle-down works."

The chairman chuckled. "Trickle-down doesn't work, Max. we just *tell* people it works."

"I know. Why do they believe us?"

"If you say something often enough, people will start to believe it, whatever the evidence. Max, this seems like a good plan."

He looked at his watch and stood up.

*

The air conditioners in the windows whirred and clunked, but had no impact whatsoever on the temperature in the boardroom. Beads of sweat appeared on Soper's brow as he brought the meeting to order, and then handed it over to Max for his quarterly report.

"I decided we need some forwards vertical integration," Max began. "So we've bought Merv's Deli across the street."

Eyebrows were raised. "You bought a *deli*?" somebody said.

"It does great business. All their customers come from us, so why should Merv get the profit? This is a win-win. Then I looked around the neighborhood and saw two other businesses that depend on the Samaritans: Temp-o, the nurses agency, and the Heavenly Peace Memorial Chapel & Memory Gardens funeral home. So we bought them both. Acquisitions. That's how you grow a business."

"Brilliant," said Soper. "Well done, Max!"

"Thank you, Mr Chairman."

"How did you pay for these acquisitions?" asked Jacqueline Goodman. "Did we have a cash reserve?"

"Very little money has changed hands so far. Just deposits and stuff. If we don't have enough cash in hand, the bank is happy to lend it to us to purchase profitable businesses. I've cleared it with them. But I think we'll be able to pay, given all the economies that we're going to make."

"Such as?"

"I've already outsourced all catering and all billing. Next, I'm outsourcing radiology to India. The entire department will be Bangalored."

There was consternation around the table. "What...? *India*...? Are you serious?"

He waited until the hubbub died down. "It's a huge saving. All our X-rays and MRIs can be viewed in Bangalore or Mumbai by Indian radiologists working around the clock for fourteen dollars an hour. With luck they'll be British trained or have American experience. If not, we'll manage. When that's organized, we'll move Pathology to Thailand and the lab to Taiwan."

"How will you send them blood counts?" called Fred Coward, the faded ginger dormouse, from the far end of the table.

"FedEx."

"How long will that take?"

"Four or five days to get the answer, probably. No more than week, anyway. Next..." Max hurried on. He didn't want to get bogged down in trivial details. "And we're closing the diabetic center. It's a total loss. Then, tomorrow, we fire thirty per cent of the nurses."

More gasps. Nervous glances were now being exchanged around the long, scratched, shiny table. "Are you crazy?" asked Jacqueline Goodman, when nobody else did.

"Wait one minute…" said Soper.

Max had forgotten to warn him about this one and the chairman was looking worried. Always a little pink in the face, he was now florid and slightly blotchy. Maybe it was the heat. "I don't think we can do that, Max."

Max didn't bat an eyelid. "I'm sure you're thinking, Mr Chairman, that we can't fire nurses for incompetence. And you're right. Union rules prevent that. But we can let them go for economic reasons."

Soper couldn't conceal his relief. He turned to the board. "You know, I think he's right about that…"

"I know I am," said Max. "I checked with a chainsaw consultant."

"A what?" said Fred Coward.

"An expert on firing people. Labor law."

"But… why?" asked Jacquie Goodman.

"Two reasons," said Max. "First, I did a budget review. We have too many nurses, too many janitors and too many housekeeping staff. We have to downsize. The nurses get paid more than the janitors, so we'll achieve much more significant economies if we keep the janitors and downsize the nurses. Also, the head nurse threatened to bring all the nursing staff out on strike. I have witnesses."

In the ensuing hubbub Max heard, "A strike…? We can't run a hospital without nurses…"

He raised his voice. "Hear me out, okay?"

They stopped talking and stared at him as if he had lost his mind. "It's not a problem. We will still have nurses. We can work around the strike. Everyone told Reagan he couldn't fire the air traffic controllers but it worked out just fine. There's a moral there. Don't worry, if necessary I'll rehire some of the outgoing nurses as temps, which makes much more sense than keeping them all on staff."

"Then why downsize them?" said Jacquie Goodman.

"We own the temp agency now. We'll get commission on every hire. We'll be transferring a percentage of their income from one of our pockets to the other. That's good business. And here's the kicker: if they're not on staff, we no longer have to pay their health benefits. The overall savings are humungous!"

"Makes sense to me," said Soper.

"But you said you'll rehire only some of the nurses. Not all?" asked Fred Coward.

"Nurses are costly," Max said. "And we have too many janitors, who cost much less and don't have enough to do. So, we'll put some of the janitors in nurse's uniforms, to help out."

"This is so smart," said Soper.

"Is it legal?" asked Coward.

"According to a Pulitzer Prize-winning article Blanche found in the *Chicago Tribune*," Max replied, as Blanche passed photocopies of it around the table, "housekeeping staff assigned to clean rooms have been pressed into duty as aides to dispense medicine under a cost-saving program in at least two Chicago hospitals. I quote: '*Earning an average of nine dollars an hour, unlicensed and unregulated aides are used to augment staffing, but they sometimes supplant higher-paid registered nurses. Up to one third of nursing staff in these hospitals consists of such aides, many of whom are not even required to have high school diplomas.*' If they can do it, why can't we?"

"But it's wrong, surely?" said Jacquie Goodman. "Depriving nurses of health benefits? We're a hospital, for God's sake!"

"Wrong?" said Max. "What do you mean, wrong? I used to work in Vegas. We had a maxim in the hotel trade: You only have a hundred per cent. You have your labor, your food, your loan repayments, your utilities, your laundry – oh, incidentally I'm reducing the laundry bill, I'm only sending the nurses' uniforms to be washed half as often. They'll be clean enough—"

"Are you sure?" she asked.

Max gave her a condescending smile. "You worry too much! Relax, Jacquie! All I'm saying is, it has to add up: the uniforms, the bedding, the paper goods, the orchestras, the show room…"

"The *show room*?"

"Not the show room, no, not here! I was talking about Vegas!" Max hated being questioned like this. "All I'm saying is, it's math: how much you spend, how much you make, it has to add up. What's your profit margin? Like I said, you only have a hundred per cent. Am I right?"

The board members looked at each other. That there is only a hundred per cent seemed unarguable. Fred Coward said nothing and stared at his blotter. Jacquie stared at the ceiling, or perhaps reproachfully at God. The mutiny was quashed.

"Next on the agenda is Medicare," continued Max. "This is our biggest problem. It doesn't pay enough and it pays by the illness, not by the length of stay. We get about ten grand for an appendectomy, whether the victim – patient, I mean – stays one night or twenty, or even forty if peritonitis kicks in. That's a financial disaster. So, consumers who are on Medicare are now being eased out of the hospital – gently, of course, and only when they're ready, but fast!"

Jacqueline Goodman didn't join the chorus of murmured agreement. And this time she did not address her comments to Max. "Mr Chairman, I am concerned about the ethics of everything that Mr Green is doing. We have responsibilities to the whole community. We can't just treat the wealthy."

"No offense, toots," Max said, "but cut the class warfare. We live in a consumer-driven society. This place was going bankrupt before I got here. If we go under, we can't treat anybody, rich or poor."

This was met by silence.

"My first quarter's numbers are looking great. I take it you don't have a problem with that? Because this hospital can't fulfill *any* community responsibilities if it fails to join the modern world."

Still nobody responded. It was time to go for the jugular. "You want me to run this place or not? Yes or no. If you don't, just say so. I'll be gone tomorrow. You can find someone else to clear up the financial mess that this board has created and tolerated."

The silence continued, but now you could cut it with a knife.

"That's a binary question," Max said.

"Meaning what?" asked Jacqueline.

"Answer yes or no."

Soper said, "Well, I – for one – definitely want you to stay."

There were more murmurs of agreement, from everyone except Fred and Jacquie.

"Fine," said Max. "Then let's do it. Let me get on with it."

"All in favor?" said Soper.

It was a walkover.

Jacqueline Goodman resigned the following day.

26

Max fired Head Nurse Sheila McIntyre and about forty per cent of her staff and rehired a few of them though the agency twenty-four hours later. Max gave a bonus to Julia Morris at Temp-o, who was delighted by the sharp increase in revenue even if she had to share much of it with Samaritans.

The nurses Samaritans didn't rehire joined Sheila's rather forlorn and rain lashed picket line outside the main entrance. Their shoes were sodden and their feet were wet. The ink ran on their cardboard placards. Max phoned the *Washington Star* and all the local TV stations, to alert them to the fact that they could get great pics of fat, smoking nurses on the picket line outside Samaritans Medical Center.

"So what?" they replied.

"Who wants to be nursed by an obese, morbidly unhealthy nurse who smells like an ashtray?"

The media gleefully jumped on the idea. The delight of the picket line at the sudden appearance of video and stills photographers turned to distress when their photos filled the papers and the local TV news, alongside headlines that lost them public sympathy overnight.

Max put out a statement saying that he had fired those nurses who were not health conscious and who filled the sluice rooms with smoke. Both the statement and more photos of the couple of nurses with damp cigarettes dangling from their lower lips went viral. Despite protestations of sympathy, the rest of the hospital staff were too anxious about their own future to lift a finger on the strikers' behalf. It was a slam dunk.

Max put some of the janitors into nurses' uniforms, called them "nurses' aides", and ordered they be given simple jobs in the wards. He made it clear it would be a rise in status but not in pay, and they were just fine with that. Status matters.

The decrease in janitors and housekeeping staff prompted Max to issue his directive about cleaning and laundry. He instructed housekeeping that henceforth all bed and window curtains would be washed half as often.

He also started work on major improvements to the front lobby and main reception. The Stephen P Murphy Revolving Door had just been a beginning. The whole entrance needed to look much more inviting. The lobby soon boasted the Marc J and Cynthia P Leventhal Elevators. At the ribbon cutting, two of them were unfortunately out of order, but one was working and Mr and Mrs Leventhal were delighted to see their names right above the Up/Down indicator, in Times New Roman gilt lettering for which they had paid so handsomely.

The Moses H Hartz Cardiothoracic Ward and the Frances di Gaetano Maternity Wing continued the brand-building process. Max had realized, after naming the former, that 'wing' sounded bigger than ward and therefore suggested a more generous gift by the donor. The only glitch came with the search for a donor for whom he could name the persistently malodorous toilets in the lobby. Samaritans' enduring drain problem was proving an insurmountable obstacle, despite the promise of large New Roman gilt lettering.

The two-storey main hall contained thousands of square feet of underutilized real estate, much of which Max leased to a florist, and a newspaper and bookshop. Get-well cards now rubbed shoulders with a range of electronic goods, stuffed toys and novelty kitsch that so appeals when you need to buy a present but are short of time or inspiration. More ATMs were installed nearby, and in the ER too, where Samaritans now provided financially voracious video games for waiting patients and their children.

With Sheila McIntyre gone, Samaritans needed a new head nurse. Human Resources asked to be present at the interviews but Max told them he had to meet the candidates in private first. HR said that was the wrong way round, so Max asked them how much revenue they generated for the hospital and that shut them up. The message was clear. Their jobs depended on his approval.

Max's first choice was thirty-eight. "Mmm. Very good," he said, checking out her slim figure, pretty face and good legs while pretending to read her resume.

"Are you interested?"

"I certainly am."

"I am too."

"Good. Tell me about yourself. Married? Kids?"

She evaded the personal questions. "I've been a nurse for eighteen years. I have a Masters in nursing, and an MBA, and I have been Deputy Head of Nursing at Johns Hopkins for the last five years."

"Wow. Sounds great to me. What do they pay you?"

It was more than he was prepared for, and she made it clear she had no interest in earning less.

"This won't work," he said, disappointed. "I have a budget. But thanks for coming over from Baltimore." As she left he asked for her number and she refused to give it to him. *Good riddance*, he thought.

After he met a few more candidates, a beautiful slim young woman entered his office, expensively blonde with natural-looking streaks, and a large mouth with a big wide smile. She didn't have an appointment, she didn't look like head nurse material, but she did look sort of familiar.

"Hi, babe," he said. "Have we met before? What's your name?"

"Yes, we have. My name's Melodie. Melodie Feather."

"Hi Melodie."

"When you made that commercial. I played a nurse. You asked me if I'd ever wanted to be a nurse."

"What did you say?"

"I asked if you meant, like, role-play?"

"That's exactly what I meant. How did you get into these interviews?"

"I didn't know there were interviews. I just dropped by to show you my portfolio."

She did. There were plenty of shots of her both in and out of uniform.

"Great. Melodie, let's make music together. Come and sit on my lap."

She did. Her emerald eyes sparkled with mischief.

As they fucked on his black leather sofa a few minutes later, Max reflected on how inconvenient it would have been if HR had attended the interviews.

*

After he met Melodie, Max got bored with interviewing head nurses and HR hired one who was said to have a great bedside manner. When he tried to put this to the test, it became clear to him that they had been talking at cross-purposes. But he didn't mind. Melodie was so cool at role-play that she could pretend to be head nurse whenever he wanted.

He prevailed upon HR to find her a day job at reception; she was great window dressing, which seemed to be therapeutic for everyone. Also, it meant he didn't have to pay her out of his own pocket. Occasional dinners, champagne and a few expensive gifts kept her more than happy, all of which he could charge to the hospital. She made a pleasant change from Blanche, every now and then, as Blanche was so intense and seemed to be becoming a little too proprietorial.

27

Mrs Jefferson's hip was presented at the next morbidity and mortality meeting to take place after the lecture room had been reopened, with Milton Weiner again in the chair.

Dr Duff stood up and surveyed the crowded lecture room. A little nervously, he cleared his throat. "Um – can we see the first picture?"

Dr Embers wheezed a "yes", coughed and flashed an X-ray up onto the screen. "This is prior to surgery," said Duff. "It shows the hip at the point of disarticulation."

Everyone stared at it, puzzled. Andrew Sharp raised his hand. "May I ask a question? I'm not an orthopedist, but that hip looks perfectly normal to me."

"Well… yes…" said Duff. "Yes, in point of fact… it *is* perfectly normal…"

"You removed a perfectly normal hip?"

"Yes." Duff cleared his throat again. "However, we choose to regard this as a positive measure. There very severe osteoarthritis degeneration, admittedly of the other hip. But when that needs replacement, next Thursday in fact, since we didn't do it this week – electively, of course – this new hip will certainly help speed up her convalescence."

People gazed at him, slack-jawed.

Andrew Sharp glanced around the room. "Anybody else here have concerns about this?"

Lori Diesel put up her hand. "I guess I do," she said. "Let me get this straight. You're pretending you replaced the wrong hip on *purpose*?"

"It seems to me," said Andrew, "that replacing the wrong hip on purpose is almost worse than doing it by accident."

"Not necessarily," said Duff.

Weiner tried to get things on track. "Please, gentlemen!"

Lori raised an eyebrow. "Gentlemen?"

"And ladies," Weiner corrected himself. "Dr Duff, I remind you that the purpose of this meeting is not damage control. It is to learn from our mistakes."

"There were no mistakes in the surgery itself," said Duff. "I did it perfectly."

There was another stunned silence. Then Weiner said, "I don't know how to reply to that."

Some people smiled, others shifted in their seats and one or two looked horrified. A few were looking at Weiner, waiting for leadership, apparently unaware that it was a quality he didn't possess. Andrew said, "Look, I know I'm new here, but I'd like to understand why."

"Why what?" said Duff.

"Why did you replace a perfectly normal hip?"

"The X-ray wasn't labeled. And we've eliminated the 'time-out', which used to be when we confirmed which hip is to be replaced."

"Why?"

"Mr Green wants another two hips per day. We don't have time for time-outs anymore."

The assembled company nodded and murmured "ah" and "cutbacks" to each other.

"I see," said Weiner. "So you're going to replace the other hip next Thursday?"

"As long as she's strong enough."

"She's remaining an in-patient?"

"Yes, to avoid a readmission loss."

"Okay," said Weiner. "That's it for today, thank you everybody. Same time next week."

*

As the meeting broke up, Emily Craven buttonholed him. "That was such a good meeting, Dr Weiner. You handled it so well, sir."

"Thank you, Emily," he said, edging away from her. Andrew watched her glance around the room and collect the papers lying on the table. She noticed him watching her.

"Hey, babe," she cooed at him. "You haven't called me. Wanna buy me a drink tonight? And then a little... you know?"

"Emily. What are you doing with those papers?"

"Dr Weiner forgot them. He shouldn't leave them lying around for just anyone to see."

"You'll give them to him?"

"What else would I do with them?"

"I don't know. What else *would* you do with them?"

"How about a little you-know-what tonight?" she said.

"Sorry. I'm busy."

She pouted. "You never call me."

"Look Emily, it was... um... very nice, and all that, but it was just a booty call, right? No strings attached."

"Oh."

"I'm a no-strings-attached guy, okay?"

"Sure." She smiled bravely, went to Dr Embers, leaned over her laptop, whispered and indicated something on the screen. Embers nodded, Emily inserted a thumb drive and Embers tapped something on her keyboard. Emily slid the thumb drive out of the USB port and slipped it into her pocket. Andrew was distracted by Dr Duff tapping him on the shoulder. "Excuse me, Sharp, may I have a word?"

"Yes? What about?"

Duff's jaw was clenched, and his eyes were pinpricks of anger. "I don't see why it was necessary for you to be so sarcastic in front of everybody."

"Bad for your self-esteem, was it?"

"If you want to put it like that, yes. It's not my fault that Max Green wants two more hips per day."

"You're the surgeon, not Max Green. You are responsible, not him. I don't give a shit about your self-esteem. This is about the patient. That was a major fuck-up and you need to admit it, at least to yourself!"

Dr Duff turned on his heel and walked away.

*

Max saw and heard it all on his surveillance system. He had tuned into the meetings as soon as the "repairs" were finished, and was watching live now. He couldn't quite hear what Emily said to Andrew but the body language had been clear enough. She was being given the brush-off.

Andrew was nearer the camera and the mic when Duff spoke to him; and Max was delighted that Andrew was defending him. The Porsche was paying off.

28

Cathy was not alone at her desk when Andrew arrived the next morning. A drop-dead gorgeous blonde holding a Starbucks turned and smiled at him. She didn't look like she had a cardio problem.

"Come into my office," he said to Cathy, and he shut the door behind her. "Who's that out there?"

"This is your lucky day."

"What do you mean?"

"Just that. If you want to get lucky, Kimberly Cummings is your girl. She's a sales rep for Berristain-Klench Pharmaceuticals."

"Well, I guess you better send her in…"

Kimberly sailed in. She was tall and elegant and would have looked good in an old sack. She sat down opposite him and crossed her legs. A high-heeled shoe dangled from her toes. "So you're the new cardiothoracic star. Congratulations."

"Thank you."

"No, thank *you*, for finding the time to see me."

"It's my pleasure," he said, and he meant it. He could have sat and looked at her all day.

"I want to talk to you about our new anti-rejection drug, HeartGraft."

"How good are the results?"

"Excellent." She opened her backpack and showed him some glossy advertising literature. "Organ rejection is far less likely on HeartGraft."

"So," said Andrew, "if I take it, am I less likely to be rejected?"

"Much less likely. We can talk about that later."

"Why not now?"

"Why not in Paris?"

"Paris?"

She smiled. "There's an upcoming five-day conference on post-operative transplant complications in Paris. Specifically, it's addressing the titration of post-op pressor amines and interactions between renal blood flow parameters and suppressor T-lymphocytes subsets in GVHD."

In spite of himself, Andrew was impressed. "You certainly know your stuff."

"I need to make my stuff attractive."

"Your stuff," said Andrew, "is highly attractive."

She smiled again. "The best thing about the conference is that it only runs from nine a.m. till noon. The rest of the time is for study, and... personal updating and networking." Somehow she made it sound infinitely seductive.

"Will you be there?"

"Of course." Her green eyes sparkled. "That's why I'm suggesting you... come. Here's my card. Call me any time."

She stood up. "By the way, Max Green is interested in making a bulk deal on HeartGraft."

"What the hell does he know about it?"

"Nothing. But we're educating him. He's going to a hospital manager's conference—"

"In Paris?"

"No. In Tahiti."

She didn't say if she'd be there or not. She strolled out of his office, confident that he would be looking at her ass as she walked away.

"Bye." She waved as she swanned past Cathy.

"Bye," called Andrew, now in his doorway.

Cathy said, "You going to date her?"

"Maybe," said Andrew. "Why do you ask?"

She resumed typing. "No reason."

"She seems like a smart saleswoman," he said.

"Oh yes. And she's good for a free sample or two. In fact, she gives free samples to most of the guys. And some of the gals."

His eyes narrowed. "Do you have a problem with Kimberly?"

"No."

"Would it bother you if I dated her?"

"Nothing to do with me. That would be your problem."

"You know I've tried to get a date with you."

"It's not a good idea, Andrew. It's dumb to date your boss."

"So, if I wasn't your boss, would you?"

"You are my boss," she said. "And I need this job."

"I think that underneath your truculent exterior you secretly want me."

"In your dreams," she said.

Andrew knew she disapproved of his money-making ambitions and he knew she had guessed about Emily. And then there was the whole matter of the Porsche. "I had a lot of fun driving into work this morning," he said provocatively.

She clicked faster on her keyboard.

"In my Porsche."

She froze. Bullseye.

"Come on, Cathy, say what you want to say."

"Okay!" She sat back and looked him in the eye. "That thing cost about ninety thousand dollars that could have been used for patient care."

"I know. I'm embarrassed about it. I was joking when I asked for it. But you know what? Now I have it, I love it. Don't spoil it for me, okay?"

"It's nothing to do with me. You brought up the subject..." She returned to her typing.

He stood there for a moment. Then, as he turned to go back into his office, she asked, "You know what she was before she worked for Berristain-Klench?"

"Who?"

"Kimberly."

"No?"

"A cheerleader."

"So?"

"Just thought you'd like to know."

"Nothing wrong with that, is there?"

"No."

He could see there was more to come.

"You want to know what she'll say to you if you date her?"

"How would you know?"

"Everyone knows. She's famous around here. She has a routine." Cathy put on a breathy, Marilyn Monroe sort of voice. "Oh Doctor, how many lives did you save today?"

"Nothing wrong with that."

"Doctor, you perform... miracles..."

In spite of himself, Andrew smiled.

"Doctor, honey – all that delicate surgery, you must have the most sensitive fingers. I bet there are other parts of you that are sensitive as well…"

Andrew thought about it for a moment. "She sounds great!" he said.

29

When Melodie Feather started her day job on the reception desk, a call came in from Mrs Jefferson's granddaughter LaTanya in Brooklyn, wanting to speak to Dr Duff about her grandma.

"Hold on," said Melodie, "I'll look him up." She consulted a list and was immediately puzzled. "Dr Duff. It says here he's in sugary… oh, I get it, surgery…"

The lobby was changing fast. The new shops had opened and Merv's Deli had started up a concession stand, like at the movies. *Merv's Moveable Feast* sold hot dogs, burgers, buttered popcorn, candy, ice cream and every possible type of milky coffee. Max, Blanche and Andrew surveyed the scene. Max and Blanche were beaming but Andrew was concerned. "Look what they're selling. Fat and sugar. Heart disease, diabetes—"

"Great!" said Max. "Both are on the increase, and both are exceedingly profitable."

"I don't get it," said Andrew. "If diabetes is on the increase, and it's profitable, why did you just close the diabetic center?"

"The diabetic center was for prevention," Max said. "Wake up, Andrew! Prevention's not profitable. But with amputations, liver transplants, transfusions, infections, eye surgery and heart attacks, diabetes is an illness that really racks up the big bucks."

"But we don't want to cause it."

Max couldn't see Andrew's problem. "It's a free country! They don't have to buy that crap. But if they want it – hey!"

"But not here, Max."

"Why should somebody else get the profit? These people are going to buy it anyway. And we need the money! That's why I'm closing the diabetic center, we can't afford to keep bankrolling it and it's valuable real estate. We're going to monetize the bricks and mortar as well as everything else around here, can't you see how great that is?"

Blanche, perched on the edge of a desk, was listening. "Andrew, I don't get it. What's your problem? You got a new Porsche!"

This sudden unexpected outbreak of hostilities took him by surprise. His phone rang. "Excuse me, it's an emergency." He hurried away to the ER where he was met by an anxious nurse.

"Thank goodness you're here," she said.

"Where's the heart attack?"

The ER nurse led him to Mrs Jefferson. Jordan was there. Mrs Jefferson had just undergone emergency treatment from the cardiac arrest team. Her heart had stopped, but some thirty seconds of pounding on her chest had got it going again.

"What's the story?" he asked.

"We admitted her four days ago and she had surgery on the wrong hip."

"Oh, yes." Andrew recognized the story. "I heard about her in the M&M meeting."

"She's in acute pain from the arthritic hip, and she has some post-operative pain after the replacement of her good hip," said the ER nurse. "But her insurance denied the claim. They said they wouldn't pay for replacing a good hip."

"So," Jordan carried on, "we got her downstairs. But when we told her she was being discharged because her insurance wouldn't pay, would you believe it, she had this heart attack?"

Andrew examined Mrs Jefferson. It had been a cardiac arrest but not a heart attack. He decided not to waste time explaining the difference. Lay people used the terms interchangeably – medical staff, he felt, should know better. But first things first. "Is she on painkillers?"

"No, her blood pressure's too low."

"So she must be suffering, what with her bad hip and the post-operative pain."

"Yes, she said the pain was eight out of ten."

Andrew turned to Jordan, who was still hovering. "How long has she been lying here?"

"Only a few hours. We're trying to send her home."

"Why?"

"We were told to."

"But she's having more surgery."

"That's not definite."

"It is. Dr Duff told us at the M&M meeting."

"It's not his decision, he's only a doctor. It's up to the insurance company. If they won't pay, no surgery. She can't afford it herself."

"I don't get it. Why won't the insurance pay?"

"They don't want to pay for surgery on a healthy hip. Why would they?"

"She didn't *ask* for surgery on a healthy hip. That was our mistake!"

"That's not been proved," said Jordan. "Blanche Nunn, the risk assessor, says Samaritans denies all liability. She says Victor Stone's legal opinion is that the complaint against the hospital is false and completely without merit."

"That's crap," said Andrew. "And you know it."

"All I know is," said Jordan, "we've already given her surgery that she can't pay for."

"On the *wrong hip!*"

"Don't shout at me, I'm just doing my job."

"Admit her for surgery on the bad hip, they'll pay for that."

"Dr Sharp, with respect, we don't know that for sure. The insurance company says that if she had surgery on a healthy hip she may have made a fraudulent claim."

"That's ridiculous. But okay – admit her for her cardio investigation and treatment. They'll *have* to pay for that."

"They may not. Not if they suspect she tried to defraud them."

"Ms Waters, we defrauded her to the tune of one hip. She didn't try to defraud anyone. I insist you readmit her, *right now*."

"You can't insist on admitting people to the hospital," Jordan said. "You're just a doctor."

"*What?*"

She stood her ground. "I'm sorry, Dr Sharp, it's up to the insurance company, you know that. I can't make the insurance pay. And I've been told to send her home until this is sorted out."

"Who told you?"

At that moment the culprit hurried in. "You paged me?" inquired Blanche.

"Blanche," said Andrew, "this woman has had a—"

"A very minor heart attack, I gather," interrupted Blanche.

Andrew was stunned by her effrontery. "You're a cardiologist now?"

"No, I've just been told…"

146

Andrew chose not to explain that cardiac arrest, also known as circulatory arrest, is merely a sudden stop in the circulation of the blood when the heart stops pumping, whereas a heart attack occurs where blood flow to the muscle of the heart is impaired and the muscle is damaged. A cardiac arrest can lead to death or a stroke within minutes, because the brain is starved of oxygen and glucose, but not necessarily – if the heart is quickly restarted, there may be no lasting damage.

"Good," said Andrew, happy that Blanche was wrongly referring to it as a heart attack. "So you also know that, as she has severe pain in both hips now, she might have another. She must be readmitted immediately!"

"Sorry. No can do," said Blanche, wringing her hands. She turned to Jordan. "You can take her upstairs until she's stabilized. Then send her home."

"Can't do that," said Jordan. "Sending her upstairs could be seen by lawyers as a readmission. If we have a readmission within thirty days we won't get paid anything."

"Blanche, you're always telling everyone you believe in the right to life," said Andrew.

Blanche was confused. "For unborn fetuses, yes. What's that got to do with it?"

"But there's no right to life for patients with crummy insurance?"

"Andrew, I don't understand what you're talking about, but I don't want you to see me as your adversary—"

"It's not about you and me." Andrew was trying not to lose his temper. "It's about this patient, who Samaritans is probably in the process of killing! You are legally obligated to admit her."

"No we're not. At this point she is uninsured, and we are only obligated to admit uninsured patients if their condition is life threatening."

"Listen, Blanche. Listen *very* carefully. I am a doctor. You – are not. I am telling you that her condition could be life threatening." Andrew did not think that her condition was life threatening at all. Her heart, now beating firmly, sounded pretty strong to him, but he could see no other way to get Samaritans to honor their responsibilities. "If this patient dies before she gets proper treatment, I'm blowing the whistle on all of you: you, Max, you Jordan, and the insurance company. Nurse, take this patient to Intensive Care. NOW!"

The nurse shrugged at Jordan and Blanche, and nodded to the two orderlies. They wheeled Mrs Jefferson in the direction of the elevators. Neither Blanche nor Jordan tried to stop them.

"If only she had died," Blanche said. "There would have been no problem."

Andrew said, "You don't think it's a problem if the patient *dies*?"

"Less of a problem than if she's readmitted."

Andrew took a very deep breath. "There's something here I don't get. It came up in the M&M meeting too. What's so terrible about readmitting patients?"

Blanche explained. It was no longer enough for hospitals to make patients healthy enough to leave. Under Obamacare, hospitals that have high readmission rates are penalized, so millions of dollars invested in patients are not coming back. "It's not a fair system. We have a lot of readmissions because we are a safety-net hospital, and so we often don't get to see patients until they are seriously ill. Seriously ill patients are readmitted more often than others.

"The government says that readmissions result from poor follow-up care, which may be true sometimes, but often isn't. But – whatever! We had to make elaborate arrangements to keep discharged patients from coming back. We call them after forty-eight hours to ask how they're feeling. We arrange follow-up appointments with doctors before we let them leave. And we make sure they know what medications to take when they get home."

"What happens if patients *are* readmitted?"

Blanche loved questions about data. "Two thirds of hospitals with Medicare patients paid penalties last year of about three hundred *million* dollars because too many patients were readmitted within thirty days of being let out."

"I see."

"That's the point, Dr Sharp: dead patients can't be readmitted."

"So… we should try and kill every patient we discharge in doubtful health?"

"It would save us a lot of money. But unfortunately we have to leave that to God, and market forces."

"You seem to be against the government making it possible for poor people to get health care."

"Yes, I am."

"Aren't you supposed to be a Christian? What about charity? What about 'love thy neighbor'?"

"I believe very deeply in those things. But it's more complicated than that. God doesn't think the government should interfere in the free market."

"How do you know what God thinks?"

Blanche gazed at him, not sure whether to be amused or annoyed. "Andrew, are you really trying to understand, or are you just debating with me?"

"I'm really trying to understand."

"Fine," she said. "But I have to be brief, I have work to do. The modern welfare state puts itself in the place of God and tries to handle everybody's needs, cradle to grave. I understand that you think there's a need for some sort of safety net, but there's a vast amount of data—" she stabbed the air with her forefinger, "—and sociological evidence, and statistics, and numbers—" she poked the air again, three times, "—all indicating that the decline of Christianity in the West can be correlated precisely with the expansion of government."

Andrew was incredulous. "Are you kidding me?"

"No, I would never 'kid' about God's will."

"How do you know what God's will is? Has he told you personally?"

"I haven't time for your stupid, blasphemous jokes." Blanche turned to go.

*

She hurried back up to Max's office to tell him about her argument with Andrew in the ER. Max was shocked. "Blow the whistle on us? Can he do that?"

"Andrew says her condition is life threatening. If it is, the law says we have to deal with it."

"But Andrew can't tell anyone anything, can he? What about medical confidentiality?"

"There is none if she dies. Then it's a homicide investigation. He can say anything."

"Truthfully, Blanche, I'm upset. I thought Andrew was my friend."

"I'm not sure that he is," said Blanche.

Max thought for a moment. "Well, we don't want to piss him off. It's not worth it."

"He's pissed off already," said Blanche.

Max squinted at the ceiling and thought for a moment. "I know what to do," he said.

Blanche was relieved. "You're so great," she said.

Max smiled, stood up from his desk, locked the door, took her by the hand and led her to the sofa. "C'mere, baby."

30

Andrew's furnished apartment in Georgetown had a large balcony off the living room with a view over the Potomac River. That evening, sitting on it trying to relax, enjoying a beer and the purple and pink stripes across the evening sky after the rain, the doorbell rang. Surprised, he went to answer it.

Max was standing there in the brown corridor, holding a gift-wrapped bottle and a box of cigars. "Hi, buddy."

Andrew tried to be gracious. "Max. This is a surprise."

Max came in and looked around. "Very nice…"

Andrew knew he didn't mean it. Everything in the place was beige, bland, drab and rented. There was nothing nice about it except that it was clean.

"It's okay. To what do I owe this pleasure?"

"Am I interrupting something?"

"No. Just chilling out with a beer after a difficult day."

"I know, I know. I brought you a bottle of great Scotch. Macallan, eighteen years."

"Thanks." Andrew put it on the flecked beige granite kitchen counter. He didn't offer any to Max and was amused when his uninvited guest found a shot glass in a cupboard, opened it, and helped himself to a snifter.

"I brought you some cigars. You want one?"

"No thanks."

"You sure? They're Cubans, Montecristo Number 4. Real good."

"Max, I don't smoke, I'm a cardiothoracic surgeon."

"Oh. Yeah," said Max. "Ok. Mind if I have one?"

"Not if we sit outside."

He led Max to the balcony.

"Balcony. Nice." Max opened the cigar box, took one out, cut it, lit it and puffed contentedly. "Lovely view. Great sunset."

Andrew waited for him to get around to the point of the visit.

"So. Blanche told me about your little disagreement today."

"It wasn't little. A patient was released too early after a botched operation and she was told she had to pay for it to be redone correctly. Either that, or the pain she was in, caused her so much anxiety that she had a cardiac arrest."

"A heart attack? How bad was it?"

Like Blanche, Max obviously thought that a cardiac arrest and a heart attack were one and the same. It helped.

"Not at all good," he said, laying it on thick. "Bad prognosis."

"Is she gonna die?"

"Definitely," said Andrew. After all, he told himself, everyone dies in the end. "But hopefully we can keep her alive for a while so that Samaritans is not blamed. But if her heart were put under any more stress I wouldn't like to predict the outcome." He puffed out his cheeks, a dismal expression on his face.

"What's her name?"

"Mrs May Jefferson."

Max made a note in his smartphone. "Look, Andrew, I see why you're concerned, you're a doctor, like you said. I understand. And I think I can help. In fact, I have something to discuss with you: how would you like to be director of the Cardiothoracic Rehab Unit. It pays five grand a month extra."

Andrew was puzzled. "But is there a Cardio—?"

"Not yet! It's at the planning stage. But we'll need a director on board pretty soon."

Andrew was almost amused. "Max, do you think you can just buy me?"

"Buy you? No! But I believe in cash incentives. And bonuses. You're doing a great job and I want you to be happy. You're my friend."

"I think you mean," said Andrew, "that you need me."

Max looked bewildered. "That's what a friend is: someone you need, who needs you. You scratch my back, I scratch yours. But if you don't want the job I'll backburner it."

"Max…"

"Look – try to understand, Andrew, Samaritans is a business."

"I know that."

"Of course you do. But let me ask you something," said Max. "What is our end product?"

Andrew had never thought about medicine in terms of an end product. "Health?"

"No!" said Max. "*Not* health. That's what everybody thinks, but they're wrong! 'Is he sick, is he well, is he dying, is he feeling better?' All wrong questions, baby! Alive, dead, so what? That doesn't change our price. There's an outcome – but good or bad, alive or dead, we charge the same. The product is the *outcome*. Good or bad, it makes no difference to us."

"It makes a difference to the patient," said Andrew. "And it makes a difference to me."

"But it makes no difference to the business model. There's a financial crisis I'm trying to solve here – you know that, right?"

"Of course."

"And I'm doing what I can to avoid putting up actual health care costs. So I've increased the cost of room service, I'm putting a minibar in each of the deluxe rooms—"

"You mean... wait a minute... liquor?" Andrew had real trouble getting his head around this one. "Scotch and stuff? In the wards?"

"Yeah. Great idea, right? Blanche thought of it, she's so smart."

"Real smart," said Andrew. "Booze mixes so well with all those prescription drugs."

Max was immediately defensive. "Look, it's a choice, okay? It's a free country. Nobody's forcing them to drink booze. There'll be Evian in the minibar too."

"For how much?"

"Eight-fifty a pop. Not much more than the Four Seasons. And macadamia nuts for twenty-seven dollars. I'm not neglecting medical matters either: I've told the Head of Nursing Services to put the price of an aspirin up to nineteen dollars."

"People will object."

"You mean patients?" Max chuckled. "Nah, they never fight us. They're too sick."

Andrew gazed at his CEO sitting back, sipping The Macallan 18 and puffing on his cigar. "Max – do you ever stop to think about why this hospital was called Samaritans?"

Max blew out a cloud of smoke and smiled. "It's not called Good Samaritans."

153

"You know something?" Andrew said. "I didn't acknowledge to myself, until this moment, that there was such a thing as a person who is entirely without a moral sense of any sort."

Max was wounded to the core. "You talkin' about me? You saying I have no moral sense? That's so unfair. And untrue! You have really hurt my feelings now."

"I thought you'd take it as a compliment."

"Andrew, you don't understand. Wealth is morality."

Andrew struggled for some moments with this concept. "What?"

"Haven't you read *The Psychology of Self-Esteem*?"

"Wealth is morality?" Andrew was laughing now. "That's preposterous."

"It's the truth," said Max. "Don't you know any Ayn Rand? None at all?"

"What's that?"

"She was a great writer..." Max shook his head and sighed. "Forget it, man. Look, all I'm doing is making health care more responsive to patient choice."

"Max, it may be hard for you to understand this, with your business school background and corporate experience, but patients are not consumers."

"Of course patients are consumers. What else are they?"

"They're patients. That's what they are. Doctor–patient relationships used to be special. Almost sacred. Something has gone terribly wrong with the art of medicine."

"Andrew, this is the situation. So far, we've been charging the consumer – or the patient or whatever you want to call him – far less than he's willing to pay. That's bad business. Lipitor costs ten times as much at Rite-Aid as it does at K-mart. Rite-Aid, CVS, Target and other chain pharmacies sell generic drugs at up to eighteen times their cost. We're going to match the top prices in future." He opened his arms wide. "I have a new slogan: Never knowingly oversold." He grinned.

"No, Max," said Andrew. "Patients are not customers, not guests, not clients and not consumers. Not everything can be decided by the marketplace."

"Whoa!" said Max. "This sounds like communism to me."

"Don't be absurd. Do I look like a communist?"

154

"I don't know what they look like. I imagine they look like everyone else. Like Bernie Sanders. Isn't that what makes them so dangerous?"

"Max, I'm trying to make you understand something... different. When the patient is lying on the operating table and I'm putting a stent into his artery, he doesn't ask the price or get online to look for lower estimates."

"Well, no... it's too late by then. The choice has been made."

"You keep talking about choice. Patients don't choose to be ill. They don't choose to pay for our services. They don't have a choice."

"Sure they do. We're not the only hospital in town." Max's patience was wearing thin. "Look, Mr Holier-than-thou, it's not my fault Samaritans Hospital can only afford to treat people who can pay. I didn't create this system. I'm just doing my job. And I notice you're quite happy to profit from it all." He gave an exaggerated look around the apartment. "These are pretty nice digs. In a pretty nice location. Then there's your gigantic salary. Not to mention the Porsche."

"I think you're telling me I'm a hypocrite. But I'm the best, I'm entitled to be the highest paid. That's just supply and demand."

"You can't have it both ways, pal. If you don't like the system, don't talk to me, talk to the politicians, talk to the voters, run for Congress, get elected."

"You said I'm happy to profit from the system?" said Andrew. "What system do you think I profit from?"

"The health care system."

"Max," said Andrew. "There *is* no system. It's chaos."

"Yes!" Max was on his feet, energized by his boundless enthusiasm. "That's what's so great about it! It's a barnburner! We can make the rules. This hospital is just a start. We can have twenty hospitals, fifty, two hundred even. This industry is like Vegas was in '45. It's like Californian real estate in the fifties. The sky's the limit! And I can take you right up there with me. We'll be partners. You'll be rich, and I mean *rich*. We can make *billions*."

Andrew, still seated, stared at Max with quiet amazement. "Whatever made you think that, coming from Vegas, you could run a hospital?"

"Why not? Health care is the ultimate lottery."

*

Shortly after Max left Andrew's apartment, Kimberly rang the doorbell. Andrew had forgotten his date with her and Max's accusation of hypocrisy had cast a dark cloud over his evening. Was Max right?

Kimberly, however, was not easily discouraged. She took her job very seriously. Her BA in biology was her chief qualification but being a cheerleader for the Washington Redskins had defined her approach to life. Every year, hundreds of former or current cheerleaders were recruited as drug saleswomen; big pharma liked their athletic looks, their tiny skirts and their tremendous upbeat enthusiasm, and they knew that most male doctors liked them too. Hiring cheerleaders had been an almost foolproof way of selling drugs for a while, but now that the medical colleges were graduating as many women doctors as men – in some cases more women than men – Kimberly had really come into her own. She had an active libido, street-smarts, and was attracted to both sexes.

"So, Doc," she began, stepping into the apartment, "is this evening business or pleasure?"

"You tell me."

"Okay. I love multi-tasking but… shall we forget business tonight?"

"Cool. Want a drink?"

She asked for a chilled vodka, straight up, while she ran her fingers through her thick blonde hair, checking herself out in the mirror. He poured one for each of them. She sat on the sofa and patted the space beside her. His heart wasn't in it but he accepted the invitation.

"You know," she said, "just being with you is so special. You surgeons, you're today's unsung heroes. You save lives every day, day after day, as a matter of course, you give life back to people who thought it was all over. Especially a heart surgeon like you. Really, you perform miracles."

There was an eerie familiarity about what she was saying. He realized it was precisely what Cathy had predicted. "Well… I wouldn't say that exactly, I—"

"Oh, I would. I'd trust you with my heart."

"You're speaking literally, right?"

"Of course." She laughed a tinkly, flirtatious giggle. "Oh. You didn't think I meant…?"

"No – I didn't."

She put her impeccable manicured fingers on his thigh. "Though, subconsciously," she murmured, so close to his ear that he could feel her warm breath, "maybe I did mean that. Tell me Doctor, how many lives did you save today?"

He heard Cathy's voice saying the same words. He saw Cathy's sneering upper lip. He saw he was the target of a sophisticated and skillful salesperson.

"You think I'm just saying this?" asked Kimberly, snuggling up. "I'm not. I mean it. I'm in awe of you, Andrew. You're godlike. That delicate surgery you perform..." She took his hand and kissed his fingers sensuously, one by one. "You must have the most sensitive fingers." She reached for his crotch. "I bet there are other parts of you that are real sensitive too."

Andrew started to laugh. He couldn't help it.

"What's funny?" she asked.

He just shook his head and laughed more. It turned hysterical, born of despair.

"What's so damn funny? Are you laughing at me? I don't appreciate being laughed at..."

"I'm sorry, I'm sorry..." He rolled off the sofa, howling.

Kimberly stood up, walked out of the apartment and slammed the door behind her. Andrew could hear her voice rceding down the corridor as she spoke into her smartphone.

"Hi Max? It's Kimberly. I was wondering if I could come see you tonight, but no problemo if you're busy. I want to talk to you about a special rate on a bulk deal for HeartGraft. Call me, babe."

31

Andrew lay awake, thinking. His two encounters that evening had had a greater effect on him than he could have imagined. His mind was filled with the awful meeting with Max and the fiasco with Kimberly. He saw with sudden clarity that he couldn't go on like this.

He arrived at Samaritans even earlier than usual next morning. He was the first customer in the cafeteria and he served himself a cup of stewed coffee that must have been brewed the evening before. As he sat in the huge, empty room, watching a desultory janitor mop the floor, he thought about Jordan's refusal to readmit Mrs Jefferson. He thought about why Victor Stone was giving advice to the hospital and how it had all come about.

And he thought about Emily collecting up the papers and images from the M&M meeting – why had she done that?

Somewhere around the third bitter sip, it all fell into place. He left the rest of the bitter, watery liquid on the table and hurried upstairs.

When Cathy appeared he greeted her warmly. "I had a date with Kimberly last night."

"How was it?"

"She walked out on me."

"She did? Why?"

"Because I was laughing at her. Everything she said was exactly what you said she'd say."

"I'm sorry," Cathy said.

"Don't be. But it was really embarrassing. If I hadn't laughed, I'd have cried."

"Oh dear," said Cathy, but without much sympathy.

"I've got a lot of stuff to deal with this morning. Get me Dr Embers in pathology, if you can."

Cathy phoned Embers and put her through.

He had a question for her. She gave him the answer he expected. He hung up and called: "Now would you please get hold of Emily Craven and ask her to come up here?"

"Can I tell her what it's about?"

"No. Just do it, please?"

*

Cathy paged Emily, who was there within five minutes.

"Hi!" Her smile arrived in his office two steps ahead of her. "What's up?"

"Cathy, leave us alone, please."

"Is this business or pleasure?" Emily asked when the door had closed.

"Dr Craven..." he began.

"Dr Craven?" she repeated. "Definitely business, then. Is that right, *Dr Sharp*?"

"Yes. Very serious business. After the last M&M meeting I saw you collecting up Dr Duff's and Dr Weiner's papers."

He waited.

"I like to be tidy," she said.

"No other reason?"

"Well, there was some confidential information in those pages. It doesn't do to leave them lying around."

"I thought that's what you were doing," he said, and she relaxed visibly. "But now I remember I saw that Dr Duff was still in the room. Why didn't you just give them back to him?"

"He didn't want them anymore."

"So why did you want them?"

"I didn't. Like I said, I was just tidying up."

"I don't think so. Because you then spoke to Dr Embers and copied the images and the X-rays from the meeting on to a thumb drive. Why did you need them?"

"I was interested. I like to take every opportunity to learn."

Andrew didn't believe a word of it. "Emily, what would happen to a doctor who reported our M&M meetings to Victor Stone?"

"Who's Victor Stone?"

"You know who Victor Stone is."

"Oh, Victor Stone."

"Yes. A doctor who leaked information from our M&M meetings to him would be fired. I would make sure of that."

"Why are you telling me this?"

"Because you are the leak."

She hesitated for a moment. "No. I'm a whistle-blower. I'm a back channel."

"You're not. You're an unethical doctor who reveals confidential information about patients to an ambulance-chasing lawyer."

Her face crumpled. "No! Not information about patients. Information about bad doctors."

Andrew doubted that her motive was so public spirited. "What does Stone pay you, Emily?"

It was a shot in the dark, but tears filled her eyes and she confessed. "Enough to cover the increase in my malpractice insurance. It's going up again and I just can't afford it. And I'm going under because of the interest on my student loan. Andrew… I'm desperate."

Andrew handed her a bad-news tissue from the box on his desk. "Insurance seems to have gone up for everyone in Samaritans. But that's because Victor Stone is suing more and more doctors. And how is he able to do that?"

She sniffled, looked at the floor and said nothing.

"He is able to do that, Emily, partly because of the incompetence of our colleagues but partly because you are leaking the information to him."

She poured her heart out to him then. It all began with the new admission forms. When Jordan Waters tried to get a reluctant patient to sign one, she asked what was in it. At first Jordan refused to show her, but Emily insisted. As she started reading, she realized that she had stumbled across something that would raise her malpractice insurance yet again.

She was already strapped for cash, and increasingly bitter about her student loan, which hung around her neck like the proverbial albatross. "I see why personal loans – real estate mortgages, car loans and even education – should be paid back by the individual who benefits from it most directly, but why do we get no help whatsoever in paying it back? Good medicine benefits the whole community. The community needs doctors."

"I agree," said Andrew.

"Other than mortgages, student loans are the largest form of household debt in the country. $1.1 trillion, larger than the nation's car loan and credit card debt combined. And instead of lending a helping hand to people like me, the federal government itself stands to make two hundred billion over the next ten years as a direct result of its own student loan scheme. And there's no way out, short of suicide: you can wipe out any other loan by going bankrupt, but not a student loan."

The tears rolled down her face as she told Andrew her fear of going bankrupt and *still* owing all the money. A student loan, like a diamond, was forever.

He said nothing. He wasn't sure how to respond.

"I asked Jordan if it was Max Green's idea and she said she couldn't discuss it; she just follows the rules and does what she's told."

She stood up and, crossing an invisible boundary, went behind his desk and knelt at his feet. Embarrassed, he tried to make her stand up but, clutching his ankles, she wouldn't. "Please don't fire me, Andrew. Please, please…"

He tried to loosen her grip. He couldn't.

"I beg you, I beg you…" She reached inside his zipper. "I'll do anything, anything—"

"Please, Emily, stop it!"

There was a knock and Cathy opened the door and walked in.

She blinked, then averted her eyes.

"Oops! Sorry."

She backed out and quietly shut the door. Andrew scowled.

"Are you going to have me fired?" Emily's tear-stained face looked up at him. "Please don't, please, please. I'll do anything you want. Do you have a secret fantasy…? a fetish…? anything kinky…? anything at all…?" Trying to look inviting, she whispered hopefully, "…anal?"

"What I want," he said, "is that you don't ever reveal confidential information again. Or you will be fired."

She stood up, hugged him and kissed him. He felt like he was being licked by a Labrador he'd rescued from the pound. "Thank you, thank you, thank you," she said. "Thank you for not firing me. I'm so grateful, I promise I'll do *anything* for you, any time. Don't hesitate to ask."

She hurried out.

Cathy came into the room a couple of minutes later.

"Don't you want to know what all that was about?"

"None of my business. Sorry I came in."

"It's not what you think? She was trying to get around me."

"Part of you, anyway," she grinned.

"No. I was trying to… Look, what happened was, I confronted her. She's the one who's been leaking patient information to Victor Stone."

"Shit! Are you sure?"

"She just confessed."

"That's awful."

"And confidential. You know that, right?"

Cathy's eyes blazed. "Of course I know that. What is she, a whistle-blower or a spy?"

Andrew thought about Emily's final offer. "An asshole," he said.

32

Andrew had no surgery that day. Cathy brought him a turkey sandwich from Merv's with lettuce and tomato and no mayo, at his desk.

"Thank you," he said. "Sit down, have lunch in here. Keep me company."

"Sure." She sat on the sofa. All she had ordered for herself was a yogurt.

"You dieting?"

"Not especially," she said. "But most women are on diets, all our lives, until we get too old to care."

"To care about what?"

"Guys. Sex."

"What do I have to do," said Andrew, "to be one of the guys you care about?"

"I care about you. You're my boss." She ate a spoonful. "A very good boss."

"You know what I mean."

"No. Well, if you mean what I think you mean – Andrew, you're a very nice person and…" She hesitated.

"You don't mean 'and', you mean 'but'."

She ploughed on. "I appreciate that you stood up for me, but…"

"Go on."

"You sure you want to have this conversation?"

"Yes."

"Well, we care about different things. You're a great surgeon – I mean, I wouldn't know, but everyone says so – but I'm a mom, with a kid. I have responsibilities. I have to be a grown-up."

"I'm a surgeon. So do I."

"Well, yes, you do, in your way, but not the same way as me."

"What are you trying to say?"

Cathy took the plunge. "You're a bit like my kid Ben with his video games. For you, medicine is like a video game. Can I be the fastest? Can I win? Can I be best? It's just… not very grown up."

"What's wrong with being best?"

"Nothing. But there's more to being a doctor than that. At least, I hope there is."

"I repair their hearts. I give them back their health…"

"Your feelings, Andrew," she said. "Where are they?"

"Feelings? My feelings are my own. I can't get all sentimental about my patients. We have to be detached, I can't take on all their suffering. That's basic. That's how we're taught."

"Okay." She shrugged. "I'll shut up then."

"You didn't see what happened in the ER the other day. When Blanche tried to send Mrs Jefferson home. You didn't see what I did."

"What did you do?"

Andrew pouted. "Oh, forget it."

"Did you talk to Mrs Jefferson? Find out how she felt?"

"Not *to* her, no."

"Why not?"

"It wasn't necessary."

As soon as he heard himself say that, he knew she was right. He could have – should have – talked to Mrs Jefferson herself.

Cathy ate a couple of spoonfuls of yogurt. "Am I fired for talking to you like this?"

"'Course not. I asked your opinion."

He let the silence stretch between them. Then, "What happened to your guy?"

"What guy?"

"Your son's father. I'm guessing Ben wasn't an immaculate conception."

"Nope." She shoveled down more yogurt and seemed disinclined to explain further.

Andrew persisted. "Were you married? Or was he just – a guy?"

"Yep. We were married." She licked the back of her spoon. "I've made a lot of mistakes in my life. Like, everything I just said to you, for instance." She tried to smile. "My husband was one of the biggest."

"So you wouldn't want to get married again?"

"I'd certainly think twice about it. More than twice."

"Maybe," ventured Andrew, "the guy you married was the mistake, rather than marriage itself."

"Maybe."

"Does he support you? Does Ben get child support?"

"No, and no."

"What happened?"

"You really want to know? Or is this just a way of being entertained while you eat your sandwich?"

"No," Andrew said. "Shit!"

"Well, it was my fault. He was a kind of free spirit. A biker. A musician. Nice guy. Charming, funny, didn't give a damn. Didn't like to be tied down. I wanted to tie him down, so I tricked him and got pregnant. He got on his bike and left. I was very stupid."

"But you've got Ben. So it's not all bad."

"No. I've got Ben, and he's wonderful."

"What does he like? What kind of things?"

"The usual stuff. Video games, candy, ice cream... math." She stopped.

"Math?"

"Yes."

"Good for him. He likes school?"

"Loves it. Loves baseball. You know, boy stuff."

She stopped. She finished her yogurt but made no move back towards her desk. The phone rang. She let it go to voicemail.

"What is it?" he asked. "What are you thinking about?"

"Nothing, really." She stood up.

He wondered if she were thinking about Ben's lack of a father. "Do you want your husband back?"

She smiled and shook her head. "It would be nice for Ben. To have his dad back. But it would never work. He's not a domestic animal."

*

At the end of the day Cathy, with some reluctance, asked Andrew if he could give her a lift home that evening, if he was going her way. Her ten-year-old Chevy was in the shop. The rusty rear bumper had half fallen off and was rattling and trailing along the street.

When they got to her front yard she asked, to his surprise, if he'd like to come in for an iced tea. He accepted immediately. A small, scruffy, bespectacled boy was scrunched up on the sofa in the living room, engrossed in a video game on a tablet.

"You must be Ben," said Andrew. "Hi."

165

Ben took no apparent notice.

"Ben!" Cathy was firm, commanding. "We have a guest. Dr Sharp is talking to you."

Ben frowned and looked up. Andrew offered his hand and Ben shook it solemnly. "I've heard a lot about you, young man. And I'm Andrew, not 'Dr Sharp'. Very pleased to meet you."

Ben said nothing and went back to his game.

"Ben," said Cathy in a warning tone, "what do you say?"

Ben mumbled something unintelligible that might have been, "Pleased to meet you too."

"So, Ben..." Andrew sat beside him on the old, lumpy couch. "How would you like to come and watch the Redskins with me sometime?"

Ben peered myopically at Andrew, and his face brightened.

"I wouldn't like it, I'm afraid," intervened Cathy. "Football's a dangerous, brutal game, and I don't approve of it."

"Oh, sorry," Andrew said. "I thought, you know, as—"

"I know," said Cathy. "I'm sorry too."

"Well... how about the zoo?"

"The zoo?" said Cathy. "Well, I don't really—"

"Before you say anything," Andrew hurried on, "I'm aware that zoos aren't cool anymore, but I can't take him on a safari, and I think he'd find the animals interesting."

"I like the zoo," said Ben. "I've been before."

"You have?"

"Lot of times. Mom takes me because it's free."

"That's not the only reason," said Cathy. "It's the National Zoo. Run by the Smithsonian." She paused. "It is free, though."

"You like it, Ben?"

"I like the reptile house!"

"The reptile house, eh?" Andrew was intrigued. "Want to go again?"

"Can I, Mom?"

Cathy couldn't resist his earnest enthusiasm. "Okay. We'll both go with Dr Sharp. On a weekend." She glanced at Andrew. "Thanks," she added.

"Great. How about this Saturday?" Andrew held up his hand. "Gimme five."

Ben gave him a cheerful high-five.

"Cool," said Andrew.

Cathy smiled at them both, but he knew she was watching him with caution.

33

Milton Weiner told Max that, as Chief of Surgery, he had no option but to share what he'd learned at the M&M meeting about Mrs Jefferson's hip. Weiner didn't know that Blanche had already briefed Max about it, following her confrontation with Andrew in the ER.

"It happened," Weiner said, "because you pressured the surgeon to fit in two more hips per day. So time is no longer allotted for necessary checks – like being sure they're operating on the correct limb—"

"But productivity has increased."

"Yes."

"And we need the revenue."

"Max, I'm not an idiot," Milton said. "I know that. But it would, in my opinion, be better to increase our charges and take more time."

"Increase charges?" Now Max was interested. "By how much, do you think?"

"A lot." Weiner produced some papers that he'd printed out that morning. "Look… we've been charging a low basic fee of $5,300 for a hip replacement. But here," he pointed at his printout, "in the Keck Hospital at USC, they charge – on average – $123,885 for a major artificial joint replacement. Centinela Hospital in LA, which is owned by Prime Healthcare Services, charged $220,881 for the same procedure. And Monterey Park, California, charged even more: $223,000. That's a hundred grand more."

"But doesn't that include all the bundling?"

"Even so, they're charging forty times what we charge here."

"My God," murmured Max.

"Now, I'm not saying that's good," said Milton Weiner. "It's not good. But it's better than operating on the wrong limb. And if we slowed down a bit, generally, in the surgical department, we might have fewer accidents, mistakes and lawsuits."

"And we'd still come out ahead?"

"Yes. These price differences can't be explained by anything: regional difference in wages, sickness of the patients… nothing accounts for a forty-fold price differential. Not that I'm suggesting you increase our charges that much. Far from it."

Max frowned. "I thought you were suggesting it."

"No. These prices are extortionate and unethical. I'm merely pointing out that we could charge a little more, enough to allow time for the proper safety checks before surgery."

Max stood up. "Milton, you need to think bigger. You need to cultivate some blue-sky thinking. Your ambitions are too limited. But thanks for the input, I get the gist, and it's been real helpful."

Max ushered Weiner out of the office and sent for Blanche immediately. "Why didn't you tell me all this?" he asked.

"I think we need to focus on the highest paid specialties," she said.

"Isn't that what I did when I hired Andrew Sharp?"

"No. Cardiologists are well paid, but not the highest paid, because some other specialties have greater volume and turnover. Andrew can probably do two bypass surgeries in a day, but he can't compete in profitability with a dermatologist."

"Even though his procedures are major?"

"Dermatologists are skilled at increasing revenues by offering new procedures – and many more of the lucrative ones."

"Like what? I know about all the cosmetic shit but, other than that, don't they just remove small lesions, most of which aren't even life-threatening?"

"Exactly. Between two and four million skin cancers are removed every year. Only a tiny fraction of them are malignant melanomas."

"That sounds like an epidemic."

"It's a *treatment* epidemic. That's the point. Minor procedures typically offer the best return on investment. Those guys can do a couple of dozen hits while Andrew does one. They can freeze off twenty pre-cancers in one ten-minute session, and bill separately for each of them. It's incredibly profitable! You have to pay top dermatology surgeons about six hundred grand basic a year. We need one."

"Six hundred grand *basic*?" Max was shocked. "We can't afford that for one doctor. That's nearly half what *I* make!"

"You have to spend money to make money. You taught me that. We need to build up this department. We should corner the market in dermatology."

Max was on board. "Sure we should. With the right advertising and marketing campaign we can make Samaritans the 'go-to' place for skin."

"Right!" She echoed his enthusiasm. "Here in DC we have thousands of politicians, and their wives, and TV political pundits, all aging, all wanting to look younger. Plus, we'd get all those facility fees as well if we buy out the dermatologists' corporations."

"Even better," said Max. "From now on, non-life-threatening skin cancers will be a major priority at this hospital."

"As for the price discrepancies across the board," she added, "you're right. We can charge massively more, especially in cardiology. In Livingstone, New Jersey, a hospital charged $70,712 to implant a pacemaker. But in Rahway New Jersey, which is close by, the cost for the same procedure was $101,945."

"Where do you and Milton Weiner find this stuff?"

"The New York Times."

"You read that liberal shit?"

"When it's useful, yes. And look—" she showed him her iPad, "— Andrew Sharp won't like this one – or maybe he will – but in Mississippi, the charge for treating patients with heart failure ranged from nine thousand dollars up to fifty-one thousand – in the same town."

"Did both patients survive?"

Blanche said, "Isn't that TP?"

"TP?"

"Their problem?"

Max grinned. "That's my girl."

34

Max and Andrew still behaved as if they were each other's new best friend but, after their chat at his apartment, Andrew knew that they had reached a fork in the road. He was pretty sure that Max had come to the same conclusion.

A week later he joined a deputation of surgeons calling on the CEO after yet another depressing M&M meeting. He didn't enjoy being allied with Duff, Plummer, Singh, Tarnisch or Weiner but he felt his obligation to the patients gave him no choice.

"How can I help you guys?" Max seemed to be in an obliging mood as they trooped into his office. "Sit down folks." He put his feet up on his desk. "Wassup?"

Several doctors arranged themselves on the squashy edges of his black leather sofa and chairs, but looked as uncomfortable as the ones who had to keep standing. They waited for their Chief of Surgery to begin.

"Uh – we've just come from an M&M meeting," Weiner said. "It was bad. Our mortality rate must be going through the roof."

Max was quite relaxed. "No, Milton, it's going down."

"I don't see how that's that possible."

"You're right, as a matter of fact, in assuming that – tragically – we are losing a few more patients each month." Max assumed an expression of what he took to be appropriate sadness. "But it doesn't show up in the stats, because we're shipping so many of the chronically sick and dying out to County General." He beamed at the assembled company. "Isn't that great? All the cost losers – strokes, MS, Parkinson's, Alzheimer's – they're gone!"

This revelation was not received with the enthusiasm that he hoped for. There was complete silence.

"Disappeared!" said Max. "Shazam! I'm a magician. I should go back to Vegas."

"You definitely should!" said Lori Diesel. Andrew smiled.

Weiner took a deep breath and tried again. "Mr Green, things can't go on like this. My department is stretched beyond the limit. It's becoming actively unsafe to have surgery at Samaritans Medical Center."

"In that case," Max snapped, "I hold you responsible, as Chief of Surgery, and I accept your resignation."

"What? I didn't resign."

"He didn't resign!" several voices chorused.

"It's not his fault," a few added lamely.

Max ignored them. "Dr Sharp, I am appointing you Chief of Surgery. Starting forthwith."

All eyes turned to Andrew. "No thank you," he said.

"I have appointed you. You are Chief of Surgery."

"Then I resign," he said. "Forthwith."

A tense silence followed.

Then Saul Tarnisch said, "My department is also hopelessly overstretched."

"Be careful, Dr Tarnisch," warned Max. "The psychiatric department is a luxury we don't need."

"You, sir, are what we don't need," countered Saul, always ready for a showdown.

"You're fired," replied Max.

"And you are a piece of shit!"

"But I still have my job," grinned Max.

Whereupon Dr Saul Tarnisch, chief psychiatrist at Samaritans Medical Center, stood up, stepped forward and in contravention of normal psychiatric practice grabbed Max Green by the necktie, pulled him to his feet with his left hand and slugged him hard on the nose with his right.

Max clutched his face, reeling back. "Are you crazy?" he gasped. "I'm from Vegas!" He hung onto his revolving chair, lurching back and forth, trying to retain his balance. Somehow he managed it, grabbed Saul, twisted his arm and hurled him to the floor. Saul's forehead hit the edge of Max's desk with a dull thud as he fell. He lay there, inert on the white shag carpet.

Andrew and Lori ran to him. The others doctors followed, slowly gathering round the fallen shrink. Max pulled a tissue from the box on his desk that he kept for when he fired employees and dumped women, and held it to his bleeding nose. Everyone else in the room just stared at him, some reproachful, some just plain scared.

"What?" said Max. "He attacked me! Completely unprovoked!"

Lori, on her knees, patted the psychoanalyst's face. "Saul, you okay?"

"U-u-u-u-ugggggghhhhh," said Saul, recovering consciousness.

Weiner stood over them. "Maybe he ought to get a scan," he suggested. "To make sure there's no brain damage."

"He's a shrink," remarked Andrew, "so that may be a little hard to tell."

Max sat down again behind his desk, stuffing tissues up his nostril to stop the bleeding. "This meeting is over," he announced.

Nobody took any notice. After a whispered discussion over Saul's prone body, Andrew stood up. "Max, my colleagues have asked me to say that, in the interests of patient care, we are prepared to continue co-operating with you only if you reinstate Dr Milton Weiner and Dr Saul Tarnisch."

Max gave a bitter laugh. "What is this, the inmates taking over the asylum?"

"No," Weiner said with new-found courage. "That happened already when the board appointed you. We insist you apologize to Dr Tarnisch."

"Apologize?" Max was incredulous. "To him? Are you kidding? He attacked me. I never apologize. What is this? Are you NUTS?"

The doctors looked at each other. Even Andrew was uncertain of their next move.

"What this is," said Weiner, further emboldened, "is the Caine mutiny. And you are Captain Queeg."

"Captain who? What the fuck are you talking about, Milton? I'm not going to apologize to him. He should apologize to me. Then I might reinstate you both. Until then, get out, all of you."

*

They filed out, in silence. Lori and Andrew helped Saul Tarnisch to his feet and sat with him on a bench in the corridor, waiting for the gurney to take him down to radiology.

"Why do you think Saul did that?" said Andrew.

"Couldn't take it any longer," said Lori. "Cuts. Threats. Wondering how to pay for college, how to pay his mortgage. Years of transference and counter-transference with patients who hate their fathers, and want to kill them, and who take it out on him instead. I think Max is like a real bad father figure to him."

"Yeah," said Andrew. "Being a shrink must be awful. All those years of listening to boring shit, trying to look interested. Must take its toll."

Lori smiled. "It would drive me mad. And you. Shall we do a few basic neurological tests while we're waiting?"

"Yes, we'd better," said Andrew. He turned to Saul. "What is your name?"

"You know my fucking name," said Saul.

"Okay. What is your birthday?"

"If I told you my birthday, could you verify that I was correct?"

"Not immediately, no," said Lori.

"Then shut up!"

"What's the date today?" asked Andrew.

"Look on your fucking computer," said Saul.

"I think he *is* brain damaged," said Andrew.

"I'm beginning to sympathize with Max," agreed Lori. "And I didn't think anyone could make me do that."

*

Two janitors arrived with a gurney and took him away. Andrew and Lori strolled over to the Marc J and Cynthia P Leventhal Elevators, took one down to street level and made a beeline for Reilly's Bar, a block away, where they treated themselves to a couple of large vodkas.

Andrew relished the prospect of drinks with Lori once more. Being out with a smart woman who could talk about something other than medicine was a welcome relief. The World Series was playing on the TV.

"Why," he asked, "is the rest of the world not invited to participate in a World Series?"

Lori didn't know or care. "America is the world, isn't it?"

She insisted on paying for the next round of Stoly while they watched a TV news story about a US ally in Central Asia denying that their elections were rigged – somebody had slipped up and announced the result the day before the election. The US Secretary of State was interviewed and lectured the same small country about the importance of a transparent democracy, just before the station ran a feature about voter suppression in virtually half of the United States.

Andrew didn't love Lori, but he liked the way they were still able to finish each other's sentences and fall back into their old and easy relationship. "Do you want to come back to my place for the night?"

"Oh, Andrew…" Her eyes glistened. "I thought you knew."

"Knew what?"

"Well, babe – things changed pretty soon after our hook-ups at Northwestern."

"Changed?"

"I'm still very... fond... of you," she said. "But I came to the conclusion that I preferred sex with women."

Andrew tried not to look too crestfallen. "I hope that's not my fault."

"You'll be staggered to hear that it was nothing to do with you. I'm much happier." She paused. "You weren't the only guy I had sex with at that time."

"I didn't think I was," he lied.

"We're best friends now," she said, squeezing his hand. "That's much better than quarreling lovers."

He felt he had to agree, but nonetheless drove home feeling that he had failed her in some way that he didn't quite understand.

35

The heatwave was over. The rain was bucketing down. The sky was dark gray, in some places almost black. It looked like a monsoon. Andrew couldn't tell whether Mrs Jefferson, in Intensive Care, had been woken by the storm or by the touch of his hand on hers. She opened her eyes.

"Hello. I'm Dr Sharp."

She mumbled something incomprehensible.

"First of all, can you tell me your name?"

"May Jefferson."

"Do you know where you are?"

"Samaritans?"

"Yes. And what is your date of birth?"

"October 19th, 1951."

"That's right," said Andrew. "You've had a cardiac arrest. Before that, they replaced your hip. The wrong hip. Do you remember any of that?"

"Yes. All of it."

"Good. I'm confident you can make a complete recovery. Are you in pain?"

"Not too bad," she said bravely.

"Is there anything you want to ask me about, Mrs Jefferson?"

"Yes. I was told I had to sign a form, just before I went into surgery."

"That's normal," said Andrew. "You have to say you agree to the surgery, and that you understand the risks, and so forth."

"Yes, but this was… strange…"

"Strange? In what way?"

"I had to agree that if anything went wrong I would not sue the hospital, but I would sue the doctor. And I was agreeing to hire a lawyer, Vince somebody…?"

"I think you may have misunderstood," said Andrew. Then he noticed the nurse trying to tell him something. "You know about this?"

"Yes, Doctor. I've not seen the forms myself because I'm post-operative, but other nurses have told me that all surgical patients are being asked to sign them now."

"Who is the lawyer the patients are referred to?" He knew the answer before she told him.

"You know, that TV lawyer."

"Victor Stone?" She nodded. "Can you get me a copy of this form?"

"Yes, Doctor. I'm surprised you didn't know about it."

"Me too." He turned back to Mrs Jefferson. "Okay. Don't worry about that form. I am putting you on painkillers for your hip. We'll keep you here in Intensive Care until we think your heart has recovered well enough for surgery. That shouldn't take long. Then they'll do the surgery on your other hip. The bad hip. Okay?"

She was not reassured. "How much will all this cost? I can't afford to pay for any of this."

"Nothing. It'll cost you nothing, I promise you. So don't worry."

Tears of gratitude filled her eyes.

*

Cathy arrived at her usual time and found Andrew sitting at his desk, cloaked in misery and depression. He stared out hopelessly at the deluge, watching huge raindrops splattering on the window sill.

She shook out her umbrella, pulled off her rubber boots and walked over to him. "What's wrong?"

"You know, Cathy, when this job came up, I thought I'd been offered a place in heaven. Washington DC, Chief of Cardiothoracic Surgery, big salary… but it turns out to be a kind of hell."

"Yes," she said.

He had nothing further to say. He just stared out of the window, deep in the slough of despond, seeing nothing.

Cathy sat down opposite him. He looked at her after a while. "You were right."

"About what?" she said.

"I saw Mrs Jefferson this morning. I spoke to her. Asked her about her feelings."

"That's great."

"Maybe."

She waited. "Did you learn anything significant?"

"Yes. I learned that not everything can be about the bottom line."

"Actually, I think it can," said Cathy.

Surprised, Andrew looked at her.

"It can be about the real bottom line," she said.

"What's that?"

"Who we are."

She's right, he thought. As he looked at himself through Cathy's eyes he wasn't sure that he liked what he saw. Perhaps she was right about him, or at least about their suitability for each other. It made him unaccountably sad. He knew he couldn't try again with her because it would surely lead to more rejection, more embarrassment for her and the kind of awkwardness that might mean an end to their working relationship. He didn't want that.

"Well, I know you don't like that I'm ambitious..." he said.

"That's not true. Ambition's good—" she searched for the right words, "—but... it depends what you're ambitious for." She pursed her lips. "The truth is, I don't really know how you feel about anything, except that lots of money is your priority and it's not mine. I just wonder... how would it be if you were ambitious to be more than a doctor?"

"More than a doctor?"

"A healer."

"That's what a doctor is. That's what I am."

"I hope so. I really do. I hope you're not just a plumber."

She stood up, returned to the cubicle outside his door, opened up her computer and got on with her work. Andrew watched her. Not until this moment, he realized, had he fully understood how sensible, how wise... in short, how generally wonderful she was.

No wonder she's not interested in me, he thought. *I don't measure up.*

He ruminated on this for a while and then pulled himself together and tackled his day. He made some follow-up phone calls to patients, spoke to the doctors who had referred them, replied to some emails. Then he left the office to do ward rounds, and tried to interest himself in what the patients were saying.

It was a quiet day. And Max did not try to contact him, for which small mercy he was grateful.

*

At about six o'clock Kimberly strode down the corridor to his office like it was the world's longest catwalk. "I'm picking up Dr Sharp," she announced to Cathy, then smoothed down her dress over her tight, well-exercised little bottom. "Can you tell I'm not wearing underwear?"

"I'll tell him you're here," said Cathy.

She went into Andrew's office. "Kimberly's here for a date. She wants us to know she's not wearing any underwear, by the way."

He groaned. "Oh God!"

"What?"

"Please – give her my apologies and say that I can't make it, whatever she isn't wearing. I'm dealing with an emergency."

"What emergency?"

"My life," he said.

"Why did you make another date with her?"

"I don't know." He couldn't tell her that he needed something to fill the space that she wouldn't occupy.

"Inexplicable," she remarked, not quite under her breath.

Andrew, unable to say anything in his own defense, could only agree.

He waited a few minutes after Kimberly was ushered away, and then, waving a goodbye to Cathy, made a furtive exit down the fire escape stairs. He hurried through the rain to the parking lot, found his Porsche and drove out into the street. As he accelerated past the front he saw a small group of nurses, huddled together, holding signs: *LOCKED OUT BECAUSE WE WANTED HEALTH BENEFITS!*

Several of them were still smoking.

Victor Stone did not welcome Leo Pfiffig's appearance in his private room on the Moses H Hartz Cardiothoracic Ward. He was not feeling well. He was not in the mood for his associate's youthful enthusiasm, and even less so when the reason for the visit became clear.

"Victor – Mr Stone, sir – I've been thinking about your deal with the hospital. Can I speak frankly?"

"Sure."

"I don't see what's so great about this deal."

"Then you're in the wrong profession, kiddo."

"No," said Leo, "Um – I think you're not well, and not thinking this through. I mean, I can see how this deal benefits you, but how does it benefit your clients?"

"The hospital gives them a twenty per cent discount if they come to me. And I'm the best. I've been winning lawsuits against Samaritans for years."

"Yes, but... now you have promised Samaritans not to sue them. And you promised to give the hospital a kickback when you sue the doctors. That's before you take your two-thirds contingency fee. And the twenty per cent discount you're promising to the patients isn't real because you're inflating your charges to cover it."

Victor stared at him. "What's your point?"

Leo struggled to find a way to express his concerns politely. "The point is – well, this arrangement doesn't seem to be in the best interests of..." He hesitated. "It just doesn't... sound... well, kosher to me."

"Let me get this straight," said Stone. "Are you saying there's something that's not right here?"

"Well... no, not... corrupt... exactly..."

Stone sat bolt upright. "*Corrupt?*" Plastic tubes and electric wires jerked him backwards. "Ow!" He sat forward again, more gingerly. "There's nothing corrupt here. Samaritans is a fine, reputable hospital, for Chrissakes!"

"That's not what you usually say."

"They're my clients now!" said Stone. "They make mistakes here, sure. And I make 'em pay for it. That's the American way. What do you mean by corrupt, anyway? I have an unimpeachable reputation. You think there's a problem with what I'm doing?"

Leo didn't quite dare to reply.

"Just remember – young lawyers are a dime a dozen, my cocky young friend."

"No. There's no problem… exactly…"

"Okay," said Stone, and sat back against his pillows.

Then Leo's conscience got the better of him. "Well… sir… yes, there is a problem. In my opinion you need to rethink this deal. At the very least, it's careless."

Stone was not taken aback by this unexpected show of gumption. "You better wise up, kid. You think I'm running a charity here?" He tried smiling at his junior, but Leo found the unexpected show of capped teeth more alarming than comforting.

"Okay," said Leo. And then, because he was even more scared of losing his career than his job, he added, "But, just in case, I think I'll run this past the Bar Council."

Stone suddenly couldn't catch his breath. The heart monitor got overexcited and began beeping rapidly. "Are you threatening me?"

"No, Victor. It's for your protection too."

"My blood pressure – my heart – fluttering – palpitations – you want me to fuckin' *die*?" Now he was yelling. "*You want that on your conscience?*"

Leo wasn't sure if this was a heart attack or a brilliant, rhetorical, grandstanding performance but either way he panicked. "I'll get somebody," he said and ran into the corridor shouting, "Nurse! Nurse!"

No nurses came running but it is fair to say that one of them, at the station at the far end of the ward, did go so far as to look up from her computer screen. He ran towards her. "Nurse, I think something's wrong."

"Sorry, we're a bit short-staffed." She was clicking busily on her keyboard. "I'll come in a minute."

Then louder alarms started going off and, realizing that she should perhaps be concerned, she hurried along to Victor's room. Another nurse glanced in, took one look at Stone and paged Andrew Sharp. He was home but he said he'd come right back.

"Meanwhile," he told her, "call the emergency team."

"They're on their way," she said.

They arrived a few moments later, but the crisis had passed. Stone's heartbeat was nearly normal by the time Andrew had raced back in his Porsche. He walked briskly to Victor's room.

"Mr Stone?" he asked. "How are you?"

"You a nurse?" said Victor.

"No," said Andrew. "I'm Dr Andrew Sharp. Head of Cardiothoracic Surgery."

"You don't look old enough."

"Aren't I lucky?"

"Why're you here? I need surgery?"

Andrew thought it likely but he evaded the question. "I'm a surgeon, so I never rule out surgery," he said. "Just like you never rule out a lawsuit. I'd like to do a thorough examination, though, if I may?"

"Sure," said Stone, resigning himself to yet another check-up. He was trying to be patient. Perhaps that's where the word came from.

Andrew checked his pulse and his blood pressure, more than once. He pressed Stone's fingernails. He asked him to breathe in, and out, and in again, and out again, and to hold his breath, and to breathe again. He studied Stone's chart. Intermittently, as Andrew listened carefully to Stone's heart, they chatted. "So I hear you met our boss, Mr Green. That's an interesting little deal you worked out with him. Breathe in."

"What deal?"

"The not-suing-the-hospital deal. Breathe out."

"I didn't make any deal."

"Hold your breath. That's funny, he told me you did."

Victor Stone had taken Leo's advice to heart and rethought his position. "Oh really? Well, for your information, I didn't make a deal. He proposed one. I discussed it with my junior partner and we think it's corrupt. I pretended to agree and Mr Max Green fell into my trap. I have Green and Samaritans by the short hairs and I'm going to go public when I sue Samaritans for failure to treat me properly. Speaking of which, Doc, you might as well tell your insurance company to get its check book ready too."

Andrew was neither surprised nor frightened by this outburst, but he couldn't ignore the burst of noisy activity in the heart monitor. "Relax. Relax," he said as Stone fell back on the bed, clutching his chest and his arm as the alarms went off once again and the two nurses hurried in. Within half a minute the emergency team burst unceremoniously through the door with their trolley, waving their paddles.

"Cardiac arrest," said Andrew, as they stimulated Stone's chest and the heart started beating once more. "But this one's a heart attack. Take him to Intensive Care. Tomorrow I'll tell him he needs a transplant."

37

Max could see that Christmas was unlikely to be a profitable time. The graphs and the numbers from previous years indicated a substantial drop in revenue between December 24th and 31st. New Year's Eve was usually busy, sometimes a high point of the year with drunks, car wrecks and shootings, but the previous week-and-a-half left a lot to be desired. He started work on a new TV commercial to boost sales.

On the day of the shoot, a Christmas tree was set up in what had been recently renamed the Hannah and David Connolly Lobby, after a donation of several million. An actor dressed as Santa was hired to stand beside it. Max was in an elegant navy-blue Italian mohair suit. The cue cards were in place. The camera rolled. Max smiled into the lens and said, "Samaritans Medical Center has some special offers: we are offering comped beds for elective surgery at off-peak times."

He strolled across the lobby to link arms with Santa and continued, "We're now taking reservations for Christmas Eve."

"Ho, ho, ho!" said Santa.

Two pretty models entered the scene, wearing abbreviated nurse costumes and Santa hats, and stood one on each side of Max. "Chanukah will also be comped!" he said. "And Yom Kippur too. What better place is there for a fast, under the care of our lovely young gentile nurses?"

"Cut!" said the director. "What was that you said?"

"What?" said Max.

"What did you just say?"

"I dunno. What did I just say?"

Santa obligingly reminded them. "You said, 'What better place than under the care of our lovely young gentile nurses?'"

The cue card PA spoke up. "It says gentle, not gentile."

"You can't say gentile," said the director. "Not in that context."

Max was irritated. "Okay! No biggie. Let's just do it again."

The director sat down again on a box beside the camera and said, "Going again. And... action."

Max said, "What better place than under the care of our young, lovely, gentle nurses? Samaritans Medical Center – *Making health care responsive to patient choice!*"

"And... cut!" said the director.

38

Shortly after Andrew promised Mrs Jefferson that she would have to pay nothing for her next hip replacement and her cardiac arrest, an uninvited guest in a cheap brown suit arrived at her bedside.

"Mrs May Jefferson?" he asked, pulling up a chair beside her bed.

"Yes?" Her voice was weak. She was too tired to turn her head to see who it was. Just one more voice, badgering her when all she wanted to do was sleep.

"I need to talk to you about payment." The occupant of the ill-fitting suit hauled a sheaf of paper from his stained and battered pigskin briefcase.

She blinked at him through a drug-induced haze. "Payment?" She could see him now and she didn't like what she saw. He sported a sprinkling of dandruff over his collar.

"I understand that you are to have more hip replacement surgery and that you require treatment for a recent cardiac arrest?"

"Yes."

"Who is going to pay for this? I gather your insurance company, American Health, refused."

"So I've been told."

"Well, I'm sure you understand that somebody has to pay."

"The doctor said it wouldn't cost me anything."

"Wouldn't cost you anything?" he said. "You believed that?"

"He's my doctor."

"He has no say over that kind of thing."

Mrs Jefferson was concerned. "Who are you?" She looked blearily in his direction.

"My name is Jedidiah Crawley." He smiled at her. It was this smile that had earned him the nickname "Creepy" Crawley in the office. He proffered a business card, which she did not accept.

"Please go away. You're upsetting me, and I don't feel too well." She turned her face away from him, her cheek on the pillow.

"I'm sorry about that, Mrs Jefferson. But I'm afraid that you can't have the hip replacement nor any further treatment for your cardiac arrest until we have some idea of how you intend to pay for it."

"I told you – I've been told I don't have to."

"If you don't agree to pay you will be asked to leave the hospital."

She looked back at him. "You a doctor?"

"No."

She was becoming agitated. "So who *are* you?"

"I'm here in an administrative capacity."

Though not feeling well, Mrs Jefferson was still a plain-speaking woman. "Okay. I've dealt with your type, all of my life. I know who you are. You're debt collector."

Crawley inclined his head. "In a manner of speaking, yes," he agreed.

Mrs Jefferson pressed the bell push on her bed. Nobody came.

"Do you have a credit card?" he asked her. "We can settle this now."

"Go away. I don't feel good." Her heart was racing. She pushed the bell again. Nobody came. She lay back, a little breathless, and stared at the gray Styrofoam ceiling tiles, trying to stay calm.

"Mrs Jefferson, I'm trying to make this easy for you. You should not have been readmitted without giving us your credit card or making a payment. Do you have a check book here?"

She made no reply and pressed the bell for a third time. She had a feeling of rising panic. There was no way she could afford all the care she was receiving. Her palpitations made her feel as though she couldn't breathe.

Jedidiah Crawley pressed her further. "Mrs Jefferson, do you understand? I am obligated to get you to make a point-of-service payment before you receive any further treatment for your hip or your heart."

"How do you know about my hip? And my heart? Who gave you my medical records?"

"That's confidential."

"Aren't my records confidential?" She was feeling unusually angry. "What sort of a dump is this? How do you know what treatment I need?"

"I was told by admissions, in the ER." He meant he had been told by Jordan. They both worked for MediReckoning.

"Who sent you?"

187

In accordance with instructions from Head Office, he refused to identify his employer to Mrs Jefferson. It wasn't any of her business.

"Why is your employer's identity confidential, but my medical records are not?"

"Within Samaritans, records are not confidential. How can they be when everyone here is trying to treat you? How could they treat you if they don't know what's wrong with you?"

"You're not trying to treat me," Mrs Jefferson pointed out.

A nurse arrived in response to the third bell. "Sorry, Mrs Jefferson," she said, "I know you've been ringing for a while, but we're very short-staffed." She glanced at the monitors, which were showing signs of cardiac discomfort, noticed Jedidiah Crawley and her tone changed. "You again? You know you're not supposed to be in here. Get out!"

"Okay." He hauled his chubby frame out of his chair. "But I'll be back."

The nurse summoned Andrew Sharp with an urgent message. But this time he was the wrong man to call. She needed a neurologist. Because by the time he reached Mrs Jefferson's bedside she had suffered a stroke and fallen into a coma. She did not recover consciousness that night.

39

The next morning Andrew strolled into Max's office without knocking. Max, lolling back in his swinging desk chair, had a faraway look on his face. "Not now, Andrew, I'm busy."

"You don't look busy," said Andrew.

Max waved him away.

"Sorry, but we have to talk. There was a debt collector in the ICU, harassing my patient Mrs May Jefferson."

"Harassing?" said Max. "Surely not."

"Without a doubt."

"Can't we deal with this later?"

"No." Andrew had done his homework. "Harassing patients for money in the hospital violates the Emergency Medical Treatment and Active Labor Act. I looked it up."

Max looked down. "Is that right, Blanche?"

An indistinct reply came from under his desk.

"What on earth are you doing down there?" he added, feigning irritation. There was the faint sound of a zip fastener and then Blanche's face emerged.

"Hi Andrew. Sorry. Looking for my... contact lens." She mimed blindness as she clambered out. "Yes, that is right, by the way," she added. "It is illegal to harass a patient here for money."

"I know," said Andrew. "And my patient Mrs Jefferson has suffered a stroke while being harassed by some creep whose job it is to extract money from people no matter how sick they are."

"Is this the same Mrs Jefferson," asked Max, "who had a heart attack you claimed we caused?"

"The very same," said Andrew. "Whose 'problem'—" he couldn't bring himself to call a cardiac arrest a heart attack when it wasn't, "— probably occurred as a result of the stress caused by another, totally unrelated fuck-up in this so-called medical center. Namely, replacing the wrong hip."

"You said the heart attack was serious?"

"I said her condition was life-threatening. Turns out it was. Now she's had a stroke. And when she's recovered from the stroke she's got to have another hip replacement on the hip that should have been replaced to start with! So stop harassing her to pay a bill."

Max held up his hand. "Stop right there. This person, whoever he is, is not employed by Samaritans. We outsource all debt collecting."

"If you think that lets you off the hook, Max—"

"Andrew, grow the fuck up! Unless you want this whole medical center to close down, *we have to get paid*."

"You're supposed to wait until she's well. Then you're supposed to give her a financial aid application if her insurance company won't pay, which – by the way – they should. But Samaritans doesn't even have any financial aid applications."

"Yes we do."

"No we don't. I just checked."

"Blanche, don't we have any financial aid applications on offer to patients?"

"Uh – not right now, no."

"That's right," said Andrew. "You've been going straight to collection agents. And if the patients don't pay up immediately, you sue them. It's incredible – you sue patients who we're trying to cure! What do you think the stress does to their health? You're such an asshole."

Max was offended. "Don't speak to me like that. I thought we were friends."

"A lawsuit should be a last resort, not a first choice."

Max decided to spell it out. "Andrew, you may be one hell of a surgeon, but you don't understand business. Now, under the recent law, bad debts are no longer treated as charity care. They just go unpaid. Therefore we make a total loss on all such cases. Therefore we are in even deeper shit than before. *Therefore* we will have to shut down many of our services to the community, including the ER. What don't you understand about this?"

Andrew felt out of his depth in an argument about finance. "Leaving that aside, I found these." He threw a pile of forms onto the desk.

Max stared at them. "What are they?"

"You tell me. I got them from reception. Patients have to sign them now when they check in, and before surgery."

"What's in them?"

Andrew was almost amused by Max's insolent pretense. "You know what's in them, Max. My patient, Mrs Jefferson, signed one. The effect is that now she's in a coma she will be legally represented by your new poodle, Victor Stone. But I have a question for you: what happens if Victor Stone decides to go public about this deal?"

"What deal?" asked Blanche. "There's definitely no deal."

Andrew was unmoved. "What if he blows the whistle, Max?"

"Why would he do that?"

"Because this is corrupt."

"I don't understand."

"I know you don't understand corrupt, Max, but trust me on that. I think he's going to say that you proposed this scheme and he refused to go along. He'll say you took no notice of his refusal and had these forms printed for patients to sign."

"But why—"

"I don't know if he was drugged when you talked him into it, but he could lose his license and he knows that. So he's going to do what he always does: he's going to blame you and sue you. He can't help himself. It's a reflex."

For the very first time since they had met, Max had nothing to say.

"But it's not all bad news," Andrew said. "Victor Stone has a low-grade cardiomyopathy."

"What does that mean?"

"He'll probably die soon."

"Oh." Max breathed a sigh of relief. "Oh, how terrible," he said.

"Yes," said Andrew. "But maybe he will want to die with a clear conscience."

"Conscience?" Max sniggered. "Victor Stone? You're a funny guy, Andrew, you know that?"

"Just think, Max! Think what would happen to you if this deal gets out."

"There is no deal. Stone's a liar!"

Blanche said, "Well, that's not quite—"

"Shut up, Blanche!"

She stood up. "You can find someone else to suck your dick," she snarled as she stalked out and slammed the door behind her.

Max gave Andrew an embarrassed grin.

Andrew waved the forms at him. "What will you do about these?"

"Who's giving them out to people?" Max asked. "Jordan? She's fired! She's history. There's no paper trail leading back to me. I made sure of that." He clapped his hand over his mouth like a naughty schoolboy.

"You made sure of it." Andrew repeated. He stood up. "The prosecution rests."

Max was incredulous. "Are you trying to threaten me?"

"No, Max," said Andrew. "I'm trying to warn you."

He left the room.

*

Max sat and thought for a while. Then he picked up his phone and pressed the mobile number for Soper.

"Oh, David, thank God I got you, we need to talk."

"Go ahead."

"No, not on the phone. Can we meet?"

"Is it urgent?"

"Yes. And important."

"I'm in my car. Not far from the hospital. See you in the boardroom in fifteen minutes."

Max hurried out of his office and headed off down the endless corridor to the Marc J and Cynthia P Leventhal Elevator bank. None came for several minutes and a small crowd built up.

"We must have missed the three thirty elevator," a nurse joked. Two or three people laughed.

"You – shut the fuck up!" said Max. "Everyone's doing their best here."

Shocked faces. Many of them knew who Max was from the TV ads, but he didn't care. A set of doors opened and Max pushed his way in, shoving nurses and gurneys out of the way, elbowing aside a patient on crutches who wobbled perilously against the *ALARM* button but somehow managed not to hit it.

40

David Soper had been enjoying his day.

"Things are looking up," he remarked to Frank, a business pal from Boeing who was part of the group who gathered regularly at the Hay-Adams. "Business hasn't been this good since the election. All the tax cuts."

"Do you like oysters?" asked Arthur. He was from the Pentagon. His friends called him "Art".

"Yes. Good idea."

"Champagne?"

"Why not?"

"You know," said Vicky, undersecretary at the State Department, "this Middle Eastern chaos is really dreadful."

"Dreadful," agreed everyone. "Really dreadful."

She mouthed "menus" silently at a waiter. "And it's getting worse," she continued. "We see very little hope for peace anywhere in the region in the foreseeable future."

"Oh dear, oh dear," said Frank. He tasted the Krug Brut Vintage champagne 1988 and nodded his approval to the sommelier.

"Thank goodness we are able to help so many people out there defend democracy," said Art. He pushed his glasses up to the bridge of his prominent nose. His eyes glinted behind them. "We recently sold eighty billion dollars' worth of weaponry to Saudi Arabia, including Patriot air defense systems."

"Cheers!" said Soper. "Tell me – don't you ever worry about the Saudis? Blowback? I mean, fifteen out of the nineteen terrorists involved in 9/11 were Saudis, and they started financing Wahhabi Islamist extremists like al Qaeda a couple of decades ago."

"That was then, David. This is now. We must rise above it."

"Okay," said Soper. He saw no need to argue.

"Business is business," said Frank from Boeing. He swirled the Krug appreciatively around in his glass.

"There wasn't any blowback in W's time," Art said. "The media were all gung-ho for the war. It hasn't really changed. If there's an issue we'll just explain that we need the Saudis – they're worried about Iran's hegemony in the region, and we are too. We have a common interest that supersedes all other concerns."

David Soper's feeling of contentment increased during the lobster, when he learned that State recently approved sales of Hellfire missiles to Egypt, rocket launchers to Jordan, M1A1 Abrams tanks to Iraq and artillery rocket systems to the UAE. Soper's corporations made parts for all of them. He asked the sommelier to pop open another bottle of the Krug.

"And a twenty-three billion dollar contract has been agreed with the Emirates," Vicky said. "Strategically necessary, I'm afraid."

"Very much so," said Art.

"Such a small, vulnerable country," said Soper.

"But with no shortage of ready money," Vicky pointed out.

"Quite so," said Soper.

"They already have Apache attack helicopters and Patriot and Javelin air-defense systems," Art interjected. "So now we're helping them make a large purchase of Boeing F-15 fighters to replace their fleet of French Mirage jets, which are aging somewhat."

Frank from Boeing chuckled. "I've heard Lockheed's hurrying to open an office there while the going's good."

"And are we making any more sales to Israel?" said Soper.

"Of course!" said Vicky. "Always."

"Israel is a bountiful market," said Frank. "Because *we* pay for their weapons systems."

They were all highly entertained.

*

Soper wasn't pleased to receive Max's panicky call as he was being driven home. Replete with lobster thermidor, profiteroles and Chateau d'Yquem, he had planned to take the afternoon off. But Samaritans was good PR. He liked the image it portrayed, a man who generously gave back to his community. He didn't have much time to devote to this run-down hospital for ordinary people but he did his best, and he was proud of his pro-bono work. Reluctantly, he directed his driver to divert the Bentley to the medical center and wait while he took a meeting. He had to find out what was wrong.

*

He was waiting quietly at the boardroom table working on his laptop when his disheveled CEO – not the slick, well-groomed employee whom the chairman was accustomed to seeing – burst in. Max's hair was no longer impeccably combed, and his tie was awry.

"Max – what on earth's wrong?"

"David, this is a heads-up." He paused. "Thanks for coming, by the way."

Soper graciously inclined his head.

"We might have a major problem with Victor Stone. He has a low-grade cardiomyopathy that could be fatal."

"What's that?"

"A problem with his ticker. He needs a transplant. But Andrew Sharp thinks Stone is planning to sue us with a concocted case, accusing us of corruption."

"Us?" Soper was taken aback. "You mean Samaritans Medical Center, I suppose?"

"Yes. And me, as I'm the CEO. I think he'll sue you too, as chairman. He'll go for the deep pockets. I'm wondering if..." He hesitated. "What I'm wondering is... uh... do you think, maybe, we can influence the outcome? Of Victor Stone's surgery, I mean?"

"How?"

"The transplant? Maybe it won't go so well," Max winked. "Know what I mean?"

Soper was immediately on his guard. "I'm not sure that I do. Sit down, Max. I really don't have any idea what you're talking about. Begin at the beginning. What is this concocted allegation?"

Max sat down and collected himself. "Okay. Remember that plan I told you about? To reduce the number of lawsuits against us."

Soper remembered it well. "No," he said.

Max sighed and explained it again. "When patients check in we now give them an extra form to sign. They agree that if anything goes wrong they will not sue the hospital, because we only provide facilities."

"I don't know anything about this," said Soper.

"Yes you do, remember? I went over it with you in private before the last board meeting. We agreed."

Soper shook his head. "I don't remember that."

"You said it was genius. Then we refer the patients to Victor Stone. It means patients sue the doctors but not us. So the doctors' insurance foots the bill."

"The board certainly never gave its approval for this. Did you approve it personally?"

Max looked hunted. "I thought we were friends," he said.

Soper responded with a cold stare. "What's that got to do with anything?"

"I thought we were in this together."

"We *are* friends," he reassured Max. "Friendly colleagues, certainly."

"Yes, friendly colleagues. On the same side."

"Same side of what, Max?"

Soper watched him regroup. Max had realized that he could be hung out to dry. Soper had seen that sick look of betrayal on the faces of many people with whom he had done business over the years. It could be a problem, if not handled right. He waited to see what Max's next move would be.

"Look," Max said. "Let's not argue about whether you knew this or not—"

"I didn't know about it," repeated Soper. "And you won't find it in the minutes that I signed."

"Just leave that aside for a moment," said Max, trying to stay calm. "I take it that you don't want this kind of lawsuit, naming the medical center."

"Of course not," said the chairman, with studied amiability. "And if he sues you, I will give you every kind of support I can, short of financial help."

"Financial help is the kind I'd need."

"Max, you of all people know," countered Soper, "that Samaritans doesn't have the money for this sort of thing. You're talking millions."

"That's my point." Max was looking bleak. He tried to explain again. "Victor Stone needs a heart–lung transplant. Transplant surgery is always very dangerous. No one," he whispered, glancing over his shoulder although they were alone in the room, "*no one* would be surprised by a bad outcome."

"That may be true."

"And if he passed away, he couldn't sue us."

"I agree he'd find it difficult. Why don't you talk to Dr Sharp about any questions you may have?"

"I don't know if I can. Right now, he's very suspicious of me."

"I see."

"Would you sound him out?"

Soper hesitated.

Max added, "He'll be really impressed by you."

Perhaps because of the Krug and the Chateau d'Yquem. the chairman succumbed to the flattery. "All right, I'll help you, if I can. But it's a hot potato. You realize he might be unwilling to oblige. If that happens, you'd better prepare the PR people if a successful outcome to his surgery means his lawsuit would be launched."

"Right. I'll set up a media room immediately, talk to the press in a couple of hours and make a statement." He stood up and punched the air like a sports champion. "Yes!"

Soper was bewildered. "Max, if what you say is true, this situation could be exceedingly difficult for you, and for the hospital. What are you so pleased about?"

"Dave, I always keep one thing in mind: every problem is also an opportunity. There is a possible upside."

"Good. I'd like to know what that is."

"Victor Stone's a celebrity. He has a show on cable. It puts us in the public eye. It makes Samaritans buzzworthy! If we can't save him, we say we tried. Heroically. And if we do save him and there's a lawsuit, I'll find a way to kick the can down the road."

"I like your attitude," said Soper, though he wasn't being strictly truthful.

"Thank you Dave."

"My name's David," said Soper. "I'll see what I can find out."

"Sorry, Dave – David. Thank you, Mr Chairman," Max added for safety. "I gotta go now."

Soper smiled graciously as Max more-or-less backed out of the boardroom. He elected to stay there, catching up on phone calls and emails until somewhat later in the afternoon there was a knock on the door. "Come," said Soper.

Andrew appeared. The chairman was sitting at the head of the long dark table in the afternoon shadows. He stood up to welcome Andrew. "Ah, Dr Sharp?"

"Yes sir."

"Thank you for coming to see me. I'm sure it's a busy day for you, but I hear there are problems with a famous patient. Can you tell me, without breaking any medical confidences of course, what Victor Stone's medical situation is?"

"It's not good," said Andrew. "But it's not impossible that we can save him. He needs a heart transplant. We need a donor who is blood group B."

"Are there any other patients in the hospital who might be potential donors?"

"Probably. It's a common blood group."

"So… what do you do about that?"

"The same as always. If someone with the same blood group dies, whether here or some other hospital, the relatives are asked if they will donate the heart. Assuming the deceased didn't die of heart disease and has a heart that is in reasonably good working order, we can use it if the relatives sign off."

"Not awfully efficient," remarked Soper.

"It often works out."

"I suppose…" said the chairman, trying to choose his words with precision, despite the Krug, "I suppose… is there a way you can disconnect somebody a little early… if it's someone with the right blood group who would be certain not to survive anyway."

Andrew surveyed him with a steady gaze. "No, sir," he replied. "We cannot harvest a heart from a living person. That's what we call murder."

"Of course, of course, I'm not suggesting…"

"Of course you're not, sir."

Soper dropped the subject immediately. He had tried to help Max and now he wished he hadn't. He would not put himself or Samaritans in jeopardy. He fixed Sharp with a basilisk stare. "I want you to understand, Dr Sharp, that neither I nor the board knew anything about these forms which have apparently come to light."

"Not 'apparently'," replied Andrew. "They have definitely come to light. I have seen them myself."

"I understand," Soper nodded. "And I understand that you were instrumental in bringing them to my attention, for which I am most grateful. Furthermore, in my view, it is imperative that Mr Stone recovers."

Andrew looked at him with curiosity. "We try to achieve a positive outcome for all patients, Mr Chairman."

"Of course you do. Thank you. You may go."

*

A few minutes later Soper slid into the soft brown leather rear seat of his Bentley. "Home, please," he murmured.

He thought about what had just taken place. His own preference was for Stone to recover. The murder of a patient on the operating table seemed reckless. There are degrees of skulduggery and Soper was becoming increasingly concerned about Max's behavior: the problem, he decided, was that when the chips were down, Max had no class and no boundaries. Max's activities had been unmistakably criminal, unlike his own. Providing parts for weapons systems might be a form of proxy killing, but it was socially acceptable. More than acceptable, in fact. It was patriotic and legal.

He was a job creator, and the jobs he created reduced poverty, led to votes which kept the right congressmen in their seats, improved the government's balance of payments and reduced the federal deficit. American lives were not lost, except occasionally, by accident, and Soper had no responsibility for foreigners unless they were wealthy enough to buy fighter aircraft. The only Americans at risk from his activities were soldiers, which was fine with him as they had voluntarily chosen to accept the risk.

Soper still had a sneaking admiration for Max's ambition, but it was getting out of hand. *How can I be in business*, thought Soper, *with someone so careless?* Someone who had not thought through the problems these wretched forms might create, who had opened himself and the hospital up to accusations of corruption and who was now foolhardy enough to be trying to facilitate a murder, one that would have to be covered up? It was always the cover-ups that got you in the end. There was no way he would allow himself to be implicated in one of those.

41

Andrew left Soper in the boardroom and went down to the parking lot, where he sat for a while in the Porsche. Realizing that he might be late, he pulled himself together, revved up the car, whipped through traffic to Rock Creek National Park and in just a few minutes he was at the zoo where he met Cathy and Ben outside the entrance off Rock Creek Parkway. They were dressed pretty much the same, in jeans, T-shirts and sneakers. They both looked adorable.

"Hi. What do you want to see first – lions, tigers, elephants?" Although profoundly disturbed by his brief encounter with the chairman, he was determined to put on a good front, and he smiled at the little boy looking up at him. "Or how about the fuzzy animals? They have pandas here."

"He likes the Reptile Discovery Center best," Cathy reminded him.

"Oh yes."

There were alligators, American and Chinese; the Cuban crocodiles, the emerald tree boas and the Everglades rattlesnakes, and cobras and vipers and pythons and the red-footed tortoise. Soon they were staring at the Aldabra tortoise, five hundred pounds in weight and more than one hundred years old. Ben stared at it intently. After a while, as the tortoise wasn't doing a lot, Andrew suggested they move on. Ben shook his head. "I want to stay."

"What am I missing?" said Andrew. "What is it about this creature that's so interesting?"

"I like it," said Ben. "I like just… wondering…"

"Wondering what?"

Ben said, "If you wanted to crack the shell, maybe by dropping a rock on it, I wonder how heavy the rock would have to be and how high up you would have to drop it from."

Andrew glanced at Cathy, looking for an explanation. She pulled a funny face.

"Why?" he said to Ben.

"Just wondering."

"Yes. Why?"

But answer came there none. He carried on watching the tortoise.

"What do you want to be when you grow up?"

"Grown-ups always ask that."

"Sorry."

"An engineer."

"Cool," said Andrew. Interesting kid. "What do you know about engineers?"

"They work things out. They calculate stuff. They fix things."

After a much briefer look at assorted furry animals and a long spell with the elephants – Ben wanted to know how heavy they were and how much weight they could pull – they went to a concession stand, found an unoccupied table and sat down. "Cathy, may I offer Ben a hot chocolate fudge sundae?"

"No," said Cathy. "Sorry. Far too much sugar. He'll be bouncing off the walls."

"Oh come on, let me at least give him something he likes."

She didn't argue. He stood in the queue with Ben and they talked about math while Cathy stayed at the table to make sure they didn't lose it. They came back with Ben's ice-cream, an iced tea for Cathy and a black coffee for Andrew.

Ben picked up Cathy's phone, googled the zoo and found pictures of the giant Aldabra tortoise. "Look," he showed them with glee.

The grown-ups had seen enough of the tortoise for one afternoon but they pretended to be interested still. Ben saw through the pretense and focused on the photos by himself.

"That's a great reptile house," Andrew said. "Reminds me of where we work."

Cathy smiled. "Who's the giant tortoise? Saul Tarnisch?"

"The chairman. Combination tortoise, cobra and American alligator. I just came from an intimidating meeting. It's not just Max. The corruption goes right up to the chairman of the board."

"Is that surprising?"

"The chairman told me that he wanted Victor Stone to survive. What an extraordinarily revealing remark. We want all our patients to survive, don't we? That's a given."

Cathy said, "What do you think he meant?"

"I think," said Andrew, "that he and Max Green have been discussing how to ensure that Stone... doesn't."

"Doesn't what?"

"Survive. They wanted my help in…"

"In making sure?"

"I think so."

"Why?"

"That's the question." He stared at his coffee. He had ordered it out of habit, and now didn't want to drink it. He didn't even have the energy to pick it up. Inertia was overwhelming him. It was becoming a worryingly familiar feeling. "I had such a fight with Blanche and Max over Mrs Jefferson. Every day we refuse to treat ordinary, innocent, sick people because they don't have high-end insurance or pots of money. When did they change the start of the Hippocratic Oath from 'First, do no harm' to 'First, get the check'?"

"But that's not what you're all about."

"No," said Andrew. "It's not."

"No. With you, it's 'first get the Porsche'."

He stood up and walked away.

"Come back," she called after him.

He stopped, and turned. "How long are you going to keep this up?"

She stood up and walked towards him, so that her back was to Ben. "I think you're trying to get to me through my son," she said, "and that's just not right."

"That was my original thought, yes." He admitted it freely, at once. She liked his honesty. "But not anymore. I like you. And I really like Ben. And I'd like to be friends with you and your kid. Is that so terrible?"

"I like you too. You're very nice to me, and you let me say all kinds of things I shouldn't in my position—"

"Please!" Even though Ben might be able to hear, he had to tell her how he felt. "You're… you're just honest. Genuinely honest."

"You want me to be honest now?"

"Of course."

"Okay. I'm afraid."

"Of what?"

"I don't want to be your plaything. I can't allow myself to get emotionally involved with an irresponsible middle-aged Lothario, however attractive."

Andrew was appalled, but not by being called irresponsible or a Lothario. "*Middle-aged*?" he said, stunned.

"What's a Lothario?" said Ben.

"You're not part of this conversation, Ben," said Cathy.

"I know what irresponsible is," Ben told Andrew. "She's always telling me I'm irresponsible too."

"And you're only seven," said Andrew. He returned to the table and sat down beside him. "Maybe that's okay in your case."

"Don't take any notice of her," Ben said. Andrew laughed. Ben went back to the phone, concentrating, changing the photos with lightning-quick thumbs. Cathy's mobile phone rang. She took it away from Ben and hit the green button. After listening for a moment she turned to Andrew. "Is your phone off? It's Dr Weiner. He says Infection Control is looking for you. It's urgent. They need you back at the hospital. Right now."

He took the phone. "Milton, I've left for the day. Is this urgent?" He listened. "Okay… okay." And hung up. "They've located a MRSA cluster in the ICU. Several patients infected."

Ben looked up. "What's a MRSA?"

"It's short for Methicillin Resistant Staph Aureus. It's what the media call a superbug. You sometimes find it in hospitals."

"What's the ICU?" asked Ben.

"Intensive Care Unit. Where we put patients who are very sick. We call them critical."

"An MRSA in the ICU?" said Ben. "That doesn't sound good."

"You're right, Ben," said Andrew. "Sorry, got to go. See you around, I hope."

"Cool," said Ben. He watched Andrew go.

"You like him?" Cathy asked.

Ben nodded.

42

When he reached the lobby, Andrew and Milton Weiner discussed the MRSA. It wasn't just one. One would have been containable with the latest antibiotics but the Head of Infection Control had reluctantly decided he was obliged to reveal the cluster of cases in the ICU in the last two or three days. They hurried over to Max's office in the admin wing and broke the bad news.

Max exploded. "Are you kidding? Intensive Care is our biggest earner! Ten beds, about fifty grand a day, totaling five hundred thousand bucks a day. You want to close it?? No fucking way!"

"There's no choice," said Weiner.

Max ignored him. "Andrew, can you operate on Victor Stone if Intensive Care is shut down?"

"Of course not."

There was a mad gleam in Max's eyes. "I think you should! It's the ideal opportunity."

"For what? What are you saying?" asked Weiner.

"I want him to survive," said Andrew. "I'm a doctor, remember?"

Max realized he had revealed too much. "Oh! Yes! I… I meant… uh…"

"Don't you want him to survive?"

"Of course I do. But we can't close the ICU. If we do, and if Stone survives, he will talk about the MRSA in every newspaper, on every TV show! Nobody will come here again, or certainly not for weeks. We'll be all washed up. There are some things you just can't reveal to the public. You want to hammer the final nail in Samaritans' coffin?"

"Max, Milton Weiner and I – and Samaritans, in fact – are responsible for the lives of our surgical patients."

Weiner nodded in vigorous agreement.

Max lost it. "I'm responsible for *all* the patients, you putz," he shouted. "Including the non-surgical ones, which means I have to keep this hospital open and running. If not, the nurses and staff will be out of a job, and the doctors, the community will have nowhere to turn."

He saw their implacable opposition and regained control of himself. "You know what? This one is a real big moral dilemma." He put his fingers to his temples, pretending to think. "What would my mother do?" He looked up to heaven for guidance. "You're right, superbug or not, we have to keep the ICU open."

"That's not what we said!" Andrew yelled. "We said we have to shut it! And I won't operate on Stone – or anyone else – till it's reopened."

"It's not your decision," said Max. "It's mine."

"No," said Weiner. "As Chief of Surgery, it's mine."

"You're both wrong," Andrew said. "It's not up to either of you. It'll be referred to the ethics committee."

Max relaxed. "Oh, well, that's fine, they won't think it's ethical to interfere. Not since I gave them all new cars. Hyundais," he added. "Not Porsches,"

"The ethics committee?" said Weiner. "You gave them cars? And they took them?"

Max ignored him.

"Let's try to be constructive," said Andrew. "There are five two-bed bays in the ICU. What if we just closed one bay, five beds, the one where the bug was found?"

"Fine," said Max. "Do it. That's a cost I'll eat. Go!"

Weiner said, "I'm not sure that's safe. I don't see how we do that."

"YP."

"YP?"

"Your problem. Figure it out."

*

As the two surgeons were hurrying out of Max's office, the phone rang. Max waved at them to wait a moment and said to someone on the line, "Find an empty room for the media people. I'll be right down to make a statement."

He listened again, then hung up. "It's leaked out to the media that Victor Stone suffered a heart attack while in Samaritans Medical Center. This is a news story that can't be avoided, so it has to be embraced. Don't talk to the media, either of you – I'll handle it."

Weiner and Andrew had no desire to talk to the media. Instead, they trudged into the doctors' common room where many of their colleagues were gathering, having heard the rumors. In his usual corner, Father Jim

O'Halloran was quietly nursing a mug of mint tea. Lori Diesel looked up from her magazine. "Hi, you two. I hear there's a secret superbug in the ICU."

"Top secret!" Andrew said.

"Listen up, everyone. Several MRSA cases have been found in the ICU," Weiner announced.

"Max Green has been economizing on the laundry," said Lori.

"Is it true you're closing the heart unit ICU?" asked Emily Craven.

"Not the whole of it, no," said Weiner. "He won't let us. Just part of it. There's one bay no one can use until Infection Control has cleared it."

"This is confidential, right?" asked Emily. "What should I call it in the paperwork?"

"The Amity Bay," said Andrew.

"That's very funny," said Emily.

"No it isn't."

"No it isn't," she agreed without hesitation. "It's not at all funny. That's one of the things I admire about you, Andrew. The clarity and force of—"

"Give it a rest, Emily," advised Lori. "Your tongue is so far up Andrew's ass, it's coming out of his mouth."

"Ee-ew!" said Emily. "How disgusting!"

"Yes it is," said Lori. "Hey, Padre, what do you think about not closing the ICU?"

"Is there any risk?" asked O'Halloran.

"Life's a risk." Saul Tarnisch wiped his eyes and slumped back into his favorite tub chair.

"Oh dear. Is he depressed again?" O'Halloran topped up the hot water in his mug and stirred around the teabag with a white plastic spoon. "Physician, heal thyself."

"Is that a quote from the Bible?" asked Lori.

"Yes..." said the priest vaguely. "Or some other book..."

Andrew focused on him. "Isn't there a moral problem here, Father?"

"Where?" O'Halloran looked around nervously, then giggled. "Oh, you had me worried for a moment."

"Keeping part of the ICU open. Someone might die."

"Yes," said O'Halloran. "But someone else might die if you don't. It's a gamble really. Or God's will, if you believe all that stuff. Which I do, I think."

"So you think we're doing the right thing or the wrong thing?"

"Um – who can tell?" He shrugged.

Andrew looked around the room. "Okay, everyone. Who thinks we should defy Max and close the whole of Intensive Care, for safety?"

"It would lead to even bigger cuts in the hospital," said Weiner. "Because we'll be losing five hundred grand a day, and that may put the whole future of the ER and the trauma center at risk."

Nobody spoke. Some doctors studied their shoes. One or two gazed out of the window or into their coffee mugs.

"Nobody want to say anything?" said Andrew.

Everyone remained uncomfortably silent. Milton Weiner sought spiritual help once more. "Father O'Halloran, do *you* think we should close the ICU down?"

O'Halloran didn't reply.

"You don't have an opinion, do you?" said Andrew.

Father O'Halloran shook his head regretfully. "No."

"But it's a moral decision, as well as a clinical one."

"Yes, indeed."

"So what use are you?" asked Andrew.

"Very little." O'Halloran chuckled, but as always his chuckle was tinged with sadness.

43

Andrew stood outside the Samaritans parking lot in a biting autumn wind, brown and yellow leaves blowing around him, watching sadly as his Porsche was picked up on a flatbed truck and driven away to the dealership.

Cathy stopped beside him, on her way back from lunch at the deli. "Problem with the car?"

"No. No problem." He handed her a check for eighty thousand dollars.

She examined it. "It's made out to you."

"I've endorsed it on the back. Donate it to the Samaritans Charitable Foundation for cardiothoracic patients. Make sure it's anonymous."

"Eighty thousand dollars? I don't understand."

"I sold it. You were right. The money belongs where it's needed. I'll get a small car instead."

Cathy gave him an impulsive hug.

"Does every hug cost eighty grand?" he said. "Because if it does, I can't afford to maintain this relationship."

"If you keep this up, the price could drop dramatically." She kissed him on the cheek.

Back in his office, Andrew asked her to summon his team to study X-rays, ultrasounds and EKGs on his computer monitor. She watched as he explained the diagnosis. "This is Victor Stone's heart," he said, when they had all arrived and settled down. "As you can all see, it's enlarged. The EKG's normal, but the echo shows cardiomyopathy. He needs a transplant, and pretty soon. We'll need the intra-aortic balloon pump. Take him up to ICU – and make sure you put him in the safe bay."

Unannounced, Max walked into Andrew's office. "Excuse me, everyone, I need to talk to Dr Sharp. Give us a minute, please."

Andrew's team all looked at him for instructions.

"Okay, everyone, that's fine," he said. "We're all done here for the moment."

Cathy showed them out.

"You can stay, Cathy," Andrew said.

"In private," said Max.

"You can go, Cathy," said Andrew.

She left the room, closing the door behind her. Andrew turned to Max. "What do you want?"

"Andrew," Max began, "this conversation is not taking place. Do you understand?" Andrew nodded. "You intend to perform a heart transplant on Stone?"

"If a heart becomes available, of course," said Andrew. "He'll die without it."

"How soon?"

"How long is a piece of string?"

"Don't fuck with me Andrew."

"Without it, he might only have days. Or weeks."

Max sighed. "That's plenty long enough for him to file his lawsuit against me."

"I guess so."

"Will any heart do for his transplant?"

"It must be healthy. And the same blood group."

"A common blood group?"

"Yes."

"What can I do to speed things up?"

"Nothing," said Andrew. "But this is a hospital like any other. We kill one or two essentially healthy people here every week. He may get lucky."

Max hesitated and then took the plunge. "Andrew, let me ask you this: honestly. Would it be so terrible if he died?"

"It would be for him."

"I'm talking about us. Would it be so terrible for us?"

"No. We'd still be alive."

"Exactly."

"If it makes you feel better," Andrew said, "it's quite possible he'll die very soon."

"Yes. It would be better – much better – if he died immediately. Better for the hospital. Better for you."

"It's not in our hands."

"Not in mine," said Max.

Andrew stared at him for a moment. "I can't quite believe it, but... you *are* asking me to kill him."

"Of course not!" said Max. "Shocking suggestion! But… as I said, I'd rather he didn't survive."

"I'm not God, Max. I can't make that kind of decision."

"Then you shouldn't have become a doctor. I'm not suggesting you kill him. Just make sure he dies, that's all. Doctors do that all the time."

"Not like this."

"Come off it. You make those decisions every day. And, you know, in medicine, we have to make hard choices, prioritize limited resources."

"We? You a doctor now?"

"Andrew, I don't have the bandwidth for this." Max was getting angry. The desperation was overwhelming him. Andrew had never seen him like this before. "Spare me the hypocrisy. We're not so different, you and I."

"I think we are."

"We need each other, buddy. We're symbiotic. That's how it works."

Andrew was firm. "Max, I intend to do everything possible to restore him to health."

"Oh yes?" said Max. "Well, just remember this: Victor Stone is going to accuse me of trying to make a corrupt deal with him. In the discovery process, other deals may come out… All the deals I made with you, for instance. Five grand a month to be the director of a Cardio Rehab Unit that doesn't exist! And then there's your Porsche. You could be committing career suicide."

"I didn't take that five grand a month."

"Didn't you? Look in your bank account."

Andrew blinked.

"If I go down, you're going with me."

"I can't do what you're asking."

"You can," said Max. "And you will, my friend. No one will ever know. And if you don't, you're toast. This is a zero-sum game."

*

The temporary media room had been set up in a small windowless office adjacent to the lobby. The platform was backed by a large blue sheet of paper with the word *Samaritans*, in white, spread across it in a repeating pattern, which Max had had prepared in the hope of just such an occasion.

Max stopped Andrew in the corridor outside and gestured at the untidy crowd of journalists clustered alongside the orange stackable chairs, dictaphones and smartphones at the ready. A few old-fashioned news cameras and crews were waiting too. "These guys will want to know what's going on."

"You want them to know?" Andrew asked. "Great. I'll be happy to tell them everything."

"Don't fuck with me, Andrew!" said Max. "I run press conferences, okay?"

"No problem. I don't share your desire for celebrity."

Scotch-taped onto the open door was a sign that had been handwritten by Melodie with a Sharpie. Andrew took out his pen and changed *MEDEA* to *MEDIA*.

Andrew was about to move into the room when Max grabbed him by the elbow. "So, tell me, before I start, what's the precise cause of Victor Stone's illness, medically?"

"It's idiopathic."

Max muttered "idiopathic" a couple of times to help him remember the word, and went straight to the dais. Andrew kept his distance. Blanche, who was waiting in the room already, followed Max and stood next to him.

He tapped the microphone and waited for the electronic whistling and feedback to stop. "Hello, can you hear me?" he said.

There were a few nods and some apathetic murmurs of acknowledgment from the hospital press gang. He gave them a big smile. "My name is Max Green and I am the CEO of the Samaritans Medical Center."

The assembled newshounds seemed entirely uninterested in that piece of information.

"Victor Stone, the celebrated attorney and TV star, is in Intensive Care and will hopefully be having his heart transplant surgery imminently. We have no other news of Mr Stone yet. When we know anything, we'll tell you."

"Why did he choose this hospital?"

"He didn't," said Blanche. "The paramedics—"

Max interrupted her. "We're the only hospital around here with an intra-aortic pump."

211

Blanche covered the microphone with her hand and whispered, "That's not true."

"So?"

"You're talking to the media."

"Oh I forgot, they never lie."

"What exactly is wrong with Victor Stone?" asked a print journalist in the front row.

"Myocardiopathy," said Max.

Andrew stepped forward and corrected him. "Cardiomyopathy."

"Cardiomyopathy. Sorry. Similar."

"What causes it?"

Max assumed a professorial manner. "It can be caused by certain viruses. Or by alcohol. But the virus tests are negative and we're told that Mr Stone doesn't drink."

"Is this condition rare?"

"Medium rare." He wasn't sure whether to acknowledge or ignore the grins and giggles. "I mean... kind of... rare." He glanced at Andrew, who nodded encouragement. "Yes, it's rare. A rare heart muscle disease." *I've got through the difficult bit*, he thought. *This is going well.*

"So what caused this disease then?"

"We definitely know, for a fact," said Max with new-found confidence, "that the cause is idiopathic."

Two or three of the journalists asked, more-or-less in unison, "What does that mean?"

Max was stuck. He hadn't thought to ask. He turned to Andrew. "Uh... Dr Sharp?"

Andrew stepped forward with a smile. "Idiopathic means nobody knows. It comes from the same Greek word as—" he smiled at Max, "— idiot."

"Is he the doctor?" the journalists chorused. "Are you Victor Stone's doctor?"

"Yes, I am his doctor."

More shouts. "What's your name?" and, "Why aren't you answering the questions?"

"My name is Dr Andrew Sharp. Mr Green here is my boss. I'm just a humble cardiothoracic surgeon."

Max had no choice but to share the limelight. He made the best of it. "This is Dr Andrew Sharp, Head of Cardiothoracic Surgery here and the brightest star in our surgical firmament."

Andrew smiled, embarrassed. Cameras clicked at him. Max ruffled his hair with a show of affection. "Aw! I've embarrassed him."

"Please!" Andrew pushed him away.

"Sorry, buddy. But, everybody, this guy is an absolutely legendary heart surgeon. Believe me."

"Anything else you can tell us, Dr Sharp?" called a voice from the crowd.

Andrew cleared his throat. "Mr Stone's prognosis is a cause for concern. His condition has become critical. He needs a transplant."

"When will his reality show be able to come back on the air?"

"I suggest you ask Fox News that."

"How would they know?"

"They wouldn't," said Andrew. "But I'm sure they'd be happy to make something up."

Max's cell phone buzzed. A text from Soper, asking him to come to the boardroom without delay. "Okay," he said. "That's it. The doctor needs to get back to work. Thank you all, no more questions."

*

David Soper and Leo Pfiffig were in an icy stand-off when Max hurried into the boardroom. "I'm trying to prevent a tragedy, Mr Soper," Leo said, ignoring Max's arrival. "The hospital has shown a clear motive to kill Mr Stone – or at least a willingness to allow him to die – in order to cover up the totally corrupt deal that Mr Green offered him, and which Mr Stone rejected."

Max said, "That's the most ridiculous crap I ever heard in my life!"

"Is it?" Leo turned to Max. "I don't think so."

Soper, at his most emollient, took charge. "Let me tell you... No, let me assure you, that Mr Stone will get the best possible medical and surgical care."

"He'd better," said Leo. "Because if he doesn't survive this surgery, I shall see to it that there is a thorough investigation." He stood up, closed his briefcase, and walked out.

Soper turned to Max. "Andrew Sharp rightly insists on doing his best to save Stone. And if Stone lives, you could be in deep trouble with the lawsuit alleging corruption. But that's just money."

"And if he dies?" asked Max.

"Much worse. A wrongful death lawsuit, negligence, and possible charges of homicide or manslaughter."

Max swallowed. His mouth had gone very dry. "What do you suggest?"

"Off the record," said the chairman, "you might want to consider doing everything you can to find a new heart for Stone, as soon as possible."

"Everything?"

Soper gave an almost imperceptible tilt of the head. "Everything."

44

Alone at his desk, in his huge, plush office, Max ruminated about betrayal. Andrew's had been bad enough. But Soper too? He saw, with dazzling clarity, that just as his chairman was prepared to make a fortune by providing parts for weapons that would bomb the crap out of Helmand Province, the Gaza Strip, Bagdad and Aleppo, he would stop at nothing to protect his health-giving, lifesaving reputation at Samaritans. If there was a risk that his image might be besmirched, someone else would have to pay. And that someone, Max now saw, would be him.

He had to find Victor Stone a heart, and fast. He booted up his computer, and accessed the hospital records.

First, he looked up Victor Stone. Blood group B.

Then he made a list of all the other current Group B inpatients. There were forty-seven. He copied and pasted the list onto a new blank document, and left it on his desktop to come back to. Then he scrolled down to check the seriousness of their conditions. It wasn't long before he came to the name "May Jefferson". *She won't do*, he thought. She's suffered a recent cardiac arrest.

And then he had a moment of inspiration: if he could somehow get Mrs Jefferson's heart transplanted into Victor Stone, a successful surgical outcome would lead to heart meltdown in a moment of stress – and that would be that. Victor Stone kaput! Lawsuit kaput! In Vegas it was what you called a win-win!

"Bingo!" he said to himself. "I'm a fucking genius."

But how to do it...?

He thought for a moment, then accessed Mrs Jefferson's data again. She had recently been readmitted to the ICU after a stroke. Perfect. He deleted the previous line. A nanosecond later, her cardiac arrest was no longer on the record. Only the stroke and the hip surgery.

He phoned Andrew. "Hey!"

"Hey," replied Andrew, but without the same enthusiasm.

"Tell me about heart transplants," said Max.

"What do you want to know?"

"Like – what happens?"

"Max, I can't do that in five minutes over the phone," said Andrew. "It takes several years of study and practice."

"I know that," said Max. "But when you are doing a transplant, do you know or care whose heart it is, or where it comes from?"

"Not always," said Andrew, guardedly. "Why?"

"Just curious," said Max and hung up.

His phone rang immediately. Kimberly Cummings, from her little daffodil-yellow Volkswagen. "Hey! I caught your press conference on Fox News. You were great."

Max couldn't disagree. "Thanks."

"I'm near Samaritans, and now this is all in the news I'd love to talk to you some more about our new heart transplant medication, HeartGraft."

"Kimberly, I'm busy right now, but—"

"I bet you are, babe. But I'll *really* make it worth your while…"

Max couldn't resist. *Maybe it will make me feel better*, he thought. *Maybe this is what I need right now.*

*

Half an hour later, Blanche hurried along the corridor towards Max's office. She had been hurt by his attitude the previous day – telling her to shut up in front of Andrew Sharp, when what she was saying was correct, was demeaning. She needed a serious talk with him about their relationship.

She stopped at Max's door, grasped the handle and was about to turn it when Melodie Feather, now promoted to Max's assistant, piped up, "Don't go in there Blanche. He's in a meeting."

"Who with?"

"That drug company representative."

"That's okay. He won't mind."

"He said it's a closed-door meeting."

"No problem. I'll open it."

Melodie stood up from her desk. "No! He said 'absolutely no interruptus'."

"That doesn't mean me." And Blanche opened the door.

It did mean her. In fact, it meant her specifically. Blanche stopped dead on the threshold, not quite able to believe her eyes. Kimberly was on his desk, on her back, her skirt around her waist, her knees behind her ears.

Max's pants and tartan underwear enveloped his brown Church's brogues.

All three of them stared at each other and froze.

"Blanche…" said Max. "This isn't what you think…"

Blanche's face crumpled. She ran out, and tore weeping blindly down the suddenly endless corridor.

*

Max sighed, and zipped up his pants.

Kimberly rearranged her disheveled clothes. "I guess that's it for this evening, right?"

"Right. Blanche is gonna be a real problem."

"Why? What's the big deal?"

Max threw open the door, strode out of his office, and snapped at a giggling Melodie, who had seen the full tableau over Blanche's shoulder, "You're fired!"

She just laughed. "Hey, Kimberly. Wanna drink?"

*

Cathy, walking through the Moses H Hartz Cardiothoracic Ward towards Andrew's office, heard a loud, wailing sound approaching at high speed, and Blanche suddenly lurched into view from around the corner, eyes red, tears pouring down her face, snot dribbling out of her nose. "Oh Cathy," she said, and fell sobbing into her arms.

Cathy didn't care for Blanche, but she had sympathy for a fellow human being in pain. "What's wrong Blanche?"

"Max. You know we've been seeing each other?"

Cathy didn't know and wasn't interested, but she thought she should ask the appropriate questions. "No. What's he done?"

"He's done Kimberly!" Blanche wailed. "I walked in on them."

"Oh. And they were…?"

"Ye-ee-es!" howled Blanche. "She was fucking him."

Cathy was unsurprised. "She works for a pharmaceutical. The pharmaceuticals fuck everyone."

"He's a dirty pig. And I've been so loyal to him." She blew her nose and wiped her eyes. "I never even told anyone about his kickbacks."

"Kickbacks?" Suddenly this was interesting. "What do you mean, kickbacks?"

"Payoffs. You know. Perks."

"No, I don't know. Who from, exactly?"

"Everybody. Merv's Deli, the Heavenly Peace Memorial Chapel, Temp-o the temp nurses' agency…"

"Have you any proof?" Cathy asked.

"I can get it. You want it today?"

Cathy nodded.

"You'll have to stay late, till he leaves."

"I will." Cathy ushered Blanche into Andrew's office, made her a cup of coffee and phoned to ask a friend to pick Ben up from school.

*

Andrew was accosted by a couple of journalists as he headed out for the night. "Have they found a heart for Victor Stone yet?"

"No."

"How long does he have?"

Andrew couldn't conceal his exasperation. "I have no idea."

"What will happen?"

"We will do our best."

"Will he pull through?"

"I'm a doctor, not a prophet."

He hurried away, past Max who was now back in the doorway of the media room, talking to another group of journalists. "Yes… yes…" he was saying, "we're still waiting for a donor. We just have to hope that somebody suitable dies soon."

As the pens came out, Max realized that what he had just said might not look good in print. "At least… er… that's not quite what I meant… We *are* talking off the record, right?"

Nobody answered.

45

Later that evening, after dark, Cathy and Blanche crept into Max's office. They didn't turn on the lights. They used the flashlight app on Cathy's iPhone to help Blanche find her way to Max's desk and turn on his computer. Tears were gone now. Revenge was her priority. She tried to keep her excitement under control.

"Do you know his password?" asked Cathy.

"Jackpot," said Blanche and typed it. Immediately, on the desktop, she saw a document that intrigued her. "Look at this!"

"That's not his kickbacks," said Cathy. "What is it?"

It was a list of patients headed *"BLOOD GROUP B"*.

Blanche stared at it. "Why would Max have a list of blood group B patients?"

"Victor Stone's blood group is B," Cathy said. "It's a hit list." She pressed *PRINT*.

When they had it in their hands, they shut down Max's computer, opened his door a crack to check that they not been seen, crept out and ran down the corridor. Once they were in Andrew's office, Cathy grabbed the phone and dialed. Blanche, on tenterhooks, perched on the edge of the desk and listened.

"Can I speak to the Chief of Security?"

This request took more than twenty minutes to fulfill.

"You have a security issue?" the Chief of Security asked when he was eventually found.

"Yes. I'm Cathy Lockhart, Dr Andrew Sharp's assistant."

"Who?"

"Catherine Lockhart."

"Whose assistant?"

"Dr Andrew Sharp."

"Who's he?"

"He is Head of Cardiothoracic Surgery."

"Where?"

"In this hospital!"

"I don't know him."

"Well, look him up!"

She waited… and waited…

"Oh yes, I see a Dr Sharp on my list here. What do you want?"

"There is an urgent security threat, to several patients in this hospital. Their lives are at risk."

"How many patients?"

"Forty-seven."

"Look, Miss Lockhart, it's a very busy time here and—"

"Yes," Cathy said. "I know it's a very busy time, but I have a list here of forty-seven patients who need special security for the next several days."

"Forty-seven? You kidding me? What makes you think they're at risk?"

"I've found a hit list."

There was another long pause at the other end of the line. "I'll have to get clearance on this. This could involve a lot of very expensive manpower."

"Who do you have to clear it with?"

"The CEO. Mr Green."

"No, don't do that. Um… forget it, okay?" Cathy hung up.

"What did he say?" asked Blanche.

Cathy told her. She tried to phone Andrew, but he didn't reply. They couldn't see what else they could do.

Then she realized that the Chief of Security was likely to tell Max about her call. She couldn't help feeling that there would no longer be forty-seven names on Max's hit list. There would now be forty-eight.

*

Max had switched off his cell phone and was purposely out of touch. The Chief of Security would have been unable to call him, even if he had wanted to, which he didn't because he couldn't be bothered. He had decided to let Max know in the morning.

Unbeknown to Cathy and Blanche, their CEO was still in the hospital. Creeping past the doctors' common room, Max heard familiar sounds. He opened the door a little and peeped in. Kimberly was sitting astride Saul Tarnisch on the old sofa and saying between gasps, "Prozac is overrated," – gasp – "yes, do me, our new selective serotonin reuptake

220

inhibiter has a better therapeutic ratio and side effect profile... yes... yes... *yes*...!"

Max slid out and closed the door quietly behind him.

The clock said 2.10 a.m. as Max entered the ICU, past a sleeping duty nurse. In the corner was a janitor, also sleeping.

He tiptoed past the nurse. Past the empty bay where the MRSAs had been found. He found Mrs Jefferson in a bed in Bay 2, still in a coma following her stroke, connected to a respirator. He picked up the chart and looked at it. Blood group B.

He looked around. The sleeping janitor had an unplugged vacuum cleaner beside him. Perfect. Max went in search of some rubber gloves and found them at the nurses' station. He pulled them on. No risk of fingerprints. He was calm now.

He wiped Mrs Jefferson's chart free of his prints, picked up the vacuum cleaner plug and followed the lead from the respirator to the wall. Taking a deep breath, he disconnected the respirator. A loud alarm sounded immediately. Slightly panicked by the penetrating noise of Mrs Jefferson's heart monitor flatlining, he jammed the vacuum cleaner plug into the socket and accelerated out of the ICU as it roared into life.

The siren was deafening, and so was the old Hoover. The nurse and janitor leapt out of their seats. The janitor switched off the vacuum cleaner, which was screaming and writhing across the floor. The nurse ran to the respirator, saw that it was no longer functioning – and had no idea what to do about it.

She realized, far too late, that the plugs had been switched. She screamed at the janitor, above the noise. "You unplugged a patient to switch on a fucking vacuum? Are you nuts?"

"What?"

"You switched off a patient!"

"No!" the janitor screamed back. "I didn't do anything!"

"What happened then?"

"I don't know. Don't *you* know?"

"I was asleep!!"

"You telling me *I'm* irresponsible? You're the nurse. I'm just the janitor!"

"I'm not a real nurse. I'm a janitor too!"

The emergency team crashed through the doors. They tried to revive Mrs Jefferson, but this time the outcome was not positive.

*

Andrew woke up abruptly, grabbed the phone and heard the excited voice of Emily Craven. "We've got a donor for Victor Stone. Surgery is scheduled in two to three hours."

"Okay. Coming in." Andrew dragged himself out of bed and, en route to the bathroom, his doorbell rang. At 3.30 a.m? He pulled on a bathrobe, hurried to the door and saw Cathy through the peephole window. He opened the door.

"Look at this!" Out of breath, she thrust the list into his hand.

Andrew glanced down it. "Possible heart donors for Victor Stone?"

"Right. It was on Max Green's computer. And one of these patients has just died. Very convenient. And under pretty bizarre circumstances." Cathy gripped his wrist. "I think it's a hit list. I think Max killed poor Mrs Jefferson to make a heart available for Victor Stone."

"Mrs Jefferson?" Andrew went cold. "They just called me. They've scheduled his transplant. I'm on my way in—"

"Andrew, I'm scared. I think he murdered her. I phoned the Chief of Security. He said he couldn't offer any protection to these patients without Max's say-so. And I told him my name—"

"I see." He thought for a moment. "Where's Ben?"

"Safe, I think. I took him to a friend's apartment."

Andrew went into overdrive. "Right. I'll get dressed. You came in your car?"

She nodded.

"You can drive me."

"You're not going to do it, are you? Not with Mrs Jefferson's heart?"

He put his hand on her shoulder. "Cathy, I can't save Mrs Jefferson. But I still have an obligation to Stone."

"Didn't she have a heart attack?"

"No. Just a cardiac arrest."

"Don't they go together?"

"Not always. A heart attack can cause a cardiac arrest – but sometimes it just… happens. Hers happened when she was in the ER, so they were able to restart it immediately. No lasting damage that I could see."

The cardiovascular team was gathering in the operating suite when they arrived. Andrew took Cathy to the ladies locker room and instructed the OR nurse to get her into some scrubs with gloves, a hat and a mask.

Emily greeted him. "Dr Sharp – Andrew – I just want to say, I'm so proud to be able to assist you, sir. Especially when it's to save the life of a celebrity—"

"We try to save all our patients, Emily, even those who are not celebrities."

"Yes I know, all I meant was—"

Lori Diesel brushed her aside. "What are the symptoms, boss?"

"A systolic of fifty and falling." Andrew turned to the cardiovascular team. "Okay, listen up. I want the intra-aortic pump primed and ready. At least one OR prepped and on standby. Notify the ICU. Notify the labs that urgent samples might be required. Put medical cardiology and X-ray technologists on standby too."

*

"We'll have an official inquiry as soon as possible," Dr Weiner told Max and Blanche as they stood beside Mrs Jefferson's empty bed in the ICU.

Max shook his head. "I don't think we need an official inquiry, Milton."

"Of course we do," said Blanche. "A patient was unplugged here. She died."

"I've been told she was dying anyway," said Max. "She'd been in a coma for days. She wasn't going to survive. Somebody made a mistake, that's all." He shrugged, palms upward. "No big deal."

"No big deal?" Weiner protested. "We don't know she wasn't going to survive. Max, we must find out how this happened so that it doesn't happen again."

"We already know what happened," Max said. "The janitor made a mistake."

"Which he denies," said Blanche.

"Sure he does. But just think what an inquiry means: bad publicity, lawsuits, shit we can't afford. Why go there?"

Weiner frowned. "So you're saying… what, exactly? We just fire the janitor?"

"I don't think we even have to do that," Max replied coolly. "Just tell him... tell him to be more careful in future. Forgive and forget. We all make mistakes, don't we, Milton?" He clapped him on the back. "Hey, let's have a more generous spirit around here."

Weiner was having trouble figuring out this new Max. "Forgive? Have you been born again, like Blanche?"

"No he has not!" snapped Blanche.

"I guess I'm just a nice guy," said Max. "Right, Blanche?"

"If you say so," she said, tight-lipped.

Max tried to catch her eye, but she wouldn't look at him. "We have to talk, babe," he said. "Okay?"

"We do," she said. "But this is not the time or the place."

"I agree. By the way," Max added, "don't forget Mrs Jefferson's bill. If the insurance company won't pay, send it to the daughter."

Blanche said, "Her daughter's in the military, serving in Afghanistan."

"That's good," said Max. "She won't be that hard to find."

"But she won't be able to afford the bill for all this."

"Come on, Blanche! What's new? If she can't pay, sue her. Isn't that what we do?"

"Yes, but—"

"Then do it." He smiled at her. "I'll phone you, babe."

And he sauntered away.

Blanche turned to Milton Weiner. "I hate him..." she said. "So much!" Her voice rose in pitch as she unleashed her previously repressed hysteria. "I feel... You know what I feel?... Flames... on the side of my face..."

*

Max came face to face with Andrew in the scrub room. He put an arm around his surgeon in what looked like a supportive hug, but Andrew knew it wasn't. "Hi buddy. Is surgery about to begin?"

"Shortly."

"You have to save him," said Max, darkly. "Do your best. Or I do my worst!"

"I'm confused." Andrew disentangled himself with some difficulty. "I thought you were hoping that Victor Stone would die."

"Things change," said Max. "Have you seen your secretary, Cathy?"

"No." Andrew steeled himself to avoid catching the eye of the suddenly rigid woman standing next to Max in her scrubs and mask. "Why?"

"Nothing," said Max. "But when you do, ask her to come and see me."

"Sure," Andrew said, showing him the door. Then he turned on his heel and ushered Cathy through to the OR.

"Anyone have anything to say before we open him up?" Andrew began.

"Dr Sharp," said Emily Craven, "I think I speak for us all when I say that we hold you in the greatest respect and we wholeheartedly support whatever you do."

"Call me old-fashioned," Lori rasped, "but I just love to watch a good kiss-ass at work first thing in the morning."

Emily turned to her. "Dr Diesel, I don't think you appreciate him fully."

"Honey," said Lori, "I've appreciated him more fully than you ever will."

"Don't be so sure of that, *honey*," said Emily.

Lori looked at Andrew, eyes wide with astonishment.

"I've appreciated you too, Lori," responded Andrew with unaccustomed gallantry, again avoiding Cathy's glance. "And you, Emily. And all of you. All the hard work you all put in here, every day. Okay. Everyone ready?"

There were general mumbles of assent.

"Is he fully asleep?"

"Yes sir!" Lori answered.

"And you're fully awake, Lori?"

"Ready to rock," she said. "In spite of serious problems with the machine this morning."

"The heart–lung machine?"

"No, the coffee machine."

"Shit," said Andrew. "That *is* serious. Emily, open him up."

"Scalpel," said Emily.

"Scalpel," repeated the circulating nurse, handing it to her.

Emily made the first incision.

"Good," said Andrew.

"Sponge," Emily said.

"Sponge."

"Clamp?"

"Clamp."

"Suction," said Emily, and snapped, "And don't say a fucking word Lori, okay?"

"Suction," repeated the circulating nurse, handing the device to Emily.

There were snorts of laughter from behind every mask but one.

46

Stone's surgery was nearly finished. Andrew snipped the last stitch. "Okay," he said. "That looks good. Ready to take him off the bypass, everyone?"

Nods all round. "Okay. Off bypass."

The switch was pressed.

Everyone waited for a tense moment... and *BA-BOOM, BA-BOOM, BA-BOOM*, the new heart kicked in.

*

Sometime later, when Victor Stone was wheeled into the safe bay of the ICU, Father O'Halloran popped in to see what was going on with the hospital's most celebrated patient. "I thought I'd drop by, just in case he needs the last rites," he said hopefully.

"He's going to pull through," Andrew said.

The chaplain didn't give up so easily. "Maybe not. Maybe the Lord has a better plan."

"You have more confidence in the Lord than I do."

"It's part of my job description."

Lori saw Stone's eyes opening. "Andrew, he's waking up."

"Mr Stone? Can you hear me?"

Stone nodded assent.

"How do you feel?"

"I saw God!" he said.

"You did?" The padre was extremely interested.

"I was in a long white tunnel with bright light."

"That would have been when his blood pressure dropped," said Lori.

"Yes," Andrew said. "That's pretty much always the cause of a near-death experience."

"I see," said O'Halloran, disappointed to learn that there was a medical explanation.

"I was flying above the operating table," Stone said. "I saw you operating on my body. I was not in my body. Then, the tunnel. The clouds opened and a beautiful golden light shone through the clouds. And I heard the voice of God."

"What did God say?" Father O'Halloran asked.

"God said to me…" Stone's voice trembled and the veins popped out on his forehead, "…I am thy thunderbolt! You are my right arm! Strike down Samaritans Medical Center! Sue the shit out of them!"

Andrew said, "Lori. Ten milligrams of Haloperidol. Double quick. He thinks he's God's right arm."

"Haloperodol's for psychosis."

"He's having a psychotic episode. Do it now!"

"Excuse me…" Father O'Halloran intervened. "He's talking about God. That's not psychosis, that's religion."

"Call it what you like," said Andrew. "But give him the medication."

Lori nodded to the nurse, who prepared the needle.

"In his condition, that much rage could kill him."

Max hurried in. "I hear the surgery's over. How's he doing?"

"He wants to sue the shit out of you." Andrew smiled at him triumphantly. "It was a total success."

*

Max called Leo Pfiffig to reassure him that Victor Stone had come through surgery and the prognosis was good. Shortly afterwards, in his media room, Max addressed the press. "So far, the surgery on Victor Stone has been a total success."

Thumbs flying, several journalists began texting.

"I should just like to add that this triumph is a tribute to everyone at Samaritans Medical Center, which shows our health care system at its finest. A great example of American exceptionalism."

*

Upstairs, in the anteroom outside the operating suite, Andrew sat alone, his head in his hands.

Cathy, still disguised in scrubs, sat down beside him. "Coffee?"

"No thanks."

She held out a cardboard cup with a corrugated cover. "It's not hospital coffee, it's from Merv's Deli. I sent out for it."

"Oh. Okay." Andrew gave it a distracted sip.

"What's the matter?" she asked.

"I sometimes wonder… if we doctors are really any different from Max."

"'Course you are. You know that!"

228

"I don't know. We prioritize, just like him. We frequently make financial decisions. Decisions to save some patients and lose others."

"But you don't do it his way." She hugged him. "Or for his reasons."

"You're hugging me again."

"Because I'm sorry I called you a middle-aged Lothario."

"I'm sorry I said you have a nice rack."

She kissed him. A nurse hurried in. "Dr Sharp?" She whispered some news. His face fell. "What's wrong?" said Cathy.

"A patient in the ICU just died from the MRSA," he said. "We should have closed all the bays."

"You saved Stone by keeping it open," she reminded him.

"Yes, but…"

"It's not your fault. You do your best." Her eyes shone. "Life is fragile."

"Max made us keep ICU open," Andrew said. "We have to do something about him."

She nodded. "We should have weeks ago. I'll talk to Blanche."

"How will that help?"

"She's on our side now."

"Are you sure?"

47

Max was in his office the next morning, when Blanche phoned. "Hi, doll," he said breezily. "I was just about to call you."

"To say what?"

"To say I'm sorry about that thing with Kimberly."

"Are you?"

"Yes," said Max tenderly. "I honestly, truly, seriously am. I love you so much."

There was a pause.

Then Blanche said, "Okay. I believe you."

"Come over and we'll talk about it."

"No. Meet me in the M&M lecture room," said Blanche. "I'm alone here, and I have something to show you. Something very naughty."

This sounded good to Max. Five minutes later he was there. "Hey, Blanche! Before you show me whatever it is – and I'm very excited to see it – we have to talk."

"I know."

"That thing with Kimberly. I'm sorry, it didn't mean anything…"

"You were tempted," she said. "I'm not a child. I understand."

"Blanche, you're a saint."

"And you're *so* smart."

"Smart? Yeah. I guess I am."

"Switching off Mrs Jefferson to get a donor heart for Victor Stone."

"What are you talking about?"

"This list of blood group B patients is on your computer." She showed it to him.

"Give that to me, please."

She did.

"Probably best I delete it from my computer." He paused. "How did you get into it, by the way?"

"I knew your password. I've seen you type it so often."

He took a deep breath, not knowing quite which of his many expressions to wear. "You know what, Blanche? We needed that heart, and she was going to die anyway. And you know what else? I've made this hospital profitable at last."

"With my help, babe."

"Right. You and me, we're two of a kind. We make things happen."

"We're great," she agreed.

"I couldn't do it without you. You are going to share in the massive profits that are coming my way. You send patients away if they're not insured. I switch 'em off. Same difference, eh? I was hired to make the hospital pay, and between us we're doing exactly that! I love you, baby."

He brushed a rogue thread off his shiny mohair lapel. "Now, what were you going to show me that was so naughty?"

The door opened and two men in cheap suits walked in.

"Your confession," she said. "On your own surveillance system."

"Mr Green," one of the men said, placing his hand on Max's shoulder, "you are under arrest for the murder of Mrs May Jefferson. You have the right to remain silent, et cetera, et cetera, and all that other stuff you've seen on TV." The cop couldn't be bothered to list all Max's rights. Nobody ever listened anyway.

"You fucking bitch!" Max screamed, his face turning puce. "You betrayed me too? How could you do this to me?"

He lunged at her, grabbed her by the throat. Both his hands tightened around her neck as he forced her back across the desk.

The two detectives grabbed him by the wrists and neck and dragged him off her. One of them forced him to the floor, put a knee in his back and somehow got the handcuffs on him in spite of his flailing arms. As Blanche gasped for breath, the other cop pulled her to safety.

"You got everything you need?" she gasped, trying to recover her poise.

"Yes ma'am. Saw and heard every word on the surveillance. It's all recorded. Great job."

Together, the cops hauled a struggling Max to his feet.

"Okay!" he yelled in a towering rage. "What if I did switch her off? So what? I didn't create this fuckin' health care system. I'm not to blame for market forces. I was hired to make the hospital pay, and I made it pay. That's my fuckin' job!"

"Mr Green, we are a nation of laws," one of the cops replied. "You appear to have broken several of them."

"A nation of laws?" he screamed. "What's so great about being a nation of laws when the laws are made by scumbags who are all on the take from the highest bidder?"

"You gotta point," said one of the detectives. "But murder is murder."

Max calmed down and thought of a new defense, the one that had worked so well on Wall Street for so many years. "Listen, I don't know anything," he pleaded. "I'm only the CEO!"

48

Andrew, Cathy, Milton Weiner, Saul Tarnisch and the heads of departments met Chairman Soper in the boardroom later that week. He had news for them. "I have talked to Mr Stone's junior partner, Leo Pfiffig. There won't be a lawsuit against us. Inevitably, since his psychosis is not yet totally under control, Mr Stone has decided to withdraw from his own law practice."

He updated them on the CEO situation. "Max is calm now, I'm told. He's still in custody, of course. No one can afford to bail him out. They set bail at five million."

"What's happening to him?" asked Cathy.

"He's in the prison hospital, under sedation," Saul Tarnisch volunteered. It was the first time Andrew had ever seen him smile. "As it happens, I'm the attending psychiatrist there. Max has a psychotic illness, we all knew that, and I'm keeping him on antipsychotic medication. He needs to be hospitalized for a long, long time."

"Sounds right to me," said Milton Weiner.

Andrew asked, "Does Max have insurance?"

"Do you need it in prison?" asked the chairman. "Because he doesn't have any. Not since I fired him."

"So who is going to pay for Max's drugs?" asked Andrew. "The government?"

"Wouldn't that be against Max's principles?" said Saul, with a still bigger smile.

"Who else would pay?" asked Cathy.

"HP," said the chairman.

Everyone looked at him.

"His problem," he explained.

To his surprise, Andrew found himself feeling sorry for Max. More empathy, he realized to his bewilderment. "Look, we can't just —"

"You're right, I know. We can't leave him stranded," said Soper. "I've spoken to a charming young drug salesperson whom I happen to know, and she'll provide him with some sort of antipsychotic medication."

"Kimberly Cummings?" Cathy grinned. "You know her too?"

"Yes. Why?" Soper's face was turning pink. "Do you?"

"Yes, as a matter of fact I do."

"Well... um, yes," said Soper, pretending badly. "I think Kimberly might have been her name. Awfully nice young woman. So helpful."

"In so many ways," said Andrew.

"I know her too," put in Saul. "She talked to me about the prescription. She's giving me a discount, as a special favor. Frankly, I'm only too pleased to be treating Max, and I'm looking forward to telling him that Ms Cummings is providing the meds."

*

The trial was long awaited. Given Max's recorded confession on the CCTV, he could do little to deny murdering Mrs Jefferson. His only option was to plead not guilty on the grounds of insanity, which he did reluctantly, on the advice of his attorney.

The prosecution laid out the facts and the defense did not dispute them. His attorneys confirmed to the media that Max Green would take the witness stand in his own defense, and everybody waited for the big day. The courtroom was crowded. The media were there in force. There was live television transmission. His mom was in the front row of the public gallery, in her Sunday best; she was upset for Max but excited to be on TV and interviewed by Jerry Springer.

"Counsel for the defense?" the judge invited.

The defense attorney stood and approached Max, who seemed strangely confident. "Mr Green, is it true that when you pulled the plug on Mrs Jefferson's respirator, you knew she would die?"

"Yes," said Max.

"And did you think that was wrong?"

"Wrong?" Max was mystified. "No. It was absolutely the right thing to do, both from the management and the accounting point of view."

"So that's why you unplugged her?"

"Of course. She couldn't pay her bill, so she had no right to be there. Someone else needed her heart. And we also had to make space for a paying customer."

"You had no moral doubts?"

"No. Why would I? What's the difference between Mrs Jefferson and all the patients who die because they can't afford dialysis or chemo or surgery or their prescription drugs? It's not a moral question. The invisible hand of the market decides who lives and dies. That's the way it is. That's the way it's always been. You don't have the money, you don't get the treatment. I didn't do anything different. I just prioritized. It's standard practice throughout America."

"Do you have anything else you wish to add?"

"Yes. I stand here accused of murder. But I am not a murderer. Sure, somebody died because of me, but I did the right thing. Our boys and girls in the military kill people every day but nobody calls them murderers. They call them patriots. That's what I am. We need some financial and emotional discipline in this country."

After the prosecutor urged to jury to convict him of first degree murder, it was the defense attorney's turn to address them. "Members of the jury, if the accused did not know what he was doing, or did not know that it was wrong, the law requires that you must find him not guilty on account of insanity. I submit to you that it could not be clearer that Max Green did not understand that it was wrong to murder Mrs Jefferson."

It didn't take the jury long to come to a verdict. After a mere couple of hours they filed back into the courtroom.

"All rise," called the bailiff as the judge entered. In the public section, Andrew and Cathy rose with everyone else. The judge sat.

"Members of the jury," said the judge, "I gather you have reached a verdict?"

"Yes, Your Honor," replied the forewoman.

"On the charge of murdering Mrs May Jefferson, what say you?"

"Not guilty by reason of insanity."

Max leapt to his feet in an uncontrollable fury. "Insane?" he screamed. "Are you all nuts? I was just doing my job."

As the lawyers and the stenographer cowered and the judge beat his gavel again and again, bailiffs ran forward to restrain him. They only partially succeeded. He staggered around the courtroom like Frankenstein's monster, dragging a bailiff on each arm, terrifying the lawyers retreating in disarray. "This means every hospital manager in America is insane," he yelled. "And half the politicians. *You're* insane! *Everyone* is insane…"

More bailiffs hurtled in and, still shouting, Max was finally dragged from the courtroom.

*

In the street outside, Andrew walked Cathy to her rusty old Chevy. "Want a lift?" she asked.

"Where to?"

"Dinner, maybe?" she suggested.

"Oh. Is this a date?"

"Yeah, how about it?"

"It's about time!" Andrew said.

They turned out into the traffic.

"Ben's coming too, I hope?"

"Of course. He'll be my chaperone."

"Then let's go to the zoo first," Andrew said. "And before your chaperone joins us, I'd just like to say you're looking very… healthy."

"Nice rack?" she asked.

"Very nice indeed."

EPILOGUE

Max Green was committed to the Cheney Memorial Hospital for the Criminally Insane. While in a locked ward, lobbyists from the Heritage Foundation, Heritage Action for America, Americans For Prosperity, the Club for Growth and FreedomWorks all took an interest in his case. With their help and the support of their fundraising he took his appeal all the way up to the Supreme Court.

The Supreme Court pronounced Max sane in a 5:4 vote. Having previously ruled that corporations are people and that donating money to political candidates was free speech, the court now concluded that in certain circumstances killing is also a form of free speech.

However, they emphasized that this judgment set no precedent. As a precedent they cited *Bush v. Gore*, another precedent that was not to be used as a precedent.

Normally, this would have led to a retrial. But Max was released because under the Double Jeopardy rule he could not be tried again for murder, and the statute of limitations prevented his being prosecuted for fraud, taking bribes or racketeering. He returned to Washington DC, where neither his sanity nor his ethics were questioned.

Now a celebrity and a perceived victim, he was offered his own talk radio spot, a column in the *Weekly Standard*, a job at the Cato Institute and eventually a TV show on Fox News on which his proud mom was one of his first guests.

Samaritans Medical Center was now on the map. It was offered up by the American Enterprise Foundation and other think tanks as a textbook example of how to reduce the cost of health care. Max was eventually appointed to the Cabinet as Secretary for Health and Human Services.

Later he ran for president.

*

At Cathy's suggestion, she and Andrew and Ben emigrated to Australia, where everybody gets health care.

ACKNOWLEDGMENTS

First and foremost, I am grateful to my friend Leo A. Gordon, MD, of Los Angeles. I couldn't have written this book without his entertaining insights into hospital practices. I am extremely grateful to my dear friend, the late Dr Robert Buckman, professor of oncology, humanitarian and stand-up comic, who originally inspired me to write this story and whom I miss a lot; to Rick Ungar, who probably knows more about Obamacare than anyone other than Obama; to my old collaborator George Layton, with whom I used to write episodes of the London Weekend Television's *Doctor* series decades ago, and to Diane Wilk with whom I spent a few afternoons, years ago, talking over this idea. Thanks are also due to many journalists and editors at the *New York Times*, from whose pages I gleaned much of the factual information in this volume.

Thank you to my son Teddy, for his insights into the world of Vegas, banks and business and for his constant encouragement; to Susan Lyons for her careful reading of an early manuscript, and to Evzen Kolar, Richard Murphy, Matthew Rowland, Nick Kazan, Larry Arnstein and my New York agent Barbara Hogenson for excellent suggestions and helpful comments.

Finally, specially thanks to my long-time friend and London agent Mark Lucas for his support, editing and persistent criticism, asking questions that needed answers and forever pushing me to do better.

My greatest thanks, as always, are to my wife Rita.